Up in Smoke

Love in Flames 1

Elouise East

Contents

List of Characters

Andrew, Oliver's brother

Ave, George's wife, foster parent, friends with everyone

Benny, homeless shelter manager

Casey, paramedic

Clark, Dean's dad

Clay, White Watch firefighter

David, Oliver's ex-boyfriend

Dean, Red Watch firefighter

Eddie, Paul and Quinn's son

Evan, Red Watch firefighter

Felix, Red Watch recruit

George, Ave's husband, foster parent

Jack, bartender at Nourris Moi

Joey, Detective

Kade, Detective

Kinton, paramedic, Matias's ex

Leona, Benny's wife, White Watch firefighter

Matias, Blue Watch firefighter

Niall, Red Watch firefighter

Oliver, Owner and Chef of Nourris Moi

Oscar, Ave and George's foster son, youngest

Paul, Cam Fire & Rescue Station Commander, Quinn's husband
Quinn, Paul's husband
Rebecca, chef at Nourris Moi
Selena, head chef at Nourris Moi
Scott, Red Watch firefighter
Stacy, Andrew's wife
Toby, Paul and Quinn's's son
Valerie, Red Watch firefighter
Vance, Ave and George's foster son, eldest
Wade, White Watch firefighter
Xavier, White Watch firefighter
Zane, Ave and George's foster son, middle
Zee, manager at a supermarket, helps Oliver

Chapter 1

Dean

"Hold it steady!"

Dean Tyrell tightened his grip and braced his legs as the water came shooting out of the hose, adding a hissing sound to the intensity of noise around him. He concentrated on the area they had instructed him to wet down while sweat dripped down the side of his face and into the top of his jacket from the warmth of the blaze as well as the mid-summer heatwave. He flicked his gaze along the building and to the windows, ensuring he couldn't see anything amiss as he continued to help put out a kitchen fire that had gone disastrously wrong.

"Clear!"

Scott's voice came through the radio clipped to Dean's shoulder, meaning the house was, thankfully, empty.

An hour later, the fire was out, and the team tidied away their equipment. It was a devastating loss for the family because the entire house had gone up in flames. Dean couldn't imagine what they were going through, but he'd seen it happen many times over the years he'd been firefighting.

"You okay?"

Dean glanced towards Jason and tried for a smile. "Yeah. I feel bad for a family whenever this happens. To lose everything that fast..." He shook his head.

"It's never an easy thing to witness." Jason lifted the hose Dean had rolled up and fitted it back into its home on the engine.

"You would've thought with ten years under my belt, we'd be used to this by now," Dean scoffed.

"In some ways, I hope I always feel for the families; otherwise, I've lost a part of myself."

Dean rolled his colleague's words around in his head and agreed. If he lost the ability to care about those who had misfortunes, he'd need to look for another job.

The clean-up took the better part of an hour, the scent of smoke lingering in Dean's nostrils, then they were on their way back to the station. The call had come in at the beginning of his first day shift, and there were still several hours to go before he could fully relax.

"How are you enjoying our station?" Valerie asked from the seat next to him. She was an inch or two shorter than he was and always had a twinkle of mischief in her eyes.

Dean grinned. "It's great. Everyone has been amazing."

"Oh, no, fellas! We're not doing our job properly! Dean thinks we're amazing! Quick, Jason, think of a hazing we can do." Valeria nudged Evan with her shoulder, and he grunted in response.

The rest of them laughed, no doubt trying to wipe away the melancholy from the call out.

"Don't even think about it, Stokes," Scott growled from the driver's seat. "You know that shit don't fly here."

Valerie raised her hands. "Woah. It's a joke. Though a slight dousing wouldn't go amiss." She winked at him.

"You take me down; you'll get it right back. I'm not a newbie." Dean smirked. His body ached, and he desperately needed a shower, but he had never felt more at ease in his skin. The crew had taken him in as if he'd always worked there, which was a feeling he hadn't *ever* had before.

When they finally pulled the pump back into the station, he was ready for some food, as well as a shower. They worked together to set the engine to rights and ready for the next call, then showered and strode to the kitchen area, which was set up for lunch. Station Commander Paul Thompson was at the hob, stirring what smelled like bolognese.

"Need any help, Chief?" Dean wandered over to him, inhaling. The name "Chief" was left over from when the job titled had changed from Chief Fire Officer, several years back.

"Nah, I'm good. It'll be ready in five minutes."

Dean trailed over to the rest of the crew, who reclined at the table, waiting for lunch. Apart from the aloof demeanour of Scott, the rest of his team was great. Jason was the go-to guy for school visits because the kids loved him, whereas Evan was better with calming adults. Valerie was the joker of the pack; she put it down to having three older brothers. The five of them worked well together. He had no idea of the crew members' sexual orientation, but it didn't matter as long as they said nothing offensive. There was no way he could put up with that again.

"Chief! I forgot to mention. I'm having a barbecue at the weekend when we're off. Do you want to come?" Jason peered at everyone else. "I might invite you lot, too."

Evan scrunched up a piece of paper and threw it at him. "You better invite me since I invited you to the one I had a few weeks ago."

"Now, now, kids. Come on, play nicely. I'd love to. Let me know the details, and I'll check with Quinn. Shouldn't be a problem, though."

Chief indicated the food was ready, and the crew stood and filled their plates with steaming hot spaghetti bolognese before sitting back down.

"You gonna come, Dean? You'll get to meet my room-mates and a few more people from the area." Jason grinned.

Dean shrugged. "Sure."

He didn't mind meeting new people, but it wasn't his favourite pastime. He did fine with people he met on the job, but social interactions were a lot harder for him. Trying to think of conversation topics was not his forte.

"I'm going to take you to Crush one day soon," Valerie said.

"That smirk doesn't bode well. What's Crush?"

Valerie shoved him. "I wasn't smirking. I was smiling, asshole. Crush is my favourite hangout. Very welcoming and an amazing place to visit. It's a regular haunt for me."

"Sounds good."

Another social thing, but he needed to get to know the people who lived here. Once he'd been there for a while, it would be easier on him. As he shovelled the food into his mouth, he felt contentment seep into his bones. This was what he had always wanted. Acceptance and camaraderie. It was a shame he'd needed to move halfway across the country to find it.

By the time his shift was over, the control centre had called the crew out twice more, once to a small campfire on the outskirts of Cambridge, which could've been a lot worse than it was, and second, to the scene of a car accident. Today must've been a lucky day because the victims only had superficial injuries.

He collected his uniform and wandered towards the changing room.

"Hey, Dean, are you coming over for dinner tonight?"

Dean glanced over his shoulder. The chief was one of the best men he'd ever had the pleasure of meeting. He and his husband, Quinn, had made him feel as welcome as a long-lost son since Dean's arrival at Cam Fire & Rescue. But Dean couldn't keep leaning on their generosity to stop the loneliness from encroaching. He'd found a place close by where he could grab a bite to eat before he went home for much-needed sleep.

"Thanks, but I have plans." As soon as he spoke, he regretted his choice of words and concentrated on putting his uniform back in its rightful place.

"Anyone we know?" Jason nudged his arm and waggled his eyebrows as he passed.

"No, I'm trying to get to know the area." He didn't want the chief to think he'd prefer somewhere else because it wasn't the truth. He refused to outstay his welcome—that was the best way to end up being transferred somewhere less inclusive.

"Anywhere in particular?" Paul cocked his head.

"Nourris Moi."

Paul nodded. "Amazing food there. Say hi to Oliver for me."

Dean let out a slow breath, glad Paul didn't seem upset. "Who's Oliver?" He grabbed his toiletries and closed his locker.

Paul smiled. "The owner and chef. He makes food good enough to die for."

"I'm glad to hear the reviews were telling the truth."

"Definitely. A local celebrity often goes there when he's in town, too. I'd go there more often if Quinn didn't enjoy cooking so much."

Dean chuckled. "You caught a decent one there, Chief."

"That I did." Paul slapped his back and strode away.

Trudging towards the showers, Dean reflected on his five weeks at the new station. From the moment he'd set foot in the place, they'd welcomed him with open arms—figuratively and literally. Paul had opened his home to him while

Dean gained his bearings, and the other men and women on the crews had been cheery at his arrival.

It was a far cry from his prior station, where he'd been ready to leave his career for a job at a supermarket. Not that there was anything wrong with anyone who worked at a supermarket, but it hadn't been his dream job since he'd been three years old.

As much as he tried not to think about his time there, Dean couldn't help the images from flitting through his mind as he disrobed and switched on the shower. He'd trained to become a firefighter since he was a teenager. His father had helped him get fit and healthy, and after going to college, Dean had applied for a firefighter position at the local station. He'd completed the training, and by the time they declared him competent, he was twenty-one and satisfied with everything except for hiding his sexual orientation.

His father had known and had recommended that Dean keep it quiet, and he was glad he had. When a colleague had stumbled across him at a club, lip-locked with a guy Dean had planned on taking home, things had become strained, and not only between him and his colleague, Chester.

At the time, Dean thought if he spoke to Chester and requested he keep it secret, it would be the end of it. Unfortunately, Chester had a semi-hidden dislike for gay people, which he made known once Dean's "secret" made the circles. He'd approached his chief but had found no help there because of the older man's own prejudices against the LGBTQ+ community.

Dean spent many long months hiding away in between his shifts, scared someone was going to set upon him, which became unbearable. As he'd contemplated leaving the service, he heard whispers of a station where they welcomed gay firefighters. He'd researched and found Cam Fire & Rescue and had applied immediately when he'd gathered as much information as he could about them.

Within days, they accepted his request, and a couple of weeks later, here he was.

Washing away as much of the dirt and smoke smell as he could, he knew he'd made the right decision in moving a hundred miles away from home. Despite missing his father, the feeling of being included and comfortable had returned, like it had been at the beginning of his career when he was hiding his genuine life. The difference now was that everything about his life was open, and the serenity was ten times better than before.

He dried off and dressed, then grabbed his belongings from his locker. He noticed Evan, still in his uniform, hovering around the room.

"Shower's free if you need it, Evan."

Evan cut a glance at him. "I don't need you lot eyeing me, Tyrell. I'll shower at home." He slammed his locker shut and hitched his bag over his shoulder before exiting, leaving Dean with raised eyebrows.

"No idea what that was about," he muttered to himself.

Goodbyes followed him out of the station—another thing he was getting used to instead of the name-calling and jeering he'd put up before. Swinging his leg over his Ducati, he turned the ignition, the rumble of the bike between his thighs a familiar, tension-releasing feeling.

Roaring out of the station car park, he aimed for the restaurant. Nourris Moi was a little above what he usually paid for takeaways, but he'd wanted to get out into the community and see how the people in Cambridge worked and lived. This was his new home, and he wanted to be part of it, which wasn't easy for someone as quiet and introverted as Dean usually was.

When he climbed back off the bike in the restaurant car park, he locked his helmet onto it and strolled to the entrance. After entering the older building, a server greeted him and took him to his table towards the back of the main room. He thanked the woman and sat, taking in the wooden table and soft fabric chairs. Picking up the menu, he saw a variety of dishes available, including vegan and vegetarian.

"Can I get you something to drink, sir?" A different server stood to the side of the table, tablet poised in his hands.

"Sure. Uh, lemon San Pellegrino, please."

"Perfect. Are you ready to order, or would you like a few more minutes?"

"I'll have the beef fajitas, please."

"All right. Your order will be with you shortly."

"Thank you."

Dean closed the menu and linked his fingers on top of the table and, finally, took a decent look around the place. The tables were all a similar design with either red or white fabric chairs, and a breakfast bar-style table was close to the bar, he assumed, for those who were dining alone. Why hadn't they seated him there? He shook his head to dispel the thought. It didn't matter where he was sitting; he was a paying customer, regardless.

There were several people seated in the room, which could hold approximately fifty patrons, maybe more. The part he loved the most about the design was the exposed brickwork and large windows that let in plenty of light. The lighter evenings made the design stand out even more, although he was sure the restaurant would have fantastic lighting in the darker, winter evenings.

It had surprised him to find that Nourris Moi was open from midday until midnight when he'd been expecting it to be an evening-only restaurant. It could have something to do with Cambridge being such a busy city with tourists, students and natives alike. If the food was as tasty as everyone said, he'd be back time and again.

The server returned with his drink, and Dean pulled out his phone to read from while he was waiting. With no one to converse with, he didn't want to spend his time staring at other people. The never-ending list of books he wanted to read was available on his phone, why not make the most of his time?

A different server interrupted him by bringing his food.

"Good evening, sir. Here's your meal. I hope you find it satisfactory. If you have any problems, please don't hesitate to ask for me. I'm Oliver."

Dean raised his eyebrows, staring into the bright blue eyes of the man for a second before remembering his manners. "Thank you. You didn't need to come out and serve me yourself. You must be busy." He sat back and allowed Oliver to put the plate down. "Um, Paul Thompson says hello."

Oliver's gentle chuckle enhanced his deep laughter lines yet softened his features, and Dean was mesmerised. Despite having a certain severity to his features, Oliver emanated ease and friendliness. Dean had never been into instant attraction before—he usually needed to get to know someone first—but there was something enticing about the man. Not that Dean would ever do anything about it. Once bitten, twice shy and all.

"I'm never too busy for my customers. Paul called me a little while ago to tell me his new firefighter would be visiting tonight and asked me to take care of you."

Dean flushed at the words and ducked his head. "He didn't need to do that."

Oliver splayed his hands, palms to the ceiling before linking them across his stomach. "But Paul wouldn't be Paul if he didn't look after his station."

Dean nodded in understanding. "Thank you. This looks delicious."

"You're welcome. I hope you enjoy it."

Oliver smiled and drifted back through the restaurant, slipping between chairs and tables with the ease of someone comfortable with their heavyset build and occasionally stopping to speak with a diner. Once Oliver had disappeared into what Dean assumed was the kitchen, he realised he'd been staring the entire time. The dim conversation returned to his ears, almost as if it had dulled for a few seconds.

He rolled his lips inwards, focusing on his food. His stomach growled. The sizzle of the hotplate sent the aroma of freshly cooked meat, vegetables, herbs and spices into his nostrils, overtaking the lingering smoke, and he closed his eyes in appreciation. Picking up a mini tortilla, he filled it with guacamole, sour cream and some of the beef mixture, folded it up and took a bite.

As the flavours burst onto his taste buds, he groaned and chewed, savouring the tang of the different ingredients. Paul wasn't kidding when he said the food was to die for. Dean couldn't remember anything tasting as good as this did, and it wasn't because he was hungry.

He glanced across at the kitchen door, catching a peek at Oliver, who had his head through the door, staring at Dean. With a nod and a smile, Oliver disappeared again. Dean stared at the space while he finished chewing, then shrugged and refocused on the food.

Eating here was going to be a regular occurrence, and not only for the food.

Chapter 2

Oliver

Oliver Collins locked the door behind the last member of staff and smiled. As usual, the day had been busy and tiring, but the excellent reviews and friendly banter between him, the staff and the customers made everything worthwhile. He didn't need to have international recognition for him to appreciate what he had. Nourris Moi had been years in the making, and for the first time in three years, the restaurant was making a profit. If he could keep it up, he might be able to expand in a couple of years.

He set about checking what the staff had done to ensure it was to the high standard he required of them. It was high-handed of him, he knew, but his blood, sweat and tears had given life to his dream, and he refused to let anything slip because he hadn't thought to check it. Every member of his staff was a tremendous benefit to his work, and he'd happily leave several in charge, but he didn't need to. He was comfortable working long hours and being a crazy obsessive person when no one else could see it.

Having finished the last checks, he ambled to the kitchen when a knock sounded. He opened the back door, smiling at Zee, who had her hands full of food bags. He grabbed a couple of them and shuffled across the short distance to his car, setting them in the boot, repeating the action several times until everything Zee had brought from the supermarket was rammed into the car.

"Thanks, Zee. I appreciate you doing this for me."

Zee shrugged. "It's the least I can do when you do so much for others. They're throwing the stuff out anyway. It's not like they're going to miss it."

He leaned forward, hugging Zee, then watched her climb into her car before drifting back to his restaurant. Once he'd locked everything up and set the alarm, he drove home. Luckily for him, he lived in a small, functional, detached house in a quiet cul-de-sac on the outskirts of Cambridge, and as it was nearing two in the morning, he didn't feel like he had as many people watching him as they appeared to during the day. Though what they were looking for, he didn't know.

Transferring the bags from the car to the kitchen took a while because he was wearing down, but he got everything into his kitchen and put away so he could start cooking first thing in the morning, like always.

"There's some excellent food in there today. It will make plenty of meals tomorrow," he mumbled to himself, wandering down the hallway and up the stairs to his bedroom.

He yawned on his way to the bathroom, yawned on the way to his bed, and yawned as he climbed between the cold sheets.

The next thing he knew, his alarm blared through the silence, and the sun streaked through the partially open curtains, blinding him, although he had his eyes closed. He reached for his phone without opening his eyes and swiped the screen several times before he found the right spot to turn the alarm off. He swung his legs off his bed and sat upright, rubbing at his face, his eyes not wanting to remain open yet. Instead of thinking about his grumbling stomach, he climbed under the shower and tried to wake himself up. He was *not* a morning person.

Finally dried and dressed, he plodded down the stairs and set about making coffee. When the mug was warming his hands, he sipped and closed his eyes, savouring the hazelnut flavour while the silence of the house seeped into him. Most mornings, he enjoyed the stillness, but other days, like today, he wished he had someone to enjoy the morning with.

He finished his first mug and topped it up again before setting it on the counter. Opening the fridge, he removed most of the food that Zee had given him the previous evening and, glancing at the clock, calculated he had three hours to cook the meals.

Inhaling, he set to work. Chopping vegetables, slicing meat and preparing sauces was second nature to him, and he allowed his mind to wander to a certain firefighter from the evening before. Paul had mentioned the new firefighter—as he usually did—before Oliver had received the call yesterday, but Oliver had not seen him. He hadn't thought about what he'd expected, but it wasn't the six-foot, muscular, military-looking guy who had turned up. Dean's square face and prominent brow gave him an almost stern expression, but when he smiled...Oliver's heart raced. Dean appeared to be shy and unsure, which Oliver would expect from someone new to the area, but he had never met a firefighter of Paul's with the same demeanour.

Oliver had been unable to keep from checking up on the guy after he'd delivered his food to him. Peering through the kitchen door several times, he found the man fascinating to watch because his face was extremely expressive. He had been immensely proud to have put that blissful look on Dean's face when he'd first tasted the food.

Oliver stared at his movements while he finished peeling the potatoes. He didn't know why he was focusing on Dean when they would only be friends. Oliver refused to get into another relationship when his last three long-term ones ended because he couldn't give them enough of his time. Nourris Moi was still his baby, and he needed to spend an excessive number of hours at the restaurant. No relationship could withstand that.

By the time he needed to leave, he'd made four cottage pies, three large chicken and bacon pies, a big pan of mashed potatoes, and a large batch of vegetable soup with croutons. He placed them in the special heat-retaining boxes he had and carried them to his car. Returning to his house, he grabbed his wallet and phone and locked up. He drove carefully, not wanting any of the food to spill, and parked outside the rundown building. Sending a message to Benny, he climbed out of the car and leaned against the boot to wait for him.

"Oliver! How are you?"

Benny was a man who looked like the slightest breeze could knock him off his feet, but he was one of the strongest men Oliver knew—on the level of the firefighters—both emotionally and physically. White streaked through his messy brown hair, matching his full beard and moustache, and freckles covered his face and neck, which darkened when he'd been in the sun too long. They had been friends for many, many years, and Oliver was immensely glad to be able to lighten a little of the burden that came with being the organiser of one of two homeless shelters in the city.

"Morning, Benny. How're things going?"

Benny tilted his head to one side and grimaced. "Not too bad. A few issues overnight, but nothing that can't be fixed. How are you?"

"I'm good. The restaurant is picking up, and things are looking great."

"I'm happy for you."

Oliver thumbed over his shoulder. "Brought some food for the masses. Not a lot, mind."

"Even if you brought one thing, it helps tremendously, Oliver. You know that."

Benny said the same thing every time, but Oliver couldn't help but feel like he could do more. He opened his boot, and Benny called for a helper, and they carried everything in one trip. Placing the meals on the counter in the kitchen, Oliver smiled at the teenage helper.

"Thanks."

The boy nodded and left the kitchen after giving a small smile to Benny.

Oliver clapped Benny on his shoulder. "Make sure you drop by the restaurant one day so I can feed you."

Benny waved his hand. "I'm fine, but I'll drop by with Leona when we can."

Oliver yawned as he made his way back to the car after saying goodbye. Checking his watch, he headed for the restaurant. Despite feeling tired as usual, his spirits lifted when the building came into view. He'd been extremely lucky that this property had been for sale when he'd been searching for something to house his restaurant.

Nourris Moi was situated at the end of a row of terraced buildings but at a place where two roads connected. It meant the entrance was on a corner, and windows covered one side of it, and the opposite side—on the other road—had partial windows too. It was difficult to explain to someone who had never seen it, but Oliver always said to imagine an inverted triangle shape, and Nourris Moi took up the lower half of the triangle to the bottom point. The floor space was more than adequate for his needs, but the location had cinched the deal in his mind.

He parked the car in the small car park to the rear, then shuffled towards his business. The pure white painted frontage rose amongst other more drab-looking buildings, and Oliver was proud of what he'd achieved. He wished his brother could see it, but Andrew was living in Dubai, working all the hours under the sun to provide for his family there. Andrew was older than him by six years, and they'd never been close, but still shared phone calls and messages occasionally and never forgot birthdays or Christmas.

Oliver unlocked the front door and let himself in, knowing Selena, his sous chef, would already be getting things prepared for the day. He had to let this part of his day go to her because he wouldn't have been able to continue making the meals for the homeless shelter. Selena was an amazing benefit to the restaurant and had been working for him since the beginning, though she'd only been sous chef since his previous one had left a year ago.

"Morning, Chef." Selena grinned.

"One of these days, you'll call me Oliver and scare the life out of me." He winked at her. "How is everything going?"

"All on schedule. Rebecca will be here in a few minutes and the rest of the kitchen in half an hour."

"Perfect, as always."

"You've taught them well."

Oliver snorted. "I pay them to turn up."

"That you do, but you're also a fair boss. No one could ask for more."

He rolled his eyes. His kitchen was busy. When he'd first decided to open from midday to midnight, his friends had thought he was crazy, but he argued that he'd be able to catch those business meetings that often happened over lunch. He'd wavered over closing from three to five but continued through, and at the moment, everything was working out well. He'd compromised a little with reducing the menu during the lull hours, as he called them. The only issue he'd come across was that he'd needed to employ more staff to cover the twelve hours, which affected his bottom line, but it was finally turning around.

Trying to balance shift patterns was a nightmare and took up most of a week when he needed to rejig them. Luckily, the staff he'd employed were proficient and rarely asked to swap shifts or hours because Oliver touched base with them regularly to see if their personal circumstances had changed and hours needed adjusting. He'd found it better to ask about it rather than wait for them to come to him, by which point, it became more difficult to balance.

Oliver set about preparing the food, and the rest of the kitchen staff joined them over the next hour. The general camaraderie was high, which Oliver put down to him being a reasonable boss. His staff had fun but did the job Oliver required of them.

By the time the doors opened at midday, everything was almost prepared with only a few pastry items that were being finished, but there was no rush for them unless someone decided to eat dessert first.

"Good afternoon, Mr and Mrs Oxford. I hope you're having a wonderful anniversary."

Oliver smiled at the older couple, who were a big part of the community. Ave and George Oxford had been foster parents for over thirty years and showed no signs of slowing down. They were a firm fixture at many of Paul's get-togethers and often brought the kids with them. The couple had focused on LGBTQ+ children who had been removed or kicked out from their childhood homes for different reasons. For that reason alone, Oliver would've loved them, but they were amazing people and often found themselves at the restaurant to support Oliver.

He waved away the maître d' and helped the couple to their table, then fussed over them before wishing them well and heading back to the kitchen.

"Ave and George are here, so we have around half an hour before they'll want dessert, I think."

"Yes, Chef," his pastry chef replied, eyes focused on what he was doing.

He had seven staff in his kitchen, including himself, but they worked like a well-oiled machine, and he rarely had any problems with the level of food they produced. On one level, he knew he could easily leave them in Selena's capable hands, but his own personality wouldn't allow him to. Sighing, he got to work alongside his team.

When the lull came around two-thirty, Oliver took a breather, leaving Selena in charge while he went to his office. Paperwork was the bane of his existence, but he had no choice about it. One day, he'd hire someone else to do this, but for now, it was his job.

His phone rang when he had his nose buried in his accounts, and he blinked rapidly to clear his gaze.

"Hello?"

"Hey, Oliver. I wanted to let you know that the food went down extremely well. Thank you again."

"You don't have to thank me, Benny. I love doing it. I'm glad they enjoyed it."

"I know you don't like thanks, but you deserve it all the same. You spend a lot of time cooking for other people, even when you don't have to, and it means a lot."

Oliver swallowed against the lump in his throat. "You're welcome."

"I spoke to Leona. Do you have space for us on Monday?"

"I'll make sure of it. What time?"

"Six?"

"I'll put it on the list."

"Thanks, man. Take care of you. I'll see you in the morning."

Oliver smiled. "As always."

He was glad to help the homeless shelter. It had come about when Benny had mentioned the shelter running out of food one lunchtime. Oliver had brainstormed how to help them but couldn't think of anything that wouldn't take a chunk out of his restaurant's bottom line. It was only when he'd mentioned it to Zee one evening when she'd come in a beer that she had mentioned how much food the supermarket wasted because it was past its best before date. They'd concocted the idea that Zee would take the food that the supermarket was only going to throw away and hand it over to Oliver to use as he could for extra meals for the shelter.

That had been about six months ago, and it was still going strong. Zee was the manager of the supermarket, which had made things a little easier, but the company itself didn't want it known that they were doing it because the legal ramifications were a little unclear. Therefore, if they ever found out, the company would pretend they knew nothing about it, and it would fall on Zee's and Oliver's shoulders.

Wonderful business ethic as far as he was concerned. The only other problem Oliver had come across was that he couldn't cook the food in the restaurant kitchen because of the food being past its best before date. It meant he had to do it at home. Luckily, he had a kitchen large enough.

"Oliver!"

The shout had him out of his seat and into the kitchen within seconds. "What's wrong?"

Selena shook her head. "Nothing's wrong, but have you seen the time?"

Oliver checked the clock on the wall, seeing it was nearing the busy period again—where had the time gone? "Shit. Give me five minutes."

"No problem."

He raced back to the computer and saved what he'd been working on, then shut it down. Smoothing down his chef's whites, he strode to the main restaurant area and mingled with the guests, ensuring they were pleased with the service they'd received. He checked in with the bartender, maître d' and the servers to ensure there were no problems, then headed back to the kitchen, where he began the other part of his job.

He was ecstatic doing what he was doing, even if he was lonely, though he wouldn't tell anyone that. Concentrating on the sounds of the kitchen, he smiled despite the slight tug against his heart. No one could have everything they wanted, and this was all Oliver could have. He needed to brush aside anything else because he had more than others did. He should be thankful.

His heart told him otherwise.

Chapter 3

Dean

"Do you want a beer?" Jason quirked a brow at Dean, who nodded in response.

Jason's place was a surprise. He lived in a large apartment with three roommates, but they had access to a communal garden area, which was how he'd been able to hold the barbecue. The building was a good size, but Dean imagined the three men could afford it between them. That was if they didn't rent it. He hadn't thought to ask before.

He grasped the bottle passed to him and removed the lid, throwing it into the plastic bucket next to the decking area, which he was told was there for that specific reason.

"Dean, what do you think of our lovely city?" Jason grinned and swigged from his bottle.

"From what I've seen of it, it's nice. I haven't done much exploring past the city centre and shopping mall, though."

And Nourris Moi, which he'd kept himself away from for the past five days. He could easily spend his entire wage at the restaurant, but he couldn't afford to. Having no dependents made things easier, but he needed to pay his bills and put some aside for a rainy day. Being frivolous with his money was not him.

"Valerie said she'd take you to Crush one day, so that's one place you'll get to know. Hmm, where else could we show you that's interesting?" Jason frowned at the ground.

"I'm not going anywhere. There's no rush to show me stuff." Dean chuckled.

"I know, but we want you to stay, and showing you all the high-quality stuff will go in our favour."

"I'm seconding that," Paul said as he came to a stop beside Dean. "You're an asset to the station. I don't want you going anywhere." He narrowed his eyes at Jason. "It also means that Jason shouldn't be pushing too hard because it will make Dean feel pressured and might have the opposite effect to what Jason wants it to."

Jason's mouth opened and closed several times before he pouted and stuck his bottle in his mouth instead of saying anything. Dean snorted.

"I'm not going anywhere," he repeated.

Paul clapped him on the shoulder and turned when someone called his name. Quinn, his husband, was waving his hand for him to go over. Paul lifted one finger, then turned back to Dean.

"I'm glad. You fit in the crew like you're meant to be there. Despite what I said to Jason, we want you to be happy and get to know the city. Make sure you take them up on some of their offers. I don't want you squirrelling yourself away in your apartment." Paul raised his eyebrows.

Dean smirked. "I wouldn't dream of it."

His words were only words. There was no guarantee he'd agree to go out with any of them, but he could agree to try. As confident and outspoken as he was when he was working, it was different in social situations. He'd been used to hiding what he was; it was difficult to get out of the habit.

Paul ruffled his hair like he was a kid, then walked off laughing. Dean rolled his eyes.

"Dean!"

He glanced over his shoulder and smiled when Ave and George strolled towards him. Whirling to face them, he opened his arms to receive a hug from Ave, trying to avoid getting hit by her enormous sun hat.

"How are you, sweetheart? We've not seen you for over a week. Have you settled in well enough?"

Dean smiled at her and guided her to a set of chairs nearby. "I'm doing good, thanks. I'm getting there. You know what it's like when moving somewhere new. I need to find my feet a little first."

"That you do." She eased into the chair with a sigh. "Oh, these warm summers remind me of my youth, but at my age, they're bothersome." She fanned her hand across her face.

Dean reached behind him for a bottle of water, which he passed to her. "Here. It might help a little."

"Thank you, sweetheart." She uncapped it and drank a little.

"Paul told us you visited Nourris Moi the other day. It's one of our favourite places to visit. What did you think?" George asked.

George's skin looked remarkably tanned. Did he work outside a lot? Dean didn't know, but he knew George worshipped the ground Ave walked on and made sure she had everything she ever wanted or needed.

"It was amazing. The food was delicious, and Oliver seemed nice." Why had he brought Oliver into the conversation?

Ave pressed a hand to her chest. "Oliver is such a sweetheart. He works hard all the time but still makes such exquisite food. I don't know how he does it with everything else he does as well."

Dean tilted his head. "What else does he do?"

"He cooks for the homeless shelter every morning and delivers it there in time for lunch, then he goes straight to his restaurant to do it all over again for the rest of the day. He also gives cooking lessons occasionally." Ave tutted. "He works too hard if you ask me, but he won't hear of it."

Dean couldn't stop the idea of asking Oliver to give him lessons because it might stop his thoughts from going in the wrong direction, but also because he couldn't cook anything that wasn't beans on toast without messing it up. He doubted he could afford the cost and put it out of his mind. Instead, the idea of having something more with Oliver flitted through his thoughts again, but if he didn't want to cause pain and potential heartache for whoever he had a relationship with because of his dangerous job, he needed to forget about it.

"Food's ready!" Evan shouted from the barbecue.

"No doubt Oliver sent something for this party, too, if I know him well enough," Ave muttered, climbing to her feet with her husband's help. "Don't be a stranger, Dean. I expect to see you for Sunday lunch soon."

"Yes, Ave."

He grinned as she shook her head at him and watched while they drifted towards the long food table that they had set up in Jason's back garden. They had covered all the food with fly nets to protect it, and the seats were filling up. Dean was more than content to watch for the moment. There had been more people invited to the barbecue than Dean had been expecting. The way Jason had explained it, Dean had assumed it would only be their firefighting crew that was invited; however, it was friends and family, too. He was sure his father would've enjoyed meeting those he worked with, but they had to be satisfied with video calls and messages, and life sometimes got in the way.

"Here."

Someone thrust a burger into his hands, and Dean hardly had a chance to rest his beer bottle between his legs and clasp it before the person retreated. He watched Evan's back as he marched back to the table and sat. Their gazes met for a brief second, and Evan's eyes narrowed before he turned away.

Dean focused on the burger, clenching his jaw. He had been right when he'd told those who asked that everyone had been very welcoming. Everyone had, but since then, Evan's demeanour had changed, and only when others weren't paying attention. Dean had a feeling he knew what Evan's problem was, but how could he work in a station where LGBTQ+ personnel were not only allowed but celebrated when he appeared to hate them. Or maybe it was

Dean he hated. Dean couldn't figure it out. He ignored it and pretended everything was okay. As usual.

Taking a bite out of his burger, he stood, making his way across the garden while he chewed. He refused to be seen as someone who didn't mingle with others, so he pushed aside his nervous energy and sat on a chair next to Valerie. Everyone spent the afternoon shooting the shit and causing havoc, but Dean enjoyed it all. He'd experienced nothing like the camaraderie he found between firefighting crews, although he was sure the police or military personnel had something similar.

After several hours, he said goodbye and headed home. It was mid-afternoon, but he'd socialised as much as he was able. Now, he needed some downtime. When he reached home, he jumped in the shower and changed into joggers and a T-shirt then dropped to the sofa to video call his dad.

"Hello, there, Dean. How are you doing?"

Clark Tyrell was a sixty-year-old former factory worker who retired the previous year. His dad had been working in different factories all his life, and his health had suffered from it. Whenever Clark filled the screen of Dean's phone, the frail, grey-haired man who had once been full of life shocked him.

"Hey, Dad. I'm doing well. How's life treating you this week?" Dean relaxed against the cushions, propping one behind his head.

"Same old, same old, son. I'm planning to watch the footie tonight. Did you go to the barbecue?"

Dean smiled, knowing his dad was checking whether he was hiding himself away or getting out and about. "Yes, I went. It was good. There were a lot more people there than I expected, but it was enjoyable all the same." He yawned. "I think I ate too much, though. I'm tired."

His father laughed. "You can never eat too much. You have hollow legs. Always have done." He rested his head on his hand. "Are things as different there as you'd hoped?"

Dean considered his answer, which should have been an immediate yes, but something held him back. Evan's face came to mind. "Mostly. It's a thousand times better than where I was, but there's at least one person who seems to have a problem, though they're not making it as obvious as I'm used to. It's making me second-guess whether it's my brain playing tricks or if they're going to start problems."

"Keep your eyes open. I trust your instincts, Dean. They've never steered you wrong before."

His father's faith in him helped Dean to relax, and once he'd finished the call, he found he didn't want to mope around the apartment. Racing up the stairs, he didn't think twice before swapping his clothes for something better and jogging to his car. Even as he parked in the car park, he shook his head and told himself he was all kinds of stupid, but he couldn't resist visiting the place again.

He entered Nourris Moi at seven that evening, and the place was heaving. There wasn't a single table left, but he wasn't there for the food.

"Hello, sir. Can I help?"

The maître d' gained his attention, and he stepped forward.

"Hi. Am I able to sit at the bar for a drink, or do I have to book a table?"

"All our tables are booked for tonight, sir, but you are more than welcome to sit and enjoy our beverages at the bar. There is no eating there, though."

Dean waved his hand. "That's fine. I'd like a drink."

"Perfect, sir. If you take this door," she pointed to Dean's right, "it will take you straight to the bar area."

"Thank you."

He entered the main area and followed the route to the bar, hitching up onto a barstool. The bartender came to stand in front of him several minutes later.

"What can I get you?"

"A beer would be nice, thanks."

"Anything in particular?" The bartender's mouth curled, and his eyebrows rose.

"No, anything you think is good."

The bartender narrowed his eyes and turned away, reaching into a fridge before presenting Dean with a bottle. He didn't recognise the brand, but he was willing to try anything once.

"Can I open a tab?"

The bartender nodded, pressed a few buttons on the screen, then Dean presented his card before taking a swig of the beer. The almost sweet taste burst onto his tongue, and he rolled the liquid around in his mouth before swallowing. He nodded at the bartender, who had been watching him.

"Not bad."

The bartender grinned and focused on the next customer. Dean transferred his gaze to the mirror behind the bar, which enabled him to watch the comings and goings of the restaurant. He was onto his second beer when he saw Oliver at one of the tables. He held a large cake with candles on top, which he laid in front of a crying woman. She held her hands over her face before rubbing at it, then stared at the person across the table from her. Dean watched as she grabbed hold of the man's hand, and they both blew out the candles. Within seconds, the restaurant filled with song. Dean smiled at the obvious birthday surprise, but his gaze froze on Oliver, who was staring back at him.

Dean swallowed hard, breathing roughly when Oliver refocused on the woman and kissed her cheek. Oliver moved between the tables until he reached Dean.

"I wasn't expecting to see you tonight." Oliver rested his elbow on the bar at Dean's side.

"Last minute decision."

"Are you not eating?"

Dean shook his head. "I ate enough at the barbecue."

Oliver smiled. "Ah, yes. I hope everyone liked the barbecue sauce."

"Did you make that?"

Oliver nodded. "I did. Special recipe."

"It tasted amazing. Everyone loved it."

"The least I could do as I couldn't be there." Oliver glanced around the restaurant, to check if anything needed his attention if Dean was to guess.

"How's business?"

"Busy." Oliver smirked and caught Dean's gaze again as he stood to his full height. "Which means I need to get cooking." He tilted his head and licked his lips, distracting Dean. "Are you staying long?"

"No plans to move on yet."

They stared at each other for a few long seconds—or minutes, Dean didn't know—until Oliver leaned closer. "Remember to say goodnight when you do," he whispered.

Dean nodded once, Oliver's lips temptingly close. He gripped his bottle hard when Oliver stalked back to the kitchen, disappearing through the door. Blowing out a breath, he finished his beer and indicated for another. Dean pulled out his phone and loaded up a book to read while he drank. He was in no rush, and for once, he didn't mind hanging out somewhere without knowing anyone.

"What are you reading?"

Dean was startled and dropped his phone to the counter when the voice spoke. Checking over his shoulder, he saw Oliver with a small smile on his face.

"What?"

Oliver pointed to his phone. "What are you reading?"

"Oh, um, a book about space." Dean felt his cheeks heat.

"Fiction or non-fiction?"

"Non-fiction."

Oliver pursed his lips. "Do you like the stars?"

Dean nodded. "I do."

"Hmm."

Oliver placed a plate with a slice of black forest gateau on it in front of Dean, then strode back to the kitchen. Dean stared after him, frowning. What was all that about? He faced the bartender.

"I thought I wasn't allowed to eat at the bar."

The bartender shrugged as he cleaned a glass. "You're not, but he's the boss."

Dean stared at the cake and pushed aside his concerns. Picking up the delicate dessert fork, he cut off a piece and slid it into his mouth, the mixture melting in his mouth. He closed his eyes and savoured the airy chocolate sponge, whipped cream and cherry combination. Dean loved food—except when it came to vegetables, which he detested, although still ate because they were beneficial to his health—but he couldn't make anything like this. He couldn't afford to eat out like this every day and often made do with packet food or ready meals, but when he got to taste something divine like this, it made it even more worthwhile.

When he scraped the plate clean, Dean heard a chuckle.

"I think he practically orgasmed at the taste of that, boss," the bartender said to someone behind Dean.

Dean lifted his gaze to the mirror, seeing Oliver standing with a look on his face that Dean couldn't decipher. "Thank you. It was delicious."

"Remember what I said earlier." Oliver turned away, waving at someone and making his way through the room.

Dean wasn't sure what Oliver meant. What had he said earlier? Unless it was the "don't forget to say goodbye." Dean hadn't planned on leaving yet, but he needed a bathroom break. He caught the bartender's gaze and told him he would only be a minute. After finishing up, he washed his hands, gazing at his flushed face in the mirror. He was sure most of it was to do with the number of beers he'd drunk, but some of it was because of the attention he received from Oliver.

Oliver was formidable. He knew what he wanted and told it like it was. Dean could relate to that, and he found he enjoyed their similarities. It was a shame nothing could happen between them, but the flirting was a pleasant change. It had been a long time since he'd been out anywhere for anyone to flirt with him. He'd forgotten about the bubbling energy that filled him when thinking about another person.

Retaking his seat, he found another beer waiting for him. Pulling out his phone again, he continued reading, not sure entirely what was keeping him there but knowing he didn't want to say goodbye yet.

It was only when the bartender, Jack, asked him for his last order that Dean realised how late it was. There were only a few straggling diners left, and servers and cleaners were tidying up the restaurant. Dean finalised his bill and pocketed his phone. He wasn't sure what to do. He asked Jack if he could get Oliver for him. Jack came back saying Oliver would be with him as soon as he'd finished in there and to wait for him, even if they closed the restaurant around him.

Dean scratched his head but settled in to wait. It was only as the front door locked and the staff members departed through the kitchen that Oliver came out.

Dean's heart raced the closer Oliver came.

Chapter 4

Oliver

"I'm glad you stayed. Sorry it took me so long." Oliver lifted himself onto the seat beside Dean.

"It's okay. I know you're busy. I should go. I don't want to interrupt."

Oliver laid his hand over Dean's arm. "Stay. If you can, that is."

He watched Dean's Adam's apple bob and his tongue peek out to wet his lips, but he nodded.

"Can I help with anything?" Dean asked.

Oliver smiled. "No, we're all set. I'll do a last walk through before I leave, but everything is ready for tomorrow."

He couldn't explain his need to have Dean wait for him. Nothing romantic would happen between them, but something was pulling him towards the man. He wished he knew what.

"Did you want to speak to me?" Dean shifted in his seat.

Oliver reached for the two bottles of water Jack had left for them, passing one to Dean before twisting the lid off his own. Several swallows later, he recapped the bottle and met

Dean's gaze again. "I want to get to know you a bit better, that's all."

Dean's cheeks darkened as he fidgeted with the label on the bottle. "There's not much to say."

"I don't believe that. What made you end up at Cam?" Oliver rested his head on his hand, facing Dean.

Dean blew out a long breath, and his shoulders rounded. "Let's say Cam is a lot more inclusive than my last station."

Oliver's heart hurt with the pain in his voice. "I'm glad you're here instead of there. Paul and the crews are a great family."

Dean smiled, the corners of his eyes crinkling. "They are. I know it, and I've only been there a few weeks." He cleared his throat. "Why did you set up here? Is this your hometown?"

"No, actually. I lived in a town in Rutland until I was sixteen, then moved away for college. Lost my mum shortly afterwards."

"I'm sorry." Oliver nodded in thanks, but before he could say anything, Dean continued, "Rutland?"

Oliver grinned. "It's the smallest county in England, hence the need to move away. I was fed up with everyone knowing everything about everyone else. I couldn't walk down the street without being pointed at as my mother's son." Dean's forehead creased, and Oliver continued, "I've been told many times we were twins. It was tedious as a teenager."

"A little more bittersweet after you lost her, I bet?"

He glanced at Dean and nodded. How had he figured that out? "Anyway, I have always loved Cambridge, and when

I started looking for somewhere to put down roots, this place came up. An offer I couldn't refuse."

"You should be proud. This place is amazing."

"Thanks."

They slipped into silence, and Oliver studied Dean from the corner of his eye. Neither seemed in a rush to leave, despite the lull in the conversation. Did Dean have a shift tomorrow? He'd be exhausted if he did.

"Are you working tomorrow?"

Dean shook his head. "I start again on Tuesday. It's nice to not have to rush around anywhere."

"What do you usually do in your spare time?"

Dean sipped his water and shrugged. "Not a lot."

"No hobbies or interests?"

Dean smirked over at him. "No, apart from finding somewhere to eat each night."

Oliver frowned. "Why? Do you not like cooking?" He couldn't understand anyone not enjoying cooking, but he knew some people didn't.

Dean stared at the bar, fidgeting once more. "I don't know how, which is an embarrassing thing to admit to a chef."

Oliver raised his eyebrows. "You don't need to be ashamed of it." He licked his lips when an idea flickered to life. "I could teach you if you want?" He didn't know when he'd find the time, but he refused to withdraw the offer.

Wide, bright blue eyes stared at him. "Are you sure? You seem busy enough without doing this, too."

A flutter began in his stomach. "I'll make time. I can't in all conscience allow someone to starve because they don't know how to cook." He winked. "We'll need to sync our schedules."

Dean caught his bottom lip in his teeth and smiled, giving him a goofy expression. "You're sure?"

Nodding, Oliver smiled at Dean's apparent excitement, vibrating on the seat as he was. "I'm sure."

"That would be fantastic! I've always wanted to learn but recipe books assume you have basic knowledge, and I don't even have that."

"How have you survived?" Oliver joked.

"Takeaway, ready meals, restaurants, Paul comman-deered my meals for a few weeks, or Quinn did. I manage as I always do."

"Well, we're definitely going to change that. How about we start on Monday morning? You can come round to my house and help me cook for the shelter."

Dean smiled, his eyes lighting up. "Perfect. What time?"

"Is eight o'clock too early?"

"No, I'll—"

A bang sounded in the kitchen, and Oliver checked the time, realising it would be Zee. "Excuse me for a moment."

He stood, jogging to the back door. Zee blew out a breath when he opened it.

"Jesus! I thought something had happened to you. You never—" Her eyes widened, then she smirked. "Never mind. Here's your stuff."

As usual, Oliver grabbed a few bags and carried them to his car, but this time, when he turned to take some more from Zee, Dean was there instead, holding out a bag.

"Thanks."

There was more than usual, and it took a few minutes to get it all. Some had to be put on the backseat. Oliver knew he'd be able to make some amazing meals from this lot. He tugged Zee into a hug and watched her get into her car, waving as she drove into the night.

"She seems nice."

Oliver glanced at Dean with a smile. "She is." He locked his car and returned to the restaurant. "I need to check everything and lock up. Do you need a lift home?"

"No, I have my car. Thanks for the lessons. I'm looking forward to it." He shoved his hands deep into his pockets and stared at the floor.

"Me too."

Neither said anything for a long minute, but their gazes met and held. Heat rushed through Oliver, and he realised exactly what he'd done by offering Dean the lessons...he'd saddled himself with a case of blue balls for the foreseeable future.

Dean recovered first, smiling at Oliver. "Thank you. I'll see you at your house at eight on Monday."

Oliver nodded, pulling out his notepad and scribbling down his address. He tore it off and handed it to Dean, their fingers touching and leaving a tingle of electricity in its wake.

Dean's mouth curled as he whirled away. Oliver had the urge to call his name and bring him close again, but he bit his lip to stop his words from escaping. He needed to get his act together and ready for Monday.

Monday couldn't come fast enough for Oliver, and Sunday night found him restless and unable to sleep, even though the day had been the busiest of his week—as it always was with people wanting Sunday roasts without having to cook them themselves. He arrived home at around one-thirty in the morning, after puzzling over a small difference in the accounts for far longer than he should have, and finally gave up trying to sleep around three o'clock. It wouldn't be the first time he'd been awake for over forty-eight hours at a time.

He made some coffee, knowing it would be his best friend that day, then set about sorting the ingredients Zee had given him the previous afternoon—with the supermarkets closing early on Sundays, it meant Zee could drop off earlier than usual.

After looking through what he had, he sat with a coffee and planned what they could make with it, taking into consideration that Dean would be helping. He wouldn't go easy on the guy, but he also wouldn't make things difficult enough that he put him off cooking for life. Once he decided on the menu, he dragged himself for a shower. Feeling a little more alert, he pottered around the house, tidying things that didn't need tidying because he wasn't there enough to be messy.

He had half an hour before Dean was due to arrive and made a start on some breakfast. Choosing a recipe his mother had favoured, he mixed the batter for banoffee pancakes, chopped some bananas and stirred the sauce. The sauce was almost ready when the doorbell chimed. He rested the spoon on the plate and strode down the hallway, flinging open the door with a smile.

"Good morning!"

"Morning. Sorry, I'm a bit early." Dean rocked from foot to foot on his doorstep.

He waved him in. "No, don't worry. Do you like pancakes?"

Dean grinned. "Who doesn't?"

Oliver couldn't see Dean but could feel him following behind. "Have a seat. They'll be ready in a minute or two." He focused on what he was doing instead of the person sitting at his table.

The batter dripped into the pan, sizzling as it cooked. The sauce was ready, and Oliver poured it into a small jug. Pulling the ingredients closer to him, he flipped the pancake to cook the other side and picked up a plate.

Sliding the first cooked pancake onto Dean's plate, he spooned another batch of batter into the pan, then focused on getting Dean's ready. He added chopped banana to a quarter of the pancake, poured a generous helping of sauce and folded it over on itself before dribbling a small amount of sauce over the top and adding a spoonful of cream to the side. It most definitely was not a healthy breakfast, but it was a delicious one.

Oliver flipped the pancake currently cooking and delivered Dean's plate to him with a flourish.

"This looks and smells amazing."

"Well, if you like them, there will be more." Oliver winked at him before returning to the stove, his stomach full of butterflies.

He didn't know what it was about Dean, but something pulled him closer. Something wanted him to grasp him and never let him go, but Oliver had too much on his hands with the restaurant at the moment. It didn't look like his situation would change soon either, and it wouldn't be fair to Dean if they started a relationship. No. Friends only. He refused to make another person unhappy when he needed to focus on his business.

"Oh, my god!"

Dean's muffled voice brought a smile to his face, and he glanced over his shoulder. Dean was inhaling the food, his eyelids fluttering closed every time he forked another bite into his mouth. Grinning, Oliver put a second pancake on another plate and fixed it the same, setting a third to cook. He removed Dean's first plate and slid the second into its place.

"What about you?" Dean frowned.

"I'll eat in a minute."

Dean narrowed his eyes but started on the second plate. Oliver would keep making pancakes until Dean didn't want anymore, then he'd eat his own. It was the way his mother had fed them when they were little. She would make a small production line in their childhood kitchen, and in turn, each child would have a pancake put on their plate, then go down the line to add toppings of their choice. Once they were full, his mother would finish cooking the leftover batter and build a stack of pancakes. When the batter was gone, she would divide the remaining pancakes into three: some for the two kids the following day, the rest for her that day. It was one memory that was most clear in Oliver's mind when he thought of his mother.

Giving Dean a third pancake, Oliver made a fourth and sat at the table, tucking into his own. The remaining batter would make some for Dean to take home with him, but he would teach Dean how to cook them as he did it.

"Thank you. They were delicious."

He finished what was in his mouth. "You're welcome. We shouldn't cook on an empty stomach."

Dean waved a hand at the piece of paper on the table. "Is this the menu?"

He nodded. "Some of it is more complex than I would usually teach a beginner, but it's not impossible. We'll take it step by step."

When he finished, he rinsed the plates and put them in the dishwasher. Turning to the fridge, he removed several items, placing them on the counter and crooked his finger at Dean.

"Time to work."

Dean slipped his shirt off, leaving him with a tight black T-shirt. Oliver swallowed hard and diverted his gaze to the ingredients. The words on the menu swam before him until he blinked rapidly and focused.

"First, we're going to go through some prep work, which means chopping basically. A lot of the food I make for the shelter is carb-loaded but also healthy. There are a lot of potatoes to peel and vegetables to chop."

"All right. Where do I start?"

"Do you know how to peel potatoes?"

Dean wrinkled his nose. "With a knife?"

"Some people do. Others use a peeler. Let's start with a peeler and see how you go."

Oliver showed Dean how to hold the peeler and use it. After a couple of false starts, Dean seemed to get the hang of it. Oliver focused on the carrots.

"When did you realise you enjoyed cooking?"

Oliver smiled over at Dean, who stood a couple of feet away from him. "I was around eight or nine, I think. I started helping Mum around the kitchen and got sucked into it. From that moment on, I knew I wanted to be a chef. It took a while to open my own business, but the experience I gained in the early years was undeniable. I don't think I would've been as prepared as I'd thought I was without spending years following someone else's orders."

Dean nodded. "I know what you mean. I've been told I could go the officer route, but I'm content following other people for now. I won't rule it out."

"Did you always want to be a firefighter?" Oliver checked Dean's progress and refocused on the carrots, throwing them into a bowl.

"Yeah. Always. Dad helped me with my training while I was a teenager, and as soon as I could sign up for it, I was there and never looked back." Dean's grin sobered, and his eyes dimmed a little.

Oliver didn't like wherever Dean's mind had gone and changed the subject, "We need lots more potatoes."

Dean's eyes widened when he took in what he'd already done. "More?"

"Yes. We're making cottage pie, roast potatoes to go with some meat, oven-baked fries, potato cakes and potato casserole—also known as funeral potatoes."

Dean raised his eyebrows. "Funeral potatoes?" His eyes were on the potatoes he was peeling while he spoke.

"They're a dish that can pretty much go with anything and were often used to take to after-funeral get-togethers, hence the name."

"Seems morbid to me."

Oliver chuckled at Dean's huffed words. "It's why I call it potato casserole. People understand what I mean."

They worked with a gentle conversation between them, occasionally brushing arms, shoulders or hands as they reached for different things. It surprised Oliver how easy it seemed. His heart calmed before another brush of skin sent it rocketing again. He needed to relax. Despite all his words from earlier, Oliver wanted Dean. Admitting it was simple. Holding back from doing anything about it was much more difficult.

"Okay. We've peeled the potatoes and cut them into different shapes depending on what we're doing with them. The roast potatoes..." He waited until Dean pointed at them before he nodded. "They need to go into a tray with some olive oil, parsley, thyme and rosemary sprinkled over the top and put in the oven." He watched as Dean followed his instructions and smiled when the oven door closed. Oliver had already put the chicken in as well as the potato casserole, and they were well on their way to being ready. "Well done. Now, cottage pie."

He spent several long minutes talking Dean through how to cook the mince, gravy and vegetables, then how to construct the cottage pie itself. When it was done, it went into the oven alongside the fries they'd made. For a beginner, Dean was doing well, although following orders must be second nature to him.

"I'm glad you have a massive oven," Dean murmured, fanning himself with the oven gloves.

"The perks of being a chef." Oliver smiled. "The last thing to do is the potato cakes. After that, you can have a rest, and I'll finish up."

"I've slowed you down, sorry."

Oliver hip-checked him. "It's not a problem. We're doing good for time." They weren't. He *was* behind schedule, but he didn't care.

Dean grinned. "I won't remember any of this, you know."

"Doesn't matter. It'll be easier to remember when you do it for yourself."

When everything was cooking or resting, Oliver made them a coffee and sat at the table facing Dean.

"Would you like to visit the shelter with me?" Oliver surprised himself with the offer.

Dean's face lit up. "Sure. Does any of the food need to still be hot when it gets there?"

Oliver sipped his drink. "No. They will warm it up as needed. People drop by at all times of the day for food. It's why I make extra for them. It saves them having to have someone on hand to cook throughout the day, which costs extra money."

He explained the situation with Zee and what happened with the food when the supermarkets couldn't sell it anymore.

"Drink up. We need to get these into containers and get going."

Once more, Oliver noticed how easily they worked beside each other. If Dean had been part of his kitchen, he wouldn't have complained about his work ethic, that was for sure.

Chapter 5

Dean

Dean had never enjoyed cooking as much as he had during his time with Oliver. It could be because of the company itself, but no matter what it was, he was excited about trying out his new skills...what little he had. He planned to practise as much as he could, so he could cook something better for the station when it was his turn. Usually, he made jacket potatoes—which were easy for him—and salad, but he was determined to make something different to surprise them all. It had become a running joke, but Dean knew it was harmless teasing.

He carried several containers to Oliver's car, waiting while Oliver stacked them in a certain order to fit in his boot without spilling. Once they were ready, Oliver locked up his house and climbed into his car. Dean climbed onto his motorcycle and followed the chef through the streets of Cambridge to the shelter. There was no car park for them to stop in, but there was a small unloading area to the side of the building, and they parked there while they carted all the containers inside.

Inside, the shelter was surprisingly homey. Dean had never visited one before and had based his ideas on what he'd seen on TV, which he knew wasn't always true. The hallways throughout the building were dark and dank, but the main areas where people seemed to congregate were bright and airy. Dean followed Oliver through a large dining area—a nod towards his school dinner hall—to the kitchen area. He placed the food where Oliver pointed, and they walked back to the vehicles. Dean stepped back when a man came barrelling towards Oliver and wrapped him in a hug.

"Good morning! What have you got for us today?"

The man was older than Dean if the white streaking through his facial hair was anything to go by, and he was covered in freckles.

"Morning, Benny. This is Dean. He's a firefighter at Cam. He helped make all this for you today." Oliver smiled at Dean, and he felt his heart trip.

"I wouldn't say I helped as much as hindered." Dean rubbed his hand over his buzz cut.

Oliver nudged him. "You did well."

Dean lowered his eyes, knowing his cheeks were flushing. He wasn't someone who needed praise, but coming from Oliver, it felt different.

"Do you know Leona?" Benny asked. Dean nodded. "I'm her husband."

"Ah, that explains why your name was familiar, but I couldn't figure out why. Nice to meet you."

Leona was another firefighter but on a different crew to him. He saw her when they did changeover sometimes.

The station comprised four crews, but because of the shift pattern, Dean rarely saw anyone from Green Watch. Despite that, the crews often socialised together as a way of allowing those who never met to see each other.

"You've outdone yourself today, Oliver. I can't believe how much there is."

Oliver squeezed Benny's shoulder. "Zee did well with the bounty yesterday."

"Still. Thank you. As always, you're a lifesaver."

"Right. I better get to the restaurant. It doesn't run itself, after all."

Benny clasped a hand to Oliver's cheek and patted. "Take care of yourself, too." He flicked his gaze to Dean, then smiled at Oliver as he left.

Oliver didn't reply. He slammed the boot shut and faced Dean. "I need to get to the restaurant. When would you like your next lesson?"

Dean rubbed his nose as butterflies took flight in his stomach. "I'm working from tomorrow and will sleep through half of Saturday. How about Sunday?"

"Sunday is a busy day at the restaurant..." He licked his plump lips. "It could work if you wanted to meet early again like we did today?"

"I don't want to put too much on you. We can make it another day. You tell me when is best for you."

Oliver stepped closer, his gaze dropping from Dean's eyes to his lips if Dean wasn't mistaken. "Sunday morning is fine," he murmured.

Dean swallowed hard, inhaling through his nose. As much as he'd been telling himself he couldn't get involved with anyone else, if he had been able, Oliver would've been his first choice. It made Dean incapable of moving, and their staring match continued for several long minutes until Oliver closed his eyes and shook his head, stepping back.

Exhaling, Dean said, "Okay. Sunday it is."

Oliver smiled, though Dean could see it was with effort. There was a pain behind Oliver's eyes that Dean wanted to get rid of. He reminded himself he was in no position to help anyone when he had his own life to sort out first.

"Sunday."

Oliver skirted around his car to the driver's door and caught Dean's gaze once more before curling one side of his mouth and climbing into his car. As the chef's car reversed into the road, Dean held up a hand to wave goodbye, dropping it to his side and leaning back against his bike when Oliver was out of sight.

He had no idea how long he stood there, his thoughts tumbling through his mind when he heard a siren. Lifting his gaze, he tilted his head, trying to identify which direction it was coming from. He turned his head to the right in time to see the engine speed around the corner. He stood upright and gave a two-finger salute as it passed him. He saw Clay Osbourne driving and Wade Stewart in the front seat, and he sent his hopes and wishes with them. It was always difficult to see others run headlong into potential danger when he could help, but today wasn't his day unless they called him in.

Dean sighed. His mind whirled with images of Oliver, but he knew nothing could come from it. His work hadn't changed; it was still dangerous. He couldn't provide a stable home life for someone else when his job had so much uncertainty around it. He'd have to go it alone as much as that thought had his stomach feeling like lead.

"Scott, Evan, get the aerial platform in the air! I want water on that roof!" Jason shouted.

Dean was holding the hose on the corner of the office building, with Valerie doing the same on the other side, both aiming for the orange flames escaping through the broken windows. The call had come in the early afternoon, and luckily, the staff had evacuated before the building became too smoke-filled. By the time the fire engine had arrived, the flames had already overtaken most of one side of the ground floor of the building.

From what Jason had told them, a vending machine had caught fire in the staff kitchen. Several staff members had been on a break and had seen it happen, giving them the chance to tell everyone to get out. Naturally, the office was full of paper, and the fire was consuming every inch it could, even with the crews from several engines present. Dean knew from experience it was unlikely they'd save the building with how fast the fire was growing.

"Scott is in place. Water starting now," Evan called through the radio.

Dean braced himself. Sometimes, adding water from the roof would divert the flames elsewhere or make it worse for a few minutes before it helped. The heat seemed to increase a few degrees, sweat dripping down Dean's face and back while he concentrated on aiming at the flames.

"Dean, aim for—"

He heard nothing else Jason said because glass exploded outwards, showering them in fragments as the second floor went up in flames. Dean kept the hose in place but ducked his head and turned his eyes away from the unexpected shower. As soon as the glass stopped falling, he refocused on the building.

"Dean, aim for the first floor. Valerie, keep on the ground floor. Scott, how's the roof looking?" Jason said.

"Not good, sir. It's going to drop any time now," Scott growled through the radio.

"Firefighters! Step back!" Jason yelled.

The crews took several steps back from where they were aiming their hoses. There was no hope of saving the building now. Orange and yellow flames licked through the windows and doors, and Dean could see part of what Scott had a first-hand view of—flames escaping through the roof.

"It's going!" Scott bellowed several long minutes later, and not even a second passed before the roof collapsed, taking several windows with it. Most of it caved inwards, but some came diving from three stories up. Dean aimed the water at those flaming missiles as they crashed to the ground, sending sparks flying in different directions. Once he had extinguished those, Dean refocused on his target.

It took six hours to finally put out the fire. When he shut off his hose, he stopped and stared at the remains of the smouldering building. Fire was a beast that took no prisoners, and every time Dean saw the result, it reminded him of that fact.

Dean, Valerie, Scott and Evan tidied their equipment while Jason spoke with the other watch commanders. When the man came over, he appeared as weary as the rest of them did.

"Let's head back."

The journey back to the station was quiet, which was the result when such a big fire happened. The positives Dean took from it was that no one was hurt, and they contained it enough to not spread to neighbouring buildings.

When Scott parked the engine, they all climbed down, meeting the crew who were taking over from them. It was an hour past his shift end, but that meant nothing when fire was involved. He removed his kit and dropped it by his locker, grabbing his shower stuff and a towel. He'd have another shower when he got home, but he didn't want to put clean clothes on over soot and smoke-stained skin.

He yawned when he strode back to his locker. At least he had a full twenty-four hours before he had to be back on shift. Tonight was for relaxing and catching up with his TV shows. He bid goodbye to everyone he saw on the way to his bike. As he flung his leg over the seat, he caught sight of two bright eyes in the bushes to the side of the station. He'd been told about the station's night-time visitor but had yet to see it. Dean started the night shift tomorrow. The inquisitive animal might come and visit.

The eyes disappeared when Dean started the engine, and he roared out of the car park. Reaching home in good time, he showered while he tried to decide which takeaway he wanted that night. He'd wanted to visit Nourris Moi but didn't want to be a stalker. Despite all his reservations about being in a relationship, his brain kept reminding him how much he wanted something with Oliver.

Brushing aside his wayward thoughts once more, he ordered Chinese food and dropped onto the sofa, dialling a number.

"Hey, Dad. How are you?"

His father coughed. "Full of cold, but I'm all right. Sadie is looking after me."

Sadie was his father's girlfriend. They had been together for the last five years, and Dean knew they were perfect for each other. He had been on cloud nine when his father had taken a chance on Sadie when she'd asked him out six years after his wife—Dean's mother—had died. Dean would never begrudge his dad the opportunity to find someone who meant the world to him.

"I'm glad. I hope you're resting up. You've taken time off work, haven't you?" Dean doubted it.

"Actually, yes. I took yesterday and today off. I'm feeling a lot better than I had been. I know I'm on the mend."

"Glad to hear it." His father's cough rattled through the phone. "Keep an eye on that cough though."

"I will. How are things with you? Still enjoying the station?"

Dean smiled. "Yeah. Everyone is great." His mind flicked to Evan, but he ignored his unease about the man. "I wish I'd known about this place years ago."

"Pfft. You knew about it when you needed it most."

Dean chuckled. His dad was all for fate and things happening for a reason. Dean wasn't sure, but he didn't argue.

"Without a doubt. I've found an amazing restaurant to take you to when you visit. The food is to die for." Paul wouldn't mind Dean pinching his phrase.

"It doesn't give you those tiny, fancy portions, does it? You know I can't stand those." His father laughed, which turned into a coughing fit. Dean's heart broke at how ill he sounded. There was silence for a minute. "Sorry about that. I needed a drink."

"Are you okay?"

"Yeah, I'm good."

Dean's doorbell sounded, and he rose, opening the door when he got there. He took the proffered food and mouthed a thank you to the delivery guy. He'd already paid online and didn't need to worry about that.

"Let me know when you can come for a visit, and I'll book us a table. And no, it doesn't have fancy portions. They're properly sized and delicious." Dean strode to the kitchen, placing the bag on the counter.

"Sounds enjoyable. I'll talk to Sadie and work out when we can get time off."

"Great." He hooked the phone between his ear and shoulder and grabbed a plate.

"I'm going to go, Dean. I need to get some more medicine and find my bed."

"All right, Dad. Get well soon, you hear?"

"Doing my best, son."

Dean put the phone in his pocket and tipped the contents of the container onto his plate. He could've eaten from the container, but it felt lazy doing that—not that ordering takeaway wasn't lazy in the first place. Shaking his head at his inner thoughts, he acknowledged he needed a few more lessons from Oliver before he'd attempt to make anything on his own.

Flicking on *Battlestar Galactica*, he settled on the sofa and devoured the greasy but tasty food. He'd lost count of how many times he'd watched the TV series, but it was his go-to programme when he was restless or couldn't decide what to watch.

It was nearing ten in the evening when his phone rang. Frowning, he answered, "Jason? What's up?"

"Hey, Dean. Do you fancy coming out for a beer? We're meeting up at Crush."

Dean leaned his elbow on his knee. "I would've thought you'd be resting up."

"Nah, I try not to go to sleep before 4 a.m. because I'll wake too early for the night shift."

Dean chuckled. "Yeah, me too." He paused. "Sure, why not."

"Woohoo! Do you know where it is?"

"No, but I'm sure I can figure it out." He strode down the hallway to his bedroom, yanking his T-shirt off and replacing the phone at his ear.

"—a few of the others, too."

"Sorry, say again."

"I've managed to get a few of the others, too. I'm sure we can make a night of it."

Dean snorted. "I can imagine you're a handful, Jason."

"Hey! Don't knock it until you've seen me in action!" Jason laughed. "I'm heading there now. I'll see you when you get there."

Dean changed into jeans and a shirt to help him fit in at a bar better than what he had been wearing. Slipping his wallet and phone into his pockets, he grabbed his keys and locked the apartment before aiming for the bar. Luckily, he found a parking space close by—it was a little easier with a motorcycle—and strode for the entrance. What should he expect from a Wednesday night? As soon as he entered, he knew it was his kind of place. Music played in the background but wasn't overwhelmingly loud. Conversation was a steady hum, and it wasn't overly crowded. The bar stood to the right of the room with tables spread out in the centre and booths set around the perimeter.

It was in one of these booths that he noticed Evan and Valerie. Sighing, he skirted the room until he reached the table.

"Dean!" Valerie jumped up and threw her arms around his neck, obviously tipsy. "See! I said you'd like Crush!"

"Hi, Valerie." He disentangled her and helped her back into her seat.

"Yo, Dean!"

He peered over his shoulder and saw Jason at the bar. Jason mimed a drink, and Dean nodded and called, "Any kind of beer!" Turning back to the table, he caught Evan's lip curl but ignored it. Scott sat furthest into the booth and

Dean didn't want to crowd him, so grabbed a chair from another table and set it at the end.

"Hey, Dean. Nice of you to join us."

He stood again and stepped closer to the booth next to theirs, holding out his hand to shake Matias's. Matias Lopez worked on Blue Watch. Glancing around the table, he saw two other firefighters—one from Green Watch, another from Blue Watch, which was surprising because Blue Watch was on an early shift tomorrow—and two men he didn't recognise.

"Glad I could get here. I didn't realise you'd be here, too. I thought with you starting early, you'd be sleeping."

"Yeah, we love it here. You know Layton and Malachi. This is Joey and Kade. They're police detectives."

Dean shook everyone's hands. "Nice to meet you."

A beer appeared in front of him, and he took it with a grin towards Jason. "Thanks. I'm sure I'll see you again." He nodded to the occupants of the booth and returned to his own crew. It wasn't that he didn't want to get to know the others, but Jason was the one who'd invited him, and he didn't want to offend anyone.

"Glad you know where you belong," Evan said.

Dean took a long swallow of his beer. It was going to be a long night if he had to put up with snide comments like that. He focused on the story Jason was telling using the salt and pepper pots, trying to ignore Evan.

Chapter 6

Oliver

The week had gone by at a snail's pace, but finally, it was Sunday morning. Once more, Oliver had not slept much. He was like a little kid on Christmas Eve. Dean had not visited Nourris Moi at all, and Oliver was disappointed. He would've loved to spoil the man. Instead, he'd needed to wait and be patient.

He had finished making some homemade croissants as the doorbell chimed. Wiping his hands on a towel, he shuffled towards the door. Dean stood on his doorstep, looking fresh as a daisy for eight in the morning.

"Good morning," he said, indicating for Dean to enter.

"Morning." Dean shoved his hands in the pockets of his jeans, and Oliver closed the door behind him.

"Are you ready for a busy morning?" Oliver winked. Dean gave a small smile, but nothing like what he had on his previous visit. "Is everything okay?"

Dean nodded. "Yes. Everything's fine. Why wouldn't it be?"

Oliver bit back his first retort. "You looked a little out of sorts. Do you still want me to show you how to cook?"

"Yes! Please. I'm sorry. Work has drained me a little this week."

Moving slowly to stop Dean from potentially recoiling, Oliver reached for his shoulder and squeezed it. "If you need to talk..." He left the end of the sentence off, knowing Dean would get the idea.

Dean met his gaze. "Thanks."

Those few moments were charged with tension, but Oliver couldn't make himself break away. Instead, he slid his hand up to the column of Dean's neck and cupped the side, his thumb rubbing along his jawline. He felt Dean swallow yet couldn't move his gaze away from his dark brown eyes. The colour reminded him of the different shades of brown found on shiny conkers. Dean's tongue peeked out and wet his lips, and Oliver's focus moved to those thin lips.

He inhaled shakily and stepped back, his hand dropping to his side. Clearing his throat, he attempted to diffuse the atmosphere, "We have a lot of work to do. Are you up for the challenge?"

Dean smirked. "Always willing to try." He slipped his jacket off and hung it on the hooks by the door.

Oliver tried not to ogle him too much and whirled towards the kitchen. Exhaling, he put the towel on the side and waited for Dean to reach him.

"We don't have as much food to work with today, but we don't have as long to do it either. Don't worry if you don't understand what I'm telling you while I do something, okay? We'll have plenty more lessons where I can explain it better."

"I don't want to slow you down." Dean rubbed his nose.

"If we get close to time, I'll take over. There's no way it will take too long because there are two pairs of hands doing the work now. If necessary, you can help with the prep, and I'll handle the cooking, but we'll play it by ear."

Dean nibbled his lower lip but nodded. "All right. Bring it on."

They worked side by side, near enough their shoulders and arms brushed regularly despite it not being necessary for them to be so close because of how big Oliver's kitchen was. The intense awareness warmed Oliver's body, and it took everything in him to shove it down and not do anything about it. He wanted nothing more than to worship the man's body, but it was time he didn't have. That was the crux of the matter.

"Why don't you grab yourself a drink while I finish these?" Oliver said.

"Do you need anything put in containers yet?"

Oliver shook his head. "They can stay where they are for the moment."

Dean washed and dried his hands before opening the fridge. "Do you mind if I have a glass of milk?"

"Go ahead."

Oliver tried to concentrate on what he was doing instead of Dean's movements, but it was difficult. When he finished the last item, he turned all the burners off as well as the oven, then twisted around to see Dean sitting at the table, his hand around an empty glass, his heated gaze on Oliver. Swallowing hard, Oliver inhaled and blew out a breath.

"All done. Now, only the delivery to do, and I can get to the restaurant. Sundays are one of our busiest days because everyone wants roast dinners."

Dean smiled. "I can imagine. Nothing beats a roast."

Oliver tilted his head. "Are you going to be dropping by today?" He couldn't help but ask.

"Not today. Paul and Quinn have invited me to their house for lunch."

"Ah, understandable. That man would do well in my kitchen. If he ever wanted a new career, I'd be delighted to hire him."

Dean chuckled. "I'll let him know."

"Oh, I've told him many times, but he insists he's not accomplished enough." Oliver began transferring some of the food to the waiting containers, Dean coming to help until everything was ready to go.

"Would you like me to deliver these for you? You could get to the restaurant quicker."

Oliver stared at him, heart racing. "No, I can't ask you to do that."

"You're not asking. I'm offering."

Oliver licked his lips and tried to decide what to do. On one hand, he wanted to deliver it because he always had, though he wouldn't have denied Dean the chance to go with him to extend their time together. On the other hand, he could do with the extra time at the restaurant.

"On one condition?"

Dean's eyes sparkled. "What's that?"

"You come by the restaurant after you've been to Paul's, and I'll give you some dessert."

He hadn't meant for the invite to sound dirty unless it was his mind that had made it seem that way. Chancing a glance at Dean's expression, it wasn't only his brain that had taken that turn.

"Deal," Dean rasped.

"Thank you. It would make my life a little...wait. Don't you have a motorcycle?" Oliver frowned at Dean.

Dean's mouth twitched. "I was going to offer to deliver the food anyway because I knew you were busy. I have a car and a bike; I prefer the bike."

Oliver raised his eyebrows and stared at the man, gobs-macked. Dean fidgeted under his scrutiny, but Oliver felt overwhelmed by the generosity. He shifted closer until they were toe to toe, then gripped the back of Dean's neck and pulled him in for a hug. He hadn't planned on doing it but was glad when Dean's arm slid around his waist and flattened against his back. Dean hadn't rested his chin on Oliver's shoulder like he'd expected him to; he'd tucked his face into Oliver's neck, and he could feel the warm breath caressing his skin.

They held each other for several long minutes. It took every piece of strength inside Oliver to step back, though he couldn't resist skimming his palm along Dean's cheek as he removed it.

"Thank you. I appreciate your help."

"You're welcome." Dean thumbed over his shoulder. "I better get all this in the car and get going."

He helped Dean fill the car, and sooner than he wanted, they had finished. They faced each other on the driveway, Dean flicking his keys in his hand.

"Thank you again."

Dean nodded, and Oliver leaned forward, aiming a kiss to his cheek, but Dean turned his head, and the kiss glanced off the corner of his mouth instead. Oliver gritted his teeth to stop him from doing something stupid and stepped back. Dean grinned, and Oliver rolled his eyes.

"Go before I make you peel three bags of potatoes as punishment."

"What did I do?" Dean held his hands out, feigning innocence.

Oliver withheld a grin and pointed at the car.

"See you later," were Dean's parting words.

Oliver watched Dean drive away, his hand reaching through the open window to wave back at Oliver. There was more between them than Oliver had expected, but he couldn't stop wondering how they would even begin to figure out the long hours and shift patterns if they ever tried for a relationship.

He shook his head and entered the house. Why was he even trying to figure anything out? Hadn't he decided he was going to stay alone to make things easier on everyone?

Twelve hours later, there was still no sign of Dean, and Oliver couldn't help but worry about whether they had called Dean into work or if he'd backed off because Oliver had come on stronger than he'd meant to. It was closing in on eleven in the evening, and Oliver's feet were aching more than they had done in weeks. He wandered through the dining area of Nourris Moi, smiling at the guests and snatching small conversations with people he knew, which were most of them.

The closer closing time came, the more dejected he felt, and he remained in the kitchen for the rest of the night, helping the others to clean up the area.

"Boss? There's someone here to see you." Jack stuck his head through the door with a smirk.

Oliver's heart skipped a beat, and his stomach churned. "Dean?"

Jack nodded and disappeared, the black door flicking back and forth until it settled.

"Go and see him. We can finish the rest of this," Selena said, pushing against his shoulder.

Oliver cleared his throat and reached into the fridge for the slice of chocolate cake he'd saved for Dean. He picked up a fork and inhaled, stepping through the door and licking his lips when he saw Dean looking divine in different clothes from what he'd been wearing that morning with a well-loved leather jacket.

"I didn't think you were going to make it," he said, nodding his head for Dean to follow him to a table at the back of the room. No one should disturb them because they had already cleaned this area.

Dean slipped into the seat opposite him, and Oliver pushed the plate towards him. The firefighter's gaze never wavered from his own.

"Are we on the same wavelength here?"

Dean's question was unexpected but to the point. Oliver stared at his hands as his fingers threaded through each other. He wasn't sure how he could explain what a relationship with him would be like without sounding bitter. Dean saved him from replying straight away by tucking into the cake and moaning.

Oliver licked his lips. "Can we see what happens? You know how busy my life is. I don't want to...put any pressure on us."

Dean studied him. "One step on a ladder at a time," he murmured.

Oliver's mouth dried up as he watched Dean devour the cake, except for the last bite, which he put on the fork and held out to Oliver. He leaned forward and closed his lips around the tines, his attention never leaving Dean. He saw Dean's breath hitch when the fork came back empty. Oliver chewed. Where were they going with this? Was he getting his hopes up for nothing?

"Stop thinking so hard."

Oliver chuckled at Dean's words. "I need to close the place up. Will you wait?"

"Longer than I should."

The whispered words sank deep inside Oliver, and he closed his eyes for a second. Sliding out of the seat, he took the plate and fork into the kitchen, washing them by hand and checking in with the staff before they left for the night. Jack came back from seeing the women to their cars—not because the women couldn't fend for themselves, but because the streets were not secure at night and there was safety in numbers as far as he was concerned—and checked in with him before Oliver locked up behind the bartender, but not before Jack had given him a cheeky wink.

As the lock clicked, he felt heat at his back. His eyelids drifted closed as hands smoothed up his back, massaging away the aches. Dropping his head forward when Dean's large, warm hands rubbed into his shoulders, he groaned.

"What else do you need to check?"

Warm air coasted across his ear, and he shivered, trying to think of his answer. "Um...oh, god...your hands are magic," he mumbled.

Dean chuckled and withdrew his hands, and Oliver stopped a whimper from escaping. He rested his head against the doorframe, then pivoted around. "I have to check over the place to make sure it's ready for tomorrow."

"I'll be waiting."

The only thing Oliver could do was push Dean to the back of his mind while he finished up. It was easier said than done, though, because Dean followed him from room to room, watching what he was doing. It was unnerving but arousing in the same breath. When he finally collected his coat from the office, his blood pressure was through the roof. What he wanted to happen that night was also what shouldn't happen, but he wasn't strong enough to stop it.

Without words, they left the restaurant through the back door, Oliver locking up behind him, the heat of the night not helping to cool his ardour. He ambled to his car, fidgeting with his keys. Normally, confident in his words, he was unable to verbalise anything that would make sense. Hands rested on his shoulders and whirled him around when they reached his car.

"Should I follow you home?"

The banked heat shone in Dean's eyes, and Oliver was helpless against it. This might be a mistake, but he wouldn't regret it.

"Yes," he whispered.

Dean stared at him for a second longer, then lowered his head, pressing a gentle kiss at the corner of Oliver's mouth. "Be careful while driving. I'll see you there." He strode to his bike, and Oliver watched as he unhooked his helmet and pulled it on. His breath exhaled in a rush as Dean swung a leg over the back of the bike. There was something about the action that was fucking sexy. Oliver could watch it all night.

Swallowing to get his mouth unglued, he climbed into his car, throwing his coat on the passenger seat. It took him a couple of tries to get the key in to start the engine. He closed his eyes for a few seconds, gripping the steering wheel until the growl of the motorcycle startled him. Oliver huffed a laugh and shook his head. How old was he? He was acting like a first-time lover.

Clicking his belt into place, he reversed the car out of the space and, without looking at Dean, drove home. If his hands slipped on the wheel more times than usual or his breathing sounded laboured, then so be it. He wanted this, but he was nervous as hell. His body was not what most people would call hot or sexy, and most of the time, he could forget about it when he scratched his itch because it was always with someone he'd never see again. He made sure of that. Doing this with someone close to home...he was extremely nervous. What if how he looked turned Dean off? He'd have to remember to turn the lights off. The only problem was he wouldn't be able to see Dean, which would be a travesty.

His home appeared before him, though he couldn't remember any of the journey. Taking another deep breath, he grabbed his coat, but before he could exit, his door opened, and Dean was there, holding his hand out for Oliver to take. The moment he slipped his hand into Dean's, his fears quietened.

"You're sure?" Dean asked, meeting Oliver's gaze.

Oliver smiled. "Without a doubt." It wasn't quite true, but his doubts were about himself, but Dean didn't need to know that.

Dean rested his hand on Oliver's lower back as they walked up to the front door and entered, Dean locking the door. They removed their shoes and coats and made their way to the stairs. Oliver's heart was racing as he pulled himself up using the bannister. He was a little out of breath by the time he reached the top, but he soon recovered, only for his breath to be taken again after Dean had followed him into his bedroom and closed the door behind them.

Oliver stepped closer to the bed, his hands wringing in front of him. He hadn't expected to have visitors and checked over for any damning evidence of his messiness. His kitchen was always spotless, but his bedroom...

He knew the moment Dean moved closer, the warmth against his back, the heat from his breathing fanning across his neck, made him a little lightheaded. When Dean's warm lips touched the side of his neck, Oliver twitched. He exhaled roughly, and a light chuckle drifted to his ears. Hands smoothed up Oliver's back, over his shoulders and down his arms, until Dean threaded their fingers together and crossed them over Oliver's stomach. Dean lowered his chin to his shoulder, and they stood, breathing together, for several long moments. Oliver wasn't sure how to begin to understand what was happening between them, but in the next moment, Dean took his focus.

Dean peppered kisses on whatever skin he could find, with Oliver leaning his head to the side, giving him more access. When Dean's mouth followed the line of Oliver's jaw, Oliver dropped his head back. One of Dean's hands untangled from his and cupped the opposite jaw, turning Oliver's head towards him. When their lips finally met, there was no stopping the explosion of heat that flowed through Oliver's body.

Dean used his lips, tongue and teeth to tease and tantalise Oliver until he was a trembling mass of bones. When his legs were ready to give way, Dean twisted him around until they were facing each other, their lips never leaving the other's.

Oliver's arms slid around Dean's waist, gripping the fabric of his T-shirt. Dean cupped the back of Oliver's head while he devoured him. The need for air warred with the need for more, but the air won. Oliver tore his mouth away, inhaling. Dean rested their foreheads together as they recovered.

Dean's hands skimmed down Oliver's chest to the hem of his T-shirt. Despite the arousal coursing through his body, Oliver tensed but didn't stop Dean from lifting it.

Chapter 7

Dean

Dean could tell Oliver was tense, but he wasn't sure why. He kissed Oliver again, softly and carefully, before pulling back to look at him.

"Are you okay with this?"

Oliver's eyes were wide, and his breath a little choppy, but he nodded. "I'm more than okay with this. It's...I know I'm not..." Oliver waved a hand at his body, his cheeks darkening, and Dean didn't think it was from lust.

"You're not what?" Dean didn't want to do anything to upset Oliver, but he wasn't sure what the man was saying.

Oliver sighed and dropped his gaze, then rolled his shoulders and stared at him again. "I don't look like you. I'm not fit nor muscular, only big and flabby. I don't want you to be disappointed," he finished in a whisper, lowering his eyes again.

Dean stopped his initial denial from leaving his lips, knowing Oliver needed more than general platitudes. He considered his words before reaching for Oliver's chin to lift his head. When they were staring at each other again,

Dean said, "I don't see you the way you see yourself. I see a man who is kind-hearted, generous, overworked and stressed. I can't be disappointed because I already know who you are. I also know you won't believe my words. Let me show you with actions."

He waited while Oliver studied him, and he saw the moment Oliver decided. "Okay. Show me."

Dean smiled and lifted Oliver's T-shirt over his head before he could change his mind—though Dean would stop if Oliver asked him to—and took his mouth in another blistering kiss. Their tongues twined and tangled, their lips sucked and sipped, their teeth nipped and bit. They came up for air again, and Oliver yanked Dean's T-shirt over his head, caressing his skin and pressing kisses to his collarbone.

"You are pure muscle," Oliver murmured against his skin.

"Hazard of the job." Dean grinned.

Oliver gave a small smile, but Dean knew doubts were lingering behind those shadows in his eyes. He leaned down a little and gripped Oliver's legs, lifting him and stalking over to the bed.

Oliver scrambled to hold his neck. "No! You'll hurt yourself! Put me down!"

Dean did, but only when they reached the bed where he had planned to lay him down anyway. "I'm fine."

He braced his hands on either side of Oliver's head, staring at him. Lowering his head, he kissed Oliver again, losing himself in the feel and taste of the man. There was a slight hint of chocolate remaining, and it went well with his own taste. Dean left his lips and journeyed down his neck, shoulder and chest, flicking his tongue over the extended nipples. Oliver hummed and whimpered beneath him.

Dean understood Oliver's fears; he was overweight, but Dean wasn't attracted to someone because of how they looked—or rather, not only because of how they looked. The person had to have a friendly personality to go with it; otherwise, all the looks in the world couldn't make Dean like them. That was what he saw in Oliver, but he doubted Oliver would believe him yet. He'd keep working on him.

The thought had him frowning, although his mouth didn't stop tasting and teasing. He always listened to other people's concerns about their bodies when he slept with them; he always told them how he saw them as he had with Oliver, but there was something about Oliver that had him wanting to give him more. There hadn't been a plan to get deeper into a relationship when he was new to the area. They could make this a regular de-stressing for them both if Oliver was on board with the idea. He'd ask him later.

Concentrating on giving Oliver as much pleasure as he could, he descended further, his lips and hands caressing Oliver's chest and sides remaining aware of any places which made Oliver tense. Dean wouldn't ignore those areas, but he'd be more careful of them.

He reached the waistband of Oliver's trousers, slid a finger inside and followed the band. Peering up at Oliver, he waited for a sign he could remove them, but it was only when he tugged at the band again that Oliver nodded. He kissed his stomach and lifted the elasticated fabric off his stomach, and pulled them down his legs, leaving Oliver in his boxers. Once he'd thrown them behind him somewhere, he lowered his head to where the waistband had been, the indents visible on Oliver's skin. Dean kissed the raised skin, then rose to tower over him.

"Are you okay?" he asked after a gentle kiss.

"Good," Oliver croaked. "I want to taste you."

Dean closed his eyes and bit his lip, his hand pressing against his groin to keep his cock from erupting at the words. "Okay."

He pulled Oliver to standing, and they swapped positions, Dean laying with his hand behind his head, propped on a pillow to see everything. Oliver crawled between his thighs, his movements hesitant. Dean slid his hand down his own chest, reaching for the button on his jeans, but Oliver slapped away his hand.

"Mine." Oliver narrowed his eyes at him, and Dean chuckled at the show but nodded.

Oliver's mouth played havoc with Dean's body. He couldn't remember the last time he'd been so aroused. It had been months since he'd last fucked anyone, and even then, it hadn't felt like this. Oliver slid Dean's zipper down and dragged the jeans from his body. His briefs contained his cock, and Dean could see a wet patch at his tip seeping through the fabric. Oliver dived straight for that patch, licking over it while his hands skimmed over Dean's abs.

Dean groaned and rested his hand on the back of Oliver's head when Oliver lifted his briefs off his dick. They disappeared in the same way his jeans had, and seconds later, Oliver's hand wrapped around his shaft. Dean pushed his head back into the pillow, his abs clenching as Oliver licked the head.

"Fucking hell."

Dean flickered his eyes open to stare at Oliver when the man engulfed his cock. His orgasm barrelled forward, and he pulled Oliver off and up, kissing him hard while he encircled both their shafts in one hand. It was awkward, and Dean knew it wouldn't work to bring them off.

"Lube?" he asked.

Oliver blinked and nodded to the bedside table. Dean reached and found a tube, then rolled onto his side, directing Oliver to lie beside him, his back to Dean's chest. After explaining his plan and getting Oliver's agreement, Dean lubed his cock, then added more to his hand and wrapped it around Oliver's dick. He stroked several times, and Oliver rolled his head to the side, panting. Dean slid his cock between Oliver's thighs, the lube easing his way, and the tip nudged against Oliver's balls.

"Oh, fuck, yes." Oliver bit his bottom lip and closed his eyes.

Dean timed his thrusts with the strokes of his hand on Oliver's cock. He mouthed at Oliver's shoulder, licking and biting at the skin the closer he came to climax.

"I'm almost there," Oliver gasped.

Dean increased his speed, sending Oliver over the edge with a shout. He continued his movements, concentrating on the feeling of his cock tunnelling through Oliver's legs, the slight catch of his tip on his balls. He shuddered when he felt something touch the underside of his cock and glanced at Oliver, who was smiling over his shoulder at him. Oliver's fingers skimmed across the nerve bundle as Dean thrust again. With the extra stimulation, it didn't take him long to empty himself all over Oliver.

He lay panting into Oliver's neck as they came down. Pulling back from him, Dean hissed at his sensitive cock, then pushed Oliver to his back and spread his legs. When Oliver gasped, Dean threaded the fingers of one hand into Oliver's hand and used his other to check that he hadn't left Oliver sore. With the amount of lube he'd used, he was sure Oliver would be fine, but he needed to be sure. He couldn't see any chafed areas and relaxed a little.

"Do you feel all right?"

Oliver smiled and nodded. "Sleepy, which is a wonderful thing."

"Do you not sleep much?"

"No. Usually only four hours."

Dean frowned. "Why's that?"

Oliver sat upright, pulling the cover over his body. "Too much buzzing around in my head, I think. It's fine. I'm used to it."

"Will a shower wake you up more or make you more tired?"

"Regardless, I'm having one," Oliver said with a grin.

Dean smiled. "I can change the covers while you do if you tell me where they are."

Oliver waved him away. "I can do it, don't worry." He licked his lips. "Do you want to stay? You could have another lesson in the morning?"

He sighed. "As much as I would love to, I think it would be better if I went home. I don't want to crowd you."

The light in Oliver's eyes dimmed, but his mouth curled upwards. "Okay."

Dean leaned forward, kissing Oliver soundly. "But...I would be glad to have a repeat of today if you decide you want to." He held up his hands when Oliver opened his mouth to reply. "Think about it first. I don't want to make things uncomfortable for you. If you decide you want to, let me know. If not, that's fine. No hard feelings."

Oliver's eyes bored into him, and Dean let him look until he nodded once, as if making a decision. "I'll think about it."

Dean pressed another kiss to Oliver's lips. "Make sure you have a quick shower, then get into bed. Get some sleep while your body lets you." He rose, gathering his clothing and dressing, while Oliver watched with a small smile. When he was ready, he stepped closer again. "I'll see myself out, and I'll put the key through the letterbox." He leaned down again, not wanting to leave him but knowing he needed to.

"Bye, Dean."

"Night."

By the front door, he pulled on his boots and leather jacket before doing as he'd said, locking the door behind him, then posting the key through the letterbox. As his bike roared through the night, he smiled. He hoped there would be more nights like tonight.

"Dean, Valerie, you're going in. Mask up," Jason shouted.

Dean slid the breathing apparatus onto his face, tightening the straps and pulling the hood over his head to protect his lower neck and head. His helmet was next. He checked over Valerie's, who then checked over his, and they were heading inside.

The building was full of thick, grey smoke, but they had some visibility. They checked the rooms of the house because a neighbour had said the owner was in there.

"I can't see anyone," Valerie stated.

"Me ne—"

A groan caught his attention, and he tilted his head to the side. Another moan took him in the direction of the back bedroom. The door was closed, and he checked the temperature of the handle before opening the door. A shadow was curled up beneath the window, and Dean rushed over.

"Sir? Can you hear me?" A groan was his only answer. "I'm going to help you out. Stand up for me."

He guided the man to his feet, though he was coughing so much, he could barely stand, no doubt from how much smoke he'd inhaled. The man lifted his gaze, frowned, then pushed away from Dean. Dean tried to grab him again to stop him from falling, but the man punched at him, dropping Dean to the floor. His mask came off, and smoke filled his lungs. His eyes watered as he scrambled to his feet.

"Dean! Are you okay?"

"I'm fine. Get him out of here." Dean leaned his hands on his knees, coughing. "Sir, we need to get out of here."

"Stay the fuck away from me! I know who you are! I don't need some gay kid like you touching me!" The man bent over, coughing again.

"Okay, sir. We won't touch you, but we need to get out of here."

Valerie signalled for the man to go first, and she stayed close by in case he fell. Dean reached for his mask, fitting it over his face before realising no air was getting in. Walking down the hallway, he saw a tube had come loose on his mask, and he shook his head, coughing and hacking. They had trained him to withstand a certain amount of smoke, but this was more than he'd ever experienced without his breathing apparatus.

He descended the stairs, holding the bannister when coughing stopped him from being able to walk, then carried on again. As he reached the last step, Valerie came back in and helped him out.

"That asshole has a lot to answer for," she muttered.

Dean couldn't reply; his throat was too sore, and he couldn't breathe properly. Valerie guided him over to the ambulance, and he sat on the step to let the paramedic check him over. They removed his helmet and hood.

"You must be new. I've not seen you before."

Dean glanced up, seeing a dark-haired guy in front of him. "Yeah," he rasped.

The paramedic shined a light in his eyes, and Dean fought to stay still. "Nice to meet you. I'm Casey."

"Dean." He dissolved into coughing again, and Casey rested an oxygen mask over his nose and mouth.

"That's it. Keep that there, Dean. You'll be right as rain in no time." Casey slid the penlight into his pocket. "What happened?"

"Yeah, I want to know that, too." Jason stopped beside the paramedic.

Dean inhaled the oxygen and tried to talk through the mask. "Guy didn't want to be touched. He punched me, knocking my mask off. I couldn't put it back on because it pulled the tube free." He coughed again, leaning forward to rest his elbows on his knees.

"Asshole!" Casey said.

"Did he say why?" Jason asked.

Dean shrugged. "Said he didn't want some gay kid like me touching him."

Jason shook his head. "We get them now and then, but it's not as bad as it used to be, thankfully. I'll speak to the chief when we get back and see what he wants to do." He squeezed Dean's shoulder. "Rest up. The fire's out. There's a damn load of smoke to clear."

Dean closed his eyes, breathing the oxygen and hacking up his lungs.

The ambulance transported him to the hospital a few minutes later, and they kept him on oxygen for a while. A doctor checked him over and deemed him fit enough to leave but impressed the importance of taking it easy for the next few days. Dean agreed. At least he had the next twenty-four hours off but would start a night shift the following evening.

The whole crew turned up, worse for wear, before they discharged him.

"What are you all doing here?"

Jason stepped forward. "When one of us gets hurt, we check in and make sure they're okay."

"Oh, thanks." Dean had never had that happen before.

"It's only a quick visit anyway because we know you're out in a few minutes. We've wheeled your bike into the station. It can stay there until tomorrow."

Paul entered the room to give him a ride home, ushering everyone else out the door with rapid goodbyes. "Do you want to stay with us tonight?" he asked once they were in the car.

Dean smiled. "Thanks, but I'll be fine. I'll sleep it off." His voice was still hoarse and would be for a few days.

"Well, make sure you ring us if you need anything." Paul sighed, resting his elbow on the car door and his head on his hand. "The world is a lot more forgiving of people's differences than it was a few years back, but it still has a long way to go. Do you want to press charges against the man?"

Dean thought about it but shook his head. "No point. It won't change his views."

"No, but it might make others think twice about doing it."

Dean watched the buildings drift by but came out of his stupor when Paul parked in front of his building. "Thanks."

"You're welcome. Rest easy tonight." Paul reached over to the backseat. "Oh, you don't have to cook tonight. I grabbed you some food." Paul passed over the bag with a grin. "Oliver says get well soon."

Dean ducked his head, his cheeks heating. "Thanks. I appreciate it."

"See you tomorrow, Dean."

He watched as Paul drove away, then entered the apartment building. By the time he'd entered his place, the only thing he wanted to do was sleep, but he needed to eat. He dropped into the chair at the table and opened the box to find beef casserole. He hadn't realised Nourris Moi did takeaway food; he thought it was sit-in dining.

As he worked his way through the food, he thought about everything that had happened since he started at Cam. Evan had been making snide comments since he'd arrived, which made him think he wasn't LGBTQ+ friendly, but then second-guessed himself because Paul was unlikely to let it slide if he wasn't. It could be *him* that Evan didn't like. Then the guy tonight being pissy because he didn't want Dean to help him—as if the man could "catch" being gay from him. Dean sighed and packed away the empty containers.

All in all, his move to Cambridge had been the best idea, but occasionally, he felt like he was back where he'd been before, and that pissed him off royally.

Paul was right about one thing: he should press charges against the man. It would make an example out of him. Dean's only reservation was that it could also bring a lot more harm to the fire station than good.

Chapter 8

Oliver

When Paul had turned up at the restaurant and asked to speak to him, he'd thought the worst. After explaining the situation and saying he was going to pick Dean up from the hospital, Paul had apologetically mentioned collecting some food from the fast-food place around the corner, but Oliver had stopped him. He'd grabbed a couple of containers and filled one with beef casserole and the other with a slice of strawberry cheesecake. The restaurant didn't have a takeaway service, but he needed to let Dean know he was thinking about him.

The knowing smirk on Paul's face made Oliver's cheeks heat, but he'd stood his ground. Paul had left with a grumbled remark about favouritism, but for the rest of the evening, Oliver felt out of sorts. Despite how late it was, he decided to drop by Dean's apartment—which he'd mentioned in passing during one of their conversations while cooking. He hoped he wouldn't interrupt Dean's sleep, but he didn't think he would because he was starting a night shift the following day. At least, he thought he would be working. From what Paul had said, it wasn't enough to stop Dean from continuing in his role.

He stood, holding a fruit salad he'd thrown together with the remainders of the fruit from that day, and inhaled several times, unsure of Dean's potential reaction. Knocking, he waited. If Dean didn't answer at the sound, he'd go home and call him the following day.

When the door opened, Dean was wearing some joggers and nothing else. Bare chest and bare feet greeted Oliver, and he was bowled over at the vision Dean provided.

"Hey! What are you doing here?" Dean's voice was raspy, which added to the sexy display.

"Hi—" He coughed to clear his throat. "Hi. I didn't wake you, did I?"

Dean opened the door further, jerking his head for Oliver to enter. Oliver's gaze roamed the small area, which was filled with furniture. It looked lived-in, but it had a comfortable air to it and wasn't at all messy—not that he'd expected it to be.

"Is everything okay?"

Oliver transferred his gaze from the room to Dean and held out the fruit bowl. "I thought something soft would help your throat. It's some fruit, but if you put it in the fridge for a little while, the coolness might help, too."

Dean stared down at the bowl. "Thanks."

"I don't want to disturb you. I'll…" He pointed to the door.

"Do you have time for a drink?"

Oliver exhaled, his shoulders loosening. "If you're sure I'm not intruding."

Dean headed through a doorway on the left, and Oliver followed, seeing the kitchen, and waited close to the door when he saw how small the space was. "Nah, I was trying to decide what to watch. I'm supposed to be resting, but if I want to work tomorrow night, I need to stay awake for a few more hours." He coughed and put the bowl in the fridge, then flicked the kettle on beside it.

"How are you feeling?"

Pulling down some mugs from the wall cupboard, Dean chuckled. "Like I could be a high-class phone sex operator and make excellent money." He winked at Oliver. "My throat is a little dry and tickly, but I'm managing. Thank you for the casserole, by the way. It was great."

"Did you get any sleep earlier?"

"A little. I ate the casserole and lay on the sofa. I slept for about an hour, then woke up coughing. The cheesecake helped ease my throat." He rolled his eyes.

Oliver had never inhaled smoke as Dean had, but he had inhaled steam enough times to know it would take a few days to settle. "Are you still able to taste flavours?" It would be his idea of hell.

"A little. I could taste the spices you used in the casserole more than anything else, but it was delicious."

Dean handed a freshly brewed cup of tea to him, and they wandered into the living room, where Dean sat on one side of the sofa and pointed to the other side for Oliver. He sat with care, not wanting to spill his drink, and settled back. It was a comfortable sofa that he readily sank into. It wouldn't be as easy to get out of, and he could easily fall asleep if left alone too long; it was *that* comfortable.

"How was the restaurant?"

Oliver chuckled. "Busy. I've had two servers hand their notice in because they're going off to university. I knew it was coming but wasn't expecting it so soon. They need to get their student accommodation sorted and find their way around campus. Don't get me wrong, I'm glad they're going to uni, but they're damn fine servers." He sipped his tea.

"You'll have no trouble finding replacements, I'm sure. You're a good boss. They'll be lining up at the door wanting to work for you."

"Hopefully." He licked his lips. "What are you going to do about the man from the fire?"

Dean sighed and stared at his mug, rubbing his thumb around the rounded edge. "I don't know. I should report him, but I don't want to cause issues for the station. Paul said it would be fine, but some of the public are already pushing back at him for being so inclusive. I don't want it to get worse for him or the other firefighters. I know not all the firefighters there are in the LGBTQ+ community personally, but they will get brought down by the same issues. And as for the LGBTQ+ firefighters? Haven't they been through enough already?"

Oliver could understand what Dean was saying. It was a difficult position to be in. "If you brought light to the situation, wouldn't it show the station in a more favourable light?"

Dean frowned. "What do you mean?"

"Well, if you highlight the scenarios you've had problems with, the public would know you won't allow it to continue. By staying silent, surely you're showing them you will let anyone take a shot at you. They might translate it as you won't stand and fight for those who can't stand for themselves."

He couldn't believe the words had come out of his mouth, but he couldn't take them back now. Dean stared off into the distance, and Oliver sipped his tea to stop his mouth from blurting apologies for sticking his nose in what wasn't his business. His words were true, but he didn't know the policies or procedures for things like this.

"You're right," Dean said finally. "I'll speak with Paul tomorrow and see what the best course of action is. Thanks." He smiled.

Oliver dipped his head, hiding his smile in his mug as he finished it. "I should go. I need to sleep before tomorrow."

He shifted forward on the sofa, right to the edge, then heaved up but sank right back down with a laugh.

"This sofa is too comfortable," he joked.

Dean grinned. "I know. Several nights, I don't make it to bed. I sleep here in a mountain of fluff."

The man held his hands out from where he was standing in front of Oliver, and Oliver took them, nearly bowling Dean down when the muscular firefighter pulled hard enough to send them toppling over. Oliver clung to Dean while they regained their balance, then realised how close they were. He lifted his gaze to meet Dean's. Dean lowered his head, inch by inch, until his lips touched Oliver's top lip, pulling at it. Dean followed it with a similar pull on Oliver's lower lip, then ran the end of his nose in a circle around Oliver's before closing the distance between their mouths once more.

Tingles flowed through him when Dean licked at his lips. Oliver opened for him, and the kiss deepened, but it didn't stop being slow and mesmerising. Oliver's eyelids fluttered closed, and his head dropped back, opening himself further. Dean's hand slid from Oliver's waist, up his chest to cup the back of his head, all the while kissing him. All Oliver could do was hold on.

It came to a slow stop, teasingly small pecks continuing for long moments before Dean pulled back fully.

"Hmm. You taste as nice as your food," Dean rasped.

With effort, Oliver dropped his forehead to Dean's shoulder, inhaling. His scent was a mixture of an earthy smell he assumed was his shower gel and the lingering smoke from the fire. He nuzzled his nose up the column of Dean's neck until he reached his ear, where the earthy scent increased. He inhaled again, his nose following the line of his jaw to his chin before he left a kiss. Opening his eyes, he saw the banked heat in Dean's eyes and knew his own reflected the same.

"I'll see you soon," he murmured and pulled back.

Dean stayed where he was while Oliver pivoted and left. He couldn't look back because he wouldn't be able to leave, and they both needed to rest. As Dean's front door closed behind him, he rested against it, blowing out a breath and staring at the ceiling.

That man was dangerous to Oliver's equilibrium.

Two days later, Oliver exhaled and swiped a hand across his forehead. The kitchen had been non-stop that day. He'd been on his feet more than ever because two of his chefs had called in sick. Rearranging the remaining staff had proved more problematic because some didn't have the skills to move around and needed to remain where they were. It meant he was working two stations and the wait time for meals was longer than he liked. He couldn't help it.

As the restaurant wound down to closing time, he stared around him. He needed help. Not only to cover for a chef who called off sick, but to help him cook for the shelter. When he thought about it, he was working at least sixteen hours a day, and he knew he couldn't continue the same way.

He cleaned up his station, then left the staff to finish setting the rest of it and the dining area to rights while he dropped into his office chair and unlocked his laptop. He brought up the restaurant's accounts and studied the figures, smiling. In a couple of years, if everything went the same as it was at this moment, he could employ someone to take the strain of the shelter work from him. Oliver knew Benny wouldn't mind if he had to stop cooking for them, but he also knew it was something Benny truly appreciated and needed. If Oliver stopped, the shelter wouldn't be open for as many hours as it was at that moment.

The figures were promising, even with the confusing discrepancies he'd been finding, but it didn't stop the issue he had now. He couldn't go on like this. Something had to give, and he was afraid it would be the shelter. If he stopped cooking for the shelter, it would also mean he'd have to stop giving Dean "lessons" because he would be back at the same problem if he continued.

Dropping his head into his hands, he closed his eyes and breathed. He couldn't see a solution for the short term.

"We're all set, Chef."

Serena entered his office and sank into the chair in front of his desk.

"Thanks, Serena. Has everyone gone?"

She nodded. "Except Jack, of course."

Jack never left until all the other members of staff had left, his big heart not wanting anyone hurt when he had a chance to prevent it.

"Great, thanks. Get yourself home and rest. I shouldn't say this, but I hope tomorrow is less busy."

Serena raised her eyebrows before standing. "You realise tomorrow is Sunday, don't you?"

Oliver's head fell back, and he stared at the ceiling. "Fuck." He chuckled. "I've lost my days."

"You need to rest up, Chef. Take a day off or something."

Oliver smiled at her. "One day, I will."

They both knew it was a lie. Oliver loved his restaurant and cooking too much to stop doing it. It was the hours on his feet that hurt. The thought of trying some sort of exercise regime crossed his mind as it occasionally did, but he brushed it aside as always, knowing it would take more time from his already packed schedule. That thought reminded him of the trip to the doctors he had coming up. He hardly ever visited his doctor because he was rarely ill, but his tiredness was becoming excessive, and he wanted a check-up to make sure anything else was eliminated, and it was only because he was working all the hours of the day.

"Night, Chef."

"Night, Serena."

He picked up his phone to check for messages and saw one from Dean.

DEAN: *Don't work too hard tonight. You need to sleep more, from what I'm hearing. I'll drop by for a bite tomorrow afternoon.*

Oliver chuckled, sending off a message back, detailing exactly how long his night had been. He closed out of the message thread and pressed the one for his brother from several hours earlier.

ANDREW: *Hey, Ollie. We might be able to come for a visit soon. As soon as I know more, I'll ring you. Hope everything is going well.*

Oliver smiled. He wasn't close to his brother, but he'd love to see him again. It had been six years since they'd met face to face because of Andrew's job and the rising prices. Oliver hadn't even met Andrew's two kids yet, except for over a video call once or twice. He closed out of the message, mentally making a note to message at a more reasonable hour for his brother. If he sent it now, no doubt he'd wake him.

Doing his nightly check of the restaurant, he finished in time for the knock on the back door. As usual, they shuffled the bags from Zee's car to Oliver's before Zee whipped off home. He always felt bad asking Zee to drop them off after the restaurant had closed, but because of the rules of having out-of-date food in the kitchen, his hands were tied. She didn't mind, thankfully.

Locking up the restaurant after collecting his belongings, Oliver climbed into his car. The engine started on the first try, and the drive home was uneventful, although he could feel the exhaustion dragging at him. Hopefully, he could sleep as soon as he was home. Carrying the bags into his kitchen, he put everything away and climbed the stairs. He needed a shower but opted for sleep instead. Undressing, he plugged the charger into his phone and slid beneath the covers, settling in.

Several moments later, Oliver's phone beeped with a message, and he groaned but rolled over and opened it to a picture of a bright pair of eyes within a hedge. Accompanying the picture was a message.

DEAN: *Foxy is back. Only the second time I've seen him.*

OLIVER: *You've seriously called it Foxy? Whose idea was that?*

DEAN: *No one is 'fessing up to that. I'm tempted to rename him Milo.*

OLIVER: *Why?*

DEAN: *Seriously? They named him Foxy! That should be enough reason.*

OLIVER: *Has he come out of the hedge?*

DEAN: *No, he's just staring at me. I've stayed in the same spot for the last half an hour, hoping he'd come out. The others are laughing their asses off at me.*

OLIVER: *I'm sure he'll visit you soon. I'm heading to bed and hoping to sleep this time. Keep messaging if you like. I'll reply either in the morning or when I decide I can't sleep.*

DEAN: *Turn your phone on silent, then you won't be disturbed.*

OLIVER: *I don't like doing that when people might need me.*

DEAN: *Well, get some rest. I'll speak to you tomorrow.*

OLIVER: *Night.*

DEAN: *Night, Oliver.*

Oliver replaced his phone on the bedside table and got comfortable once more. Well, as comfortable as he could. His back and feet ached, but that was nothing new. His hands and shoulders were screaming at him, though. He'd forgotten how bad it could get when a kitchen was extremely busy. Having worked in several restaurants that didn't employ enough staff to cover what they expected to sell, he had been like this before, but since he'd opened his restaurant, he had sworn he wouldn't do that to his staff. He couldn't help staff being sick, though. In the morning, he would need to contact an agency to see if they had two staff they could spare for a couple of days. Oliver couldn't go through that again.

His eyes drifted closed, but his thoughts were still circling. Things with Dean were getting complicated. The kiss they'd shared after they'd released Dean from hospital had been intense. Oliver had needed to see for himself that Dean was in one piece, which is why he'd used the fruit as an excuse, even to himself. The sensual turn the soft kiss had taken surprised Oliver. He'd needed to "feel" Dean in a way he'd not before. It could've been the close call Dean had, but something had made Oliver feel like he needed to memorise as much as he could.

The plan had been to have some light fun with Dean, but Oliver's mind was telling him he had already taken it further than he should have. There was no future for them. Oliver couldn't change the amount of work he was doing, not any time soon, and he knew it would be the end of any relationship he tried to have. Who wanted someone in their lives they hardly saw?

He blew out a breath, trying to calm his thoughts enough to sleep. One thought stayed with him...he didn't want anything to come between him and Dean, but he couldn't see a solution.

Chapter 9

Dean

"Can't you do anything right? It must be those pansy-ass hands," Evan groused in a voice meant only for Dean's ears.

Dean tried to ignore it, but it was becoming harder and harder to do. He didn't know what to expect from Evan anymore, but one thing was for certain...Evan did *not* like gay people. His mind wandered back to a time when other people made similar comments daily, and images of his bike pinning him down flashed before his eyes. He briefly closed his eyes, then refocused on the training exercise they were taking part in. Being partnered with Evan for this activity had worn him down before they'd even started, but he'd been determined to put up with his attitude. Unfortunately, it was dragging up memories best left submerged.

"Jesus, Dean! For god's sake, concentrate on your job instead of someone's ass!" Evan barked.

Dean flipped his hose off and dropped it to the floor, stalking away from Evan and ignoring the shouts at him. The changing rooms greeted him, and he removed his outer uniform, getting it ready to put near the engine to be prepared if Control called them for a fire. Opening his locker, he gritted his teeth when he heard the door slam open behind him.

"What the fuck are you playing at, Tyrell? If that had been an actual fire, you would've killed us all!"

Evan advanced towards him, but Dean held his ground. He was sick and tired of dealing with this shit. For once in his life, he had a station he loved working at and only one person who made his life a misery. He was not transferring without a goddamn fight.

"Well?" Evan pressed a finger into his chest.

"Well, what?" He played dumb.

"Why are you being such an asshole? Or is that the only thing you can be? Something for someone to stick their dick into?" Evan sneered, looking him up and down and finding him wanting.

"Takes one to know one, Evan," he said.

Evan stepped closer, red mottling his face. "I don't take dick from anyone, you shithead! Only you fags do that. Why they let you into the service, I don't know. You can't do anything except bend over and take what you're given."

"And that's exactly what you'll be doing now that I know how you really feel, Evan."

Paul's hard voice startled them both, and Dean glanced over, seeing his red, mottled face. Evan stepped back, holding his hands out in front of him.

"Now, now. I'm angry because he messed up our training and was only running my mouth. You know I don't feel that way."

"Nice try, Evan. My office. Now! Dean, check in with the others to see what's left to be done." Paul turned and walked away.

Evan whirled on him. "If I get fired, you'll be sorry." He stormed out of the changing rooms, and Dean dropped to the bench.

His heart raced, his palms were damp, and sweat poured down his back. It wasn't from the training, either. No one had ever had his back before, but he had a feeling this station was different in more ways than one. He rested his head in his hands and tried to ignore the memories flashing behind his eyelids, but it was pointless.

Dean finished at the station and aimed for his bike. It was the middle of winter, but the weather was holding steady with plenty of rain but no snow. He wandered to the back of the car park and started up his bike, straddling the engine while he pulled on his helmet and gloves. Other crew members exited the building, and Dean's heart increased. He needed to get out of there before they targeted him again. At least words only left emotional scars, not physical ones, and Dean would prefer it stayed that way.

He roared off into the night and aimed for his father's house; he'd promised to visit that night. Cornering onto a stretch of empty road, he increased his speed a little, still mindful of the wet road.

A roar came out of nowhere, and lights flashed behind him. Checking his mirrors, he saw headlights closing in on him. He pulled over as far as he dared, giving them space to overtake, but they didn't. The first sign he had things were going wrong was when the car bumped his back wheel, causing him to fumble to keep the bike upright. He sped up a little more, eyeing the road ahead for his turnoff.

The car bumped his bike again and sent him careening off and sliding across the asphalt with his leg trapped beneath his bike. He came to a stop when his bike slammed into the opposite side of the road, and the car raced off. He lay there for several minutes, regaining his breath, then tried to slide his leg from beneath his bike. He couldn't, so he tried to use his other leg to brace against the bike and push it off. When that didn't work, he tried to move out of the way of the road in case an unsuspecting vehicle came around the bend and didn't see him.

Nothing worked. Dean panicked when he heard a vehicle approaching. He scrambled to do anything to get him out of harm's way but could do nothing except sit upright and hope the occupants saw him before they crashed into him.

The car rounded the corner, and the headlights blinded him. He lifted his hands to shield his eyes, expecting a collision, but none came. Removing his hands, he saw the car idling close to him, and his stomach churned. Though he hadn't been able to see the make and model of the car that had run him off the road, he was sure this was the same vehicle. He began scrambling harder to remove himself from the bike, but his foot was caught in something on the bike.

The car's engine roared, and the wheels spun as it gunned towards him. There was nothing he could do except brace for pain. He leaned as far over his bike as he could to make him as small as possible.

Pain scraped across his back, and it flung him to the side as it dragged his bike across the road for a second. Then all Dean *heard was the disappearing sound of the car. He stayed still, not wanting to move and cause any more damage to himself than had already happened, but he needed to get himself up. Sitting upright once more, pain screaming through his body, he realised the car had done something else—it had moved the bike enough to free him from it. He scooted further back from the road and propped himself against the side, leaving his bike where it was.*

Pulling his phone from his pocket, he called for breakdown recovery. He'd go to the hospital afterwards to get himself checked out—he needed to know if he could work the next day or not. When the recovery guy got there, he called an ambulance for Dean. He was in worse shape than he thought.

The sound of the door opening had Dean's eyes blinking, and he dashed his hand across his face to remove any evidence of tears.

"Hey, are you okay?" Valerie entered, a frown etched onto her face.

He gave a half-hearted smile. "Yeah, I'm good. I was coming to see what else needed to be done."

"We're all set at the moment. What happened?"

"Nothing I can't put up with." He reached into his locker and picked up his phone.

"Are you sure you're okay?"

"Yep, I'm fine. I'm coming out now."

He could tell he hadn't dissuaded Valerie from her questions, but she chose not to say anything else, and he followed her through the station, dropping his kit at the engine, to the break room, where he grabbed a coffee.

"This is fucking shit! I don't deserve any of this, you fuck!"

Evan's voice echoed through the station, and seconds later, a car roared out of the car park.

Valerie went to the window. "Why is Evan leaving?"

Dean gritted his teeth. Evan's last words to him from the changing room circled his head. He could only hope Evan wouldn't do anything about it; Dean had too many brushes with death already, and that didn't include his daily job.

Jason strode into the break room with a grim expression, Paul and Scott following him.

Paul slid his hands into his pockets and stared at Dean. "Are you all right?"

Dean nodded, biting his bottom lip, then lowered his gaze, not wanting to see anyone's face.

Paul cleared his throat. "I have suspended Evan. He will not be working back at this station. Tonight, I will join you on any call-outs we have. Luckily, it's our last shift. By the time we come back on Thursday, we'll have a new crew member."

"What happened?" Valerie asked.

Paul sighed. "Evan had hidden his extreme dislike for the LGBTQ+ community. Dean withstood the worst of it, though why he chose Dean, I have no idea. Am I right?" Dean glanced up and saw Paul's gaze on him. He nodded once. "For how long?"

Dean worked his jaw. "From the beginning. It's become worse."

Paul stared at him. Disappointment and, if Dean wasn't mistaken, hurt radiated from him. "I'm sorry. I should've seen it."

"It's no one's fault but his," Scott stated. He leaned against the back wall with his arms crossed over his chest. His lips were white, and his jaw tight. Dean would hate for that to be aimed at him at any point.

"How did he—"

The alarm blared through the station, and they raced to the engine. With Evan gone, Paul stepped up to take his place, and despite Paul outranking Jason, he allowed Jason to continue. It was how they worked at this station. Paul would only interfere if he thought Jason was making the wrong call.

"Report of a burning car on Madingley Road. No occupants, a single empty car on the side of the road," Jason said after climbing into the engine.

No one said anything as they dressed in their uniform. Dean would no doubt be hearing from Paul about not telling him what was happening with Evan, but work came first, as always. He wasn't upset that Evan was gone, but why had he chosen to aim his vitriol towards him and no one else? Not that he wanted anyone else to suffer.

They moved like a well-oiled machine, following Jason's directions, and before long, the car fire was out. There was a group of bystanders who watched them work, but none of them were witnesses to how it started. The crew stayed to ensure the fire was out and wouldn't be a danger any longer, then passed the event over to the police to wrap up and investigate.

When they arrived back at the station, Scott immediately disappeared to start their meal, and the others set about getting the engine back to rights and cleaning up before heading to the break room to enjoy the chicken, potatoes and veg Scott had made. While they ate, they joked and messed around as they always did, but no one spoke of the incident from earlier.

In some ways, Dean was glad they were able to brush it off, but he couldn't. He'd moved to Cambridge to get away from that shit—at least where he worked, he knew the public opinion was a different matter, and that didn't concern him as much—but to put up with it again at work had riled him up.

"Dean, can I see you, please?"

Paul voiced it as a question, but Dean knew it was an order and followed him to his office after they'd eaten. He sat in front of his boss's desk and stared at his hands, linked as they were on his lap.

"Why didn't you tell me?"

Dean stood, moved to the window and crossed his arms as he watched the lights over the city. "Habit, possibly. I don't know. I didn't think it would make a difference. Evan had been here long enough; I thought you knew about his opinions."

"Seriously?" At Paul's angry tone, he glanced over his shoulder. "You think I would've allowed this to happen in my station? After everything I've told you about how it works here?" Paul shook his head and slumped back in his chair.

Dean felt ashamed and lowered his arms, leaning back against the windowsill to face Paul. "Sorry, Chief. I know you wouldn't, but it's hard to..." Dean sighed. "I don't know, unlearn the behaviour, I suppose. I've spent the last ten years hiding everything I am and whatever happened to me. I guess I dropped back into that way of thinking."

"What happened to you?"

Dean stared at the floor. "Too many things to count." He grimaced.

"Shit, Dean. I knew things had been bad for you, but I didn't know the extent of it."

"While I think about it, what do you want to do about that guy from the other day? Oliver says we should press charges because it will give a show of strength to the station, but I'm worried about it backfiring."

Paul exhaled. "It's a tough call. As much as I hate to say it, it's your word against his. I think it will bring down more scrutiny than we need. Especially with this Evan situation, too."

They stayed silent, Dean shutting away the images wanting to creep further into his consciousness. He needed them locked away again. He needed to forget and build his new life once more. Standing, he started for the door, even though Paul hadn't dismissed him.

"Dean?" He glanced at his friend. "Go and see Oliver, okay? Remind yourself of the pleasant things in the city."

The edges of Paul's mouth curved, and Dean smirked back but said nothing. His small smile didn't diminish as he finished his shift. As soon as he handed over to his replacement and showered, he was gone, flying across the roads to his destination. Paul seemed to know him better than himself because Dean wouldn't have interrupted Oliver's cooking this morning, but he *needed* to see him.

He'd only rested the bike on its stand before he was off and jogging to Oliver's front door. It was Sunday again, and he knew he'd be busy, but he promised himself he wouldn't stay long.

"Dean? What's wrong?"

Oliver stood with his hair mussed, hands being wiped on a towel, chef's trousers already in place with a white T-shirt and a frown on his face. Dean's brain went on hiatus. He stepped forward, cupping Oliver's jaw and slanting his mouth to take Oliver's gasp into his lungs. Coffee was the most prevalent flavour, with Oliver's unique taste in second place. Dean closed his eyes and sank into the feelings this man evoked from him. The need to be closer, the ache to be one, the butterflies in his stomach and the beat of his heart. Of both their hearts.

Slowing, he peppered kisses along Oliver's jaw and took a bite at the muscle running down his neck, the place below his ear that made Oliver shiver. Dean's cock was rock hard, but he made no move to the bedroom, content to revel in the chef's company. The hand cupping Oliver's jaw slid from his neck, his thumb tracing a path down the front until his hand spanned around the side. His face pressed into the opposite side of Oliver's neck, and he paused, inhaling.

A hand cupped the back of his head and another between his shoulder blades, smoothing up and down his spine. Several long minutes later, he pulled back, skimming his nose along Oliver's skin until he could see his face.

"Hi," he whispered.

"Hi," Oliver replied with a small smile and a bemused expression.

"I couldn't wait to see you." He kept his voice low; he didn't want to break the spell between them.

The beaming smile he received was enough to slam the door shut on the memories refusing to be banished.

"You're welcome to see me whenever you want to. Would you like a drink?"

Dean shook his head. "No, I need to get home and sleep." He exhaled through his nose.

Oliver licked his lips, and his eyes gleamed. "Do you want to sleep here? You can lock the door behind you when you wake."

"I won't disturb you?" The idea of having to drive home was less and less appealing the longer he stayed. He was tired.

"No, you'll be fine."

Dean dropped his lips to Oliver's in a sweet, soft kiss, then pulled back. "Thank you." He stepped away, although he wanted to get closer. "I need to lock my bike up."

"I'll sort the bed for you."

Within minutes, he climbed the stairs and entered the bedroom, watching Oliver pull the cover back for him.

"I won't stay." Oliver shuffled past him, but Dean caught his arm.

"Why?"

Oliver smiled. "You won't get any sleep, otherwise."

Dean clenched his jaw and shook his head. "Tease."

Oliver slid his hand to the back of Dean's neck and dragged him down the couple of inches needed to make their mouths meet. When Dean went to deepen it, Oliver pulled back, laughing.

"Go to sleep."

Watching Oliver leave the room and smile before shutting the door had Dean wanting to follow him, but he knew he'd be no use without sleep. He undressed, dropping his clothes beside the bed, then climbed under the covers. Unable to smell Oliver on the pillow, he rolled over and inhaled on the other pillow, Oliver's sweet scent filling his lungs. He held the pillow close, resting his face on it, and closed his eyes. Falling asleep had never been as easy as with the scent of Oliver and the sounds of cooking surrounding him.

Chapter 10

Oliver

Cooking while Dean was asleep in his bed was a distraction, but Oliver got everything done with enough time to deliver it before continuing to the restaurant. How long was Dean likely to stay? Would he be there when Oliver arrived home that evening? He shook his head, chuckling at his stupidity. Of course, Dean wouldn't be waiting for him.

Serena greeted him when he arrived, and they set to work prepping their stations. Other staff joined them as it grew closer to opening until the kitchen was bustling with activity and laughter. Nourris Moi opened, and lunchtime came and went for the public. As the number of customers declined into the early afternoon, Oliver stepped into his office to focus on some paperwork.

Sighing, he settled himself into his chair and opened his laptop. He had enough work to last him several hours, and luckily, enough staff to allow him to do it. Food orders, accounts, staff appraisals and arranging interviews for the new employees were some things he needed to get through.

His phone beeped an hour later.

DEAN: *Thank you for letting me sleep. I didn't want to post the key through the door like I did last time because you're not there. I'll bring it to you in a few hours if that's okay.*

Oliver smiled and let his eyes close. Opening them again, he replied,

OLIVER: *You're welcome. I'm glad I could help. Sure, there are some beef fajitas with your name on them if you want them.*

He returned to his work, finishing the food order for the following day before his phone chimed again.

DEAN: *Sounds good. What time is best?*

OLIVER: *Any time you want.*

DEAN: *I mean, when is best for me to visit when there's also the opportunity to share dinner with you?*

He grinned, then it dimmed when he wondered if Dean was asking him on a date. Trying to remind himself of all the reasons this was a bad idea did nothing to stop him from replying with a time when he could step away from his role for a short time.

For the rest of the afternoon, he distracted himself with the endless paperwork, then jumped back into the kitchen to help with the cooking for the evening.

"Serena, I'll be in the dining area between eight and nine tonight. Are you okay to take over the kitchen while I'm out there?"

"Yes, Chef."

He saw her frown but ignored it, continuing to go through the motions that were second nature to him after so many years. As his hands worked through the muscle memory movements, his thoughts turned to Dean. Oliver was getting in deeper, and he couldn't seem to stop himself. It would be beneficial for him to use this evening's meal to explain a few things to Dean, to make him understand exactly what they were getting themselves into—long hours and little to no time together.

When Jack let him know Dean was there, Oliver still had a few meals to finish up before he could join him, but he was only fifteen minutes late, and at least he could bring their food with him.

Sliding the beef fajitas in front of each seat, Oliver slipped into the chair opposite Dean.

"Hey." Dean smiled and reached for Oliver's hand, covering the back of it with his own. "I'm glad you could get away."

Oliver grinned. "I'm the boss, and I have an amazing staff who can handle the kitchen for me."

"Good. You need to rest a little."

If that didn't segue into Oliver's topic of conversation, nothing did. "I do, but life doesn't always allow it." He exhaled. "Dean, our lives are different in some aspects and similar in others. I would love nothing more than to see where a relationship between us could end up, but when would we get to see each other? I've had too many people leave because I can't give them the time they deserve. I don't want that to happen to us."

Dean stared at his plate for several minutes, the sounds of the restaurant surrounding them. Oliver concentrated on the hum of conversation, the clink of plates and cutlery, the occasional boom of laughter. It soothed him as few other things did.

Dean rested his elbows on the table and cupped his hands in front of his mouth. His gaze rose to meet Oliver's, and Oliver could see the pain behind them. "The life I had before moving here was...problematic. People I hooked up with only wanted to sleep with a firefighter—they liked the danger. I wasn't wanted at the station I worked at, which caused many issues that the bosses didn't deem worth their time to investigate. I became a shell of the man I was, staying home between shifts, hiding out." He gave a huff of derisive laughter. "I don't need all the bells and whistles of a relationship because I know that's not possible. But could we try? Could we work around the issues with our conflicting shifts and see if there is a chance of more? Are you willing to take a chance on someone whose life is in danger every day?"

Oliver could see where Dean was coming from, but he needed to explain a few things. "My life is crazy hectic; you've seen it. It won't change anytime soon. I would love to give us a try, but I don't want to ruin our friendship if things don't work out. I can't offer you more hours than I already have, which is a few in a morning while I'm already cooking, or a few minutes here and there when we're here. It was too much for everyone else I've had a relationship with."

Dean sighed. "Could we at least see if we could make it work? If you want to try, let's work out what hours we can do. People have worked through worse situations."

Dean had a point. Oliver wanted nothing more than to have everything Dean was willing to give him, and in return, Oliver would give Dean everything he had, which admittedly wasn't a lot.

He nodded. "Let's try."

The smile Dean gave him lit up the restaurant, and Oliver focused on his food, hiding his answering one.

Dean finished a mouthful of fajitas. "Okay, you work the same hours every day, even if we include the cooking for the shelter, right?

Oliver nodded. "Yeah. I work seven days a week."

Dean pulled out a pen and began writing notes on a napkin. "And I work shift patterns." He wrote the days of the week, then added in the times for each of them. "Obviously, this won't be the same day every week, but it gives us an idea." He scribbled a few more things down, then spun the napkin to face Oliver.

He'd worked out which days they could see each other and which they couldn't. When Dean was on days, they should be able to snatch some time at the restaurant like they were doing now. On the switchover from days to nights, possibly a little time when Oliver returned from the restaurant and when Dean needed to stay awake. Then on nights, a brief meet-up at the restaurant and maybe joining up in the morning while Oliver was cooking. It was only on Dean's days off they could meet up whenever. It wasn't undoable, but it wasn't easy either.

"Nothing worthwhile is," Dean replied when Oliver voiced that fear.

"You might get fed up with being second place to the restaurant."

"You might get fed up with knowing I'm in danger every day," Dean countered.

Oliver stared at Dean, heart pounding. Could he jump off the edge and hope Dean would catch him? Dean never broke their locked gaze but reached forward to clasp Oliver's hand, waiting. He licked his lips and nodded, knowing he had no other choice because he would regret it if he didn't try. Dean beamed, then changed the subject, asking about the restaurant.

Oliver explained his plans for extending into the next building and to employ some people to take over the shelter cooking but made it clear it wouldn't happen for a couple of years. His schedule, as it was then, would be it for the foreseeable future.

"Stop trying to talk yourself out of this," Dean said, squeezing his hand as they finished their desserts.

"Sorry. It's difficult."

Oliver knew Dean wasn't the same as the other guys he'd dated, but it was hard to forget about what had happened previously. It would take time to figure out where they were going with this and whether they'd be able to work it out or not.

"I know, but we'll work it out. If you're sure you want this, then we'll sort it."

"I want this. I'm...apprehensive, I suppose. I don't want things to get bad between us if we have to part ways." Oliver played with his leftover cake.

Dean put his fork down. "All I can say is that I promise I'll still be civil if it ends. I can't promise more." He grinned. "I won't be much help with your restaurant plans except if you need a taster. I could always try my hand at cheerleading, too, if you need one."

Oliver laughed. "I'm sure you would be great, but a physical cheerleader is not a requirement. An emotional one, however..."

"I'll be with you every step of the way. If not in person, then in spirit."

"Thanks." He glanced at the time. "I have to get back to the kitchen, I'm afraid."

"No problem. I'll head out and leave you in peace." He called for the server, but Oliver waved her away.

"It's on the house."

"You don't need to do that." Dean stood. "Oh, here's the key." He held out the silver item.

Oliver paused. "Why don't you keep that. You can use it when you need to." He licked his lips, wanting nothing more than to kiss Dean right there in the middle of the dining room, but unsure if it was a safe idea.

"Are you sure?" Oliver nodded. "I want to kiss you," Dean murmured.

"Hmm."

Dean leaned forward, aiming for Oliver's cheek, but Oliver smiled and turned his head. The kiss caught the edge of his lips, like had happened previously. Dean pulled back and chuckled, brushing his knuckles over Oliver's cheek.

"Tease," he repeated the word he'd said earlier that day.

Oliver smiled. "Have a good evening."

"See you soon."

He watched Dean weave his way through the tables and chairs, noticing several people's gaze on both Oliver and Dean, some with smiles, others with frowns. He refused to hide who he was, and everyone would have to put up with it, but he hadn't been visible about his affections before, especially in the restaurant itself.

Entering the kitchen once Dean had left, he received a smirk from Selena, who he ignored. He washed his hands and approached his bench, ready for the next part of his evening. His feet were already hurting, as was his back. There and then, he decided to jump into a bath when he got home that evening, no matter how tired he was.

"Did you enjoy your date?" Selena asked from beside him.

"Very much." He wouldn't give more information than she asked for. He wasn't stupid; he knew gossip spread like wildfire in places like these.

"Good."

They said nothing more about it, and he dropped into his chef role, getting his kitchen up to speed and ready for the night. He was glad to have his full staff back and fighting fit. Some customers were extremely picky that evening, and he'd lost count of how many comments they had made about the food. It didn't bother him as much because the food didn't come back to him to be remade.

"Don't worry about it, Chef. Everyone is having a bad day," Rebecca said as she finished cleaning her station.

"Yeah." He finished his work, then shuffled down the hallway to his office. There were a few things he could get done before everyone else finished up.

Selena knocked on his open door. "Are you okay, Chef?"

He nodded. "I don't think it had anything to do with the food, Selena."

She frowned and sat on the seat in front of his desk. "What do you mean?"

"Dean and I almost kissed in the dining room before he left. You could see from the reactions from some customers that they weren't pleased about it. I think it was more that display they didn't like rather than the food."

Selena raised her eyebrows, shrugging. "You'll never be able to please everyone, Chef. There will always be someone who has opinions about what others should or shouldn't be doing. It's life. The main thing is to not let it affect your own life. Their opinions are just that...theirs. You need to be content living your life as you want to live it without worrying about what others think or say. If you care about Dean, everyone else can go to hell."

Oliver chuckled. "When did you get so wise?"

"I caught it from you." She winked and slid out of the door, closing it behind her.

He shook his head, his smile unwavering. She had a point. He couldn't live for other people, and he never had before. Why was he nervous about what people thought now? It could be because of the issues he knew Dean had been facing. He wanted Dean's life to be better than his previous station, and if being in a relationship with Oliver would make things more difficult for him, then he'd give Dean up.

By the time he'd finished his routine and was in his car driving home, he was second-guessing the idea of a bath. He was shattered again. When he pulled up at his house, he frowned at the windows. Light was streaming through the living room and main bedroom windows. He didn't remember leaving the lights on, and he was sure Dean wouldn't have forgotten to turn them off. At the thought of Dean, Oliver cocked his head. Would Dean…?

Oliver climbed out of the car, wrestling with the shopping bags of food, and fumbled with the front door. When it opened, Dean was standing before him in joggers and a T-shirt, looking like he had painted it on. Did he even own any that were loose fitting? Not that Oliver minded. Dean grabbed several of the bags, then stepped back for Oliver to enter.

"I didn't realise you'd be here," Oliver said.

"I thought I'd spoil you after a long week working." His voice was still a little raspy and hoarse.

They wandered to the kitchen and put away the food that needed refrigerating. Oliver turned to Dean. "What do you mean?"

Dean stepped closer, caging Oliver against the counter. "I have a bath with your name on it."

Oliver raised his eyebrows. "Yeah? Thanks. I had planned to have one earlier, then as I drove home, I decided I was too tired to run one."

"Good job I'm here." He leaned down and joined their mouths in a soft, sweet caress. "Let's get you out of these clothes," he murmured.

Heat and butterflies flowed outwards from his stomach, leaving him trembling for several reasons. Dean threaded their fingers together and tugged Oliver towards the stairs and the main en-suite, where a steaming bath with plenty of bubbles awaited. Dean faced Oliver, sliding his hands up Oliver's arms and over his shoulders to the buttons on his chef whites, never once moving his gaze from Oliver's. There was something about the stare that soothed the edges of Oliver and settled the nerves. It was open, honest, and Oliver couldn't ask for more.

When Dean threw his chef jacket and T-shirt to the floor, Oliver trembled, nerves reigniting at being bare in the bright lights. If Dean noticed his increased breathing, he couldn't tell, but Dean kissed down his chest before dropping to his knees, undoing Oliver's trousers and removing them with no mention of what Oliver knew his body looked like. His boxers went the same way, and Oliver closed his eyes in mortification.

Hands cradled his face, and he blinked open to see Dean's frown. "You're gorgeous, Oliver. I know you don't see it but let me see it for both of us."

Oliver nodded once, trying to believe that Dean liked how he looked. He lifted his chin, requesting a kiss, which Dean obliged. They kept it light, Dean keeping his hands on Oliver's face as if he knew Oliver would baulk if they wandered anywhere else, then he helped Oliver into the bath and crouched beside it once he was settled. His bath wasn't particularly big, and his hips and thighs rested against the side, but it was deep enough that the water covered him to his waist. Throwing caution to the wind, he ignored his issues and closed his eyes, laying his head back.

"Thank you, Dean," he whispered.

"You're welcome. Rest easy for a while. I'll grab you a drink and be back in a few minutes."

Oliver cracked an eye to watch Dean exit the room, ogling his ass and tight muscles. How he wished he could look like that. He'd always wondered why he never lost weight with the number of hours he worked. When he was younger, other people had cruelly said he ate all the food he made. He didn't, but no one else would believe that. It was something he could ask the doctor when he went. The appointment was in five days, so he didn't have long to wait. Although if they did tests on him, then he'd have longer to wait for the results. He probably had an iron deficiency or something. Wasn't that what it was called when he was feeling tired all the time?

Whatever it was, whether or not he had something wrong with him, he wished he could change how he looked. It was not as easy as eating healthy and exercising, no matter what anyone said.

Chapter 11

Dean

Dean understood insecurities ran deep in many people, and it was hard to brush aside everything they had always believed and trust that another person was being truthful. Oliver's weight played on the man's mind, but Dean didn't see it as anything to be ashamed of. Oliver's personality shone brighter than anything else, his caring side, his need to look after others, his perfectionism. The latter was probably a reason Oliver hated his weight—he saw it as an imperfection.

When he'd decided to surprise Oliver, he'd crossed his fingers, hoping it would be a nice gift and not seen as stalking. He chuckled to himself at the thought.

He filled a glass with milk, rummaged through some drawers to find a straw and carried it back up the stairs to where Oliver was soaking with his eyes closed. Smiling at the utter relaxation of the pose, Dean crouched beside the bath.

"Hey, sleepyhead. Drink this for me."

He spoke quietly to stop Oliver from jumping at his appearance, but the slight curve of the man's mouth advertised he knew he was there. Oliver blinked at him and smiled.

Dean put the straw in the glass and held the end to Oliver's lips. "Drink."

Closing his lips around the straw, Oliver stared at Dean, heat warring with sleepiness. Dean wasn't there for anything except to help Oliver relax enough to sleep earlier than he usually would, then he'd let himself out of the house again and go home. Though he would've loved to have the chance to sleep wrapped around the person who was becoming more to him than he'd expected in such a short amount of time. He'd only met Oliver three weeks prior, but those three weeks felt like a hell of a lot longer.

Oliver released the straw and rested his head back again. Several minutes of silence later, he murmured, "As much as I love this, I can't stay here too long; otherwise, I'll be asleep."

"That's a good thing. It means you're tired enough to sleep." Dean stood, pulling a towel from the hook. "Let's get you out and straight into bed, then you can sleep all night."

"If you say so."

Oliver's disbelief was apparent. "I do say, and you'll do as you're told." Dean winked at him. He stuffed the towel under his armpit, then held out his hands. "Come on. Up."

"It's okay. I can do it."

"Let me help." He grabbed Oliver's hands and pulled, holding tight while Oliver got his feet underneath him. "There we go," he said once Oliver was standing on the bathmat. Dean dried him off before tucking the towel around him.

Wandering into the bedroom, Dean pulled the covers back from the bed as Oliver had done for him that morning—or yesterday morning, as it was past midnight—and pointed to the bed. Oliver smiled and drifted closer, his gaze never leaving Dean's face. He stopped in front of Dean and smoothed his hands up Dean's chest until his hands cupped his neck and head, respectively, pulling him down to meet lips. It was a soft, slow exploration, different from their first kisses but just as powerful, if not more. There was no hurry, but Dean could feel the heaviness of Oliver's arms and knew he was out of energy. Dean pecked another kiss on his lips, pulled the towel free, then guided the man to the bed, tucking the covers over him.

"Stay?"

"Not tonight," he whispered with a kiss to Oliver's forehead. "I'll come and see you tomorrow, and we can talk more."

"'Kay."

Dean smiled at the breathy word, Oliver already slipping towards slumber. He inhaled, watching him while he slept. He crept out of the room, closing the door firmly behind him, then double-checked that the food which needed putting away had been. Once he was certain everything was in its place, ready for Oliver the following morning, he left the house, locking the door behind him.

His bike sounded loud in the early morning, and he mentally apologised to anyone he might wake. Not particularly tired, even though it was nearing half-past two in the morning, he settled in front of the TV and flicked through the channels until something caught his attention. He'd give himself another hour before trying to sleep. That was the problem with working night shifts—his body didn't want to revert again afterwards.

When four o'clock came and went, he knew he needed to try. Turning everything off, he strode down the hallway to his bedroom and dropped face-first to the bed, using his hands and feet to drag the rumpled covers over him.

A flash of light followed by a crash woke him. Disorientated, he reached for his phone, only to realise it wasn't on the bedside table. He rubbed his face, squinting at the clock. Other people would be starting their days now, including Oliver, but when another flash and crash happened, Dean was glad he had no plans. The thunderstorm was right overhead, and even though the sun was up, it was extremely dark outside his window. Rain clattered against the windows, but nothing else stirred.

He rubbed his face and contemplated climbing back into bed, but he didn't. Frowning at his bedside table, he tried to remember where he last had his phone when he realised he was still wearing yesterday's clothes. He rolled his eyes; his phone was in his pocket but, luckily, remained intact. Checking the display, he found a message from Oliver.

OLIVER: *Thank you for last night. I appreciate it more than you know. I slept for six hours, which is a record for me. See you soon x*

Dean smiled, glad Oliver had managed to get a decent night's sleep for a change. The thunder reverberated once more, and Dean made a split-second decision. Oliver usually drove to the shelter at around ten o'clock, and in this weather, transferring the food from the car to the shelter would soak them all.

Decision made, Dean rushed around, ducking in and out of the shower and dressing in record time. At his door, he slid on a waterproof coat, shoved his feet into boots and grabbed two large umbrellas. He raced from his building to his car and climbed in, laughing.

"Typical British weather," he huffed.

He parked a few streets away from the shelter and strolled over to the entrance to wait for Oliver with an enormous umbrella to keep the rain from drenching him. He didn't know how long he'd been waiting when Oliver finally pulled up, but he was cold. Oliver reversed into the space, putting the boot closest to the door and switched off the engine.

Dean stood by the driver's door, holding the umbrella over it. Oliver had a bemused expression on his face when he climbed out, pulling on his coat.

"What are you doing here?"

Dean smiled sheepishly. "I thought you might struggle to keep yourself and the food dry while holding an umbrella. I thought I'd help."

"You should be sleeping. I bet you didn't sleep much last night, did you?" Oliver pointed a finger at him as he opened the boot of the car.

Dean held the umbrella over them both while Oliver grabbed two trays and slammed the boot closed again. He put his hood up to allow him to hold the umbrella over Oliver instead of trying to keep them both underneath it.

"You'll get soaked!"

"I'm fine. Keep you and the food dry. That's more important."

Oliver huffed but didn't argue again. Benny waited at the door with a volunteer, who took the trays while Oliver and Dean went back for more. It would've taken less time if Dean could've helped carry the food, but he concentrated on making sure Oliver and the food kept dry. After four trips, the final food pots were headed for the kitchen, and they stepped into the foyer for a few minutes.

"Thank you for this. On a day like this, I didn't expect you to cook," Benny said.

Oliver sighed. "Of course I'll cook, Benny. You're not in this alone, remember."

"I know, but sometimes, I feel like I'm asking too much of you."

Oliver squeezed the man's shoulder. "You're not asking; I'm offering. Now, go sort out the food before it gets eaten sooner than it should."

Benny smiled and tugged Oliver into a hug. He held his hand out for Dean to shake. "Thank you again." He strode off.

"He doesn't like asking for help, does he?" Dean murmured.

Oliver shook his head. "He believes he should be able to deal with all this himself, but with the limited funding he's provided, it's touch and go if the shelter will continue."

Dean frowned. He needed to speak with Paul, but they might be able to do a fundraiser for the shelter to help a little. He was sure they could think of something.

"Right, I need to get to work," Oliver said.

Dean opened the door, uncurled the umbrella and held it ready for Oliver. Oliver linked his arm through Dean's, and side by side, they both huddled under the canopy until they reached Oliver's car.

"Do you have an umbrella?" Dean asked.

"No, but I'll be fine. It's not a long walk from my car to the restaurant."

Dean put the handle into Oliver's hand. "Take this one. I have another in the car."

"No, honestly. I'll be fine."

"Take it in case of emergencies then."

Oliver pursed his lips but nodded. "All right."

Dean leaned closer, advertising his intentions, but he needn't have worried. Oliver grabbed the front of Dean's coat and dragged him closer, their mouths meeting with laughter before morphing into something else. Dean pressed Oliver back against the car, gripping his upper arms as they kissed with the sounds of rain around them. They only stopped when the rain started splashing on them, and Dean realised Oliver had tilted the umbrella too far to keep them dry.

"Sorry!" Oliver pulled it over them again with a chuckle. "Stop kissing me like that, and I won't lose my head."

"I quite like you losing your head," Dean said.

Oliver kissed him once hard, then opened his car door. Dean pulled his hood up again, and the rain drowned him as Oliver climbed in and shut the door behind him, but he didn't care. Oliver waved and drove off. Dean stood with the rain soaking through every part of him, and he'd never felt more fulfilled.

"Dean, are you free for dinner tonight?"

Ave caught his arm as he wandered down the street, avoiding the large puddles and staying away from the edge of the paths where cars were spraying water without a care in the world. He hadn't seen Ave until she'd grabbed hold of him, but he didn't mind the interruption. He hadn't been going anywhere exciting, only to the supermarket to get some food.

"Hi, Mrs Oxford. I'm sure you have other things to be doing without feeding me." He didn't mind visiting them but didn't like the idea of being a bother to them.

Ave swiped his arm. "You know we love having you around. I hear you have a sweetheart on your arm now. It'll give me a chance to get all the gossip. Anyway, Jason, Paul, Quinn and several of the other men are coming too. You know how the kids love you all. It's no bother at all."

"Well, if you're sure. What time do you want me there?"

"Any time you like. We sit down at six tonight because Billy has football practice."

"Okay, count me in. Do you need me to pick anything up? I was nipping to the shop."

Ave shook her head. "No, thanks, dear. I have everything I need. Just bring yourself and your appetite, which I know won't be a problem." She winked at him and waved as she continued down the street.

Although Dean now didn't need to cook for the evening, he still needed a few essentials, including milk for his tea, so he carried on to his destination. The weather had calmed a little since the torrential downpour of the morning, and now the sun was trying to peek through the cloud cover. It wasn't succeeding, but at least it was trying.

After he'd bought his few items, he returned home, putting everything away. He didn't know what time to go to Ave's house and pulled out his phone.

DEAN: *What time are you getting to Ave and George's house?*

PAUL: *We'll be there around four. I told her we'd keep the kids occupied while she cooked.*

DEAN: *I bet Quinn isn't happy about not cooking.*

PAUL: *Ha, he's already cooked today. He'll be fine for a few hours. I'm assuming you're joining us?*

DEAN: *Yeah, I saw Ave, and she invited me.*

PAUL: *Good. Will be nice to catch up before the next shift. I am bringing the new guy with me, too.*

DEAN: *Okay. See you there.*

Dean wasn't sure what to expect of the new guy, but he couldn't be much worse than Evan was. It surprised him he had heard nothing from the man. Each time he stepped out his door, he expected to find his tyres slashed or his car spray painted, but up to now, nothing. He was worried about nothing. It didn't stop the fear from being there, though.

As the poor weather had subsided, Dean took the bike. People were driving like maniacs, but he could stay out of their way, mostly. When he pulled up to the Oxfords' house, he spotted Paul's car along with Jason's and a car he recognised from White Watch, Xavier's car. He knocked on the door.

"Hey, Dean! Come on in. It's a bit crowded in here, even for Ave's house, but we'll find room."

Matias, from Blue Watch, clapped him on the shoulder and strode through the house to the large, open plan living room, which he had been told on a previous visit had once been three rooms that they'd knocked into one. Ave and George were foster parents to LGBTQ+ teens, although they took in the occasional younger or older child. They opened their house to everyone, past and present, and Dean had often visited when one or more of their previous foster kids had been around too. He loved what they did for the community. There were too many kids thrown out of their homes for being "different," and it annoyed Dean.

He had always wanted to help but had no idea where to start. At least until he'd met Oliver. With him cooking for the shelter, it had re-energised Dean to help however he could.

"Chief, when you have a minute, can I talk to you?" He waited until his boss had finished playing with the child.

"We can now."

They grabbed a drink and took it out onto the rear decking, which ran the full length of the back of the house. It was enclosed—something Dean had never seen in person before—and held several chairs and a small table, along with a swinging loveseat. Dean dropped into an armchair.

"What's in that brain of yours, Dean?"

"I want to do a fundraiser or something for the LGBTQ+ shelter. Is that something we could do as a station?"

Paul's forehead creased, and he stared into the garden for a minute. When his expression cleared, he faced Dean. "I don't see why not. We have a couple of charity events we do each year, but they are for different causes. Depending on what you wanted to do, I don't see why we couldn't arrange something. Do you have any ideas?"

"Not really. Nothing concrete, anyway. It would be nice to do something for the kids, but it might not work. I don't know." He chuckled. "Sorry, I haven't thought this through much. It only came to me earlier today, and I wanted to talk it through with you first."

"It's okay. We can't do anything on short notice, anyway. We'd need to get some sort of plan in place before we begin. I'll mention it to the other guys and get their input, too. It won't hurt to get everyone on board. I'll also speak with the other commanders and see if they want to join in."

"That would be great, thanks."

"Not a problem. How are things with Oliver?" Paul tried to hide his smile behind his beer bottle, but Dean saw it.

His cheeks heated, and he ducked his head. "Good, thanks. I certainly never expected him, but we've...decided to give things a go and see what happens."

"I'm glad. You both deserve happiness."

"Who does?" Jason asked, joining them on the seats. Matias and another guy trailed behind him.

"Dean and Oliver," Paul said before Dean could answer.

"Woohoo! Way to go, Deano!" Jason lifted his beer in a toast.

"Dean, you've not met Niall yet. Niall, this is Dean."

Dean stood, reaching through the gap to hold out his hand, which Niall shook without hesitation. So far, so good. "Nice to meet you. I hope you enjoy being here."

"I'm not disappointed yet." The Irish accent didn't surprise Dean as much as how deep Niall's voice was. "I'm more than happy to see more of the world than the corner I was born in." He grinned, the move making him seem much younger than Dean would've originally thought. Niall's light blond hair and blue eyes would make many a woman or man swoon for him. He doubted he'd feel out of place for long.

"Ain't that the truth," Xavier agreed as he exited the house, followed by four other firefighters Dean knew from White Watch. "Look, Chief! I got a full house." Xavier threw his hands wide, showing his entire team.

"Not bad going, Xavier." Paul grinned and stood. "I'm going to see if Ave needs any help. Don't forget to keep the kids occupied, you lot."

"On it," Dean said, following Paul inside.

The sound of laughter and giggling made Dean smile. One day, he might want a family of his own, but not yet. At the minute, he enjoyed being able to give them back at the end of the day.

Chapter 12

Matias

Matias, who had only managed to come to the meal because he'd happened to have booked the day off work, followed Paul and Dean back into the house but redirected to the living room instead of the kitchen. There, he found three boys shouting and roughhousing, and he winced when they fell precariously close to the display cabinet.

"Boys!" he called. They stopped and stared at him. "How about we take this outside? If you have a frisbee or a ball, we can mess around, maybe beat the rest of the crews at dodgeball or something?"

The eldest at fourteen, Vance herded his brothers into the garden, a watchful eye on each of the men they passed. Matias didn't know the reason they had fostered the boys, but from that evidence alone, it didn't look good.

"Jason, Xavier, get your men together. You have opponents to face," Matias said with a grin.

Jason jumped up. "Sir, yes, sir!" He turned to the firefighters sitting on the porch. "Team, come on. Let's win this thing!" They stepped off the porch, and Jason moved closer. "What exactly are we playing?"

Matias snorted. "No idea yet, but it has to be better than breaking all the china in the living room."

Jason winced. "Good call."

Matias faced Vance, Oscar and Zane, crouching down. "Fellas, what are we playing?"

Vance glanced at his brothers, who nodded. "Dodgeball."

Matias nodded seriously. "All right. Do you want to pick who's on your team, or do you want me to pick?"

Vance stood taller. "I'll pick."

"Okay." He stood, calling the men to order. "Leona, you are team captain for the white team. Vance is the team captain for the blue team and is going to pick first." He came to a stop next to Vance, crouching again. "You get to keep your brothers on your team as extra players, but shh, don't tell anyone." He winked, receiving a small smile in return. He stood behind the younger boys, and while Vance was studying the men, he caught Leona's gaze and sliced his hand near his neck to tell her not to pick the boys.

They went through each player, and Vance ended up with his two brothers, Matias, Jason, Clay, Xavier and Leona had Dean, Niall, Kaleb and Wade. Oakley, White Watch's watch commander, offered to keep score. They stepped to either side of the garden and faced the other team.

"Ready, Vance?" he asked. Vance grinned at him, and Matias whistled through his teeth to start the game.

They had two balls, which began the back and forth, trying to hit the opposing team. Matias got Kaleb out, but Wade hit Clay, which he good-naturedly grumbled about.

Before long, there was only Vance, Oscar, Zane, Jason and Niall left, and Vance's team had both balls in their hands. They formed a semi-circle around Niall, and Jason grinned and waggled his eyebrows. Matias snorted. He was such a goofball.

Niall waved his hands in the air. "White flag! I surrender!"

Vance yelled and punched his fist into the air, while Zane bounced around shouting, "We won! We won!" Jason high-fived the boys and dropped into a chair beside Matias.

"You're valuable to have around kids," Jason said.

"I love them. Hope to have a house full one day," Matias replied.

"With Kinton?"

Matias winced. Kinton was a paramedic he'd been seeing on and off for a few months. The most recent goodbye was final, and though Matias was sad, he knew it was for the best. They were their own worst enemies when they were together, and their conflicting schedules meant they went weeks without seeing each other for more than a few minutes.

"No. Kinton and I are finished. For good, this time."

"Sorry to hear that, man." Jason clasped his shoulder. "You'll find someone."

He watched Paul and Quinn, as well as Ave and George, and wanted what they had.

"Boys and girls, it's time for food," Ave shouted.

One day.

Chapter 13

Oliver

"**I** want to know how long you've been taking money from me?"

Oliver stared into the dark brown eyes of twenty-nine-year-old Rikki, wanting to see if what he'd figured out was true. His accounting had been off by a few pounds here and there for weeks, but Oliver thought nothing of it. It happened, human error, whatever. It was when the discrepancy had widened that Oliver checked the CCTV cameras to see what was happening. To find Rikki palming coins and notes regularly had been upsetting, to say the least. She had been with him for over a year.

"Six months, give or take," she said, eyes hard and unrepentant, different from usual.

It was worse than he'd thought.

"Why?"

"It was easy enough to do. I needed the extra for rent one month, then when you didn't notice, I didn't think I was harming anyone."

"Jesus, Rikki." He rubbed his hands over his face. "How much?"

"In total?" Oliver nodded at her. She shrugged. "Eight hundred maybe. Might be more."

"You don't sound like you care that you've stolen from me. That's not the Rikki I know."

Rikki shook her head, her hands appearing to tremble. "Life sucks, Chef. I have to adapt to the shit thrown my way. I'm not the same person I was last year."

"I can agree with that." Oliver sighed. "You're gone, Rikki. As of now. I will pay you what you've worked up to today, but you won't get any notice period payments."

Rikki's mouth dropped open. "What the hell? No way, Oliver. Come on! It was only a little money."

"A little money that's needed for my business, not to line your pockets. I should call the police." He didn't know what to feel about Rikki's stealing, but he knew he could no longer trust her. "Jack!"

He'd asked Jack to wait nearby while he had this conversation. Jack opened his office door and ducked his head in. "Yes, Oliver?"

"Can you please escort Rikki to her locker and ensure she leaves only with the items that belong to her?"

Jack's eyebrows rose, but otherwise, he appeared unruffled. "Sure thing."

"You'll regret this, Oliver," Rikki said, fire burning in her eyes.

When the door shut behind them, Oliver leaned back in his chair, his head resting on the back while he stared at the ceiling. Why hadn't he seen what she was like? Was she that skilful of an actor, or did he not want to see what was right in front of him? How could he have been so blind? The money wasn't a devastating loss because it was only a small amount overall, but that someone he trusted could do that to him…was unnerving.

A knock sounded. "Come in!"

Jack entered. "Rikki has cleaned out her locker and left."

"Thanks, Jack. You can head home now. I appreciate you staying for me."

"Not a problem. You wouldn't want anything to come back and bite you."

Oliver sighed. "Let's hope she doesn't find some other way to pay me back." He grimaced. "Night, Jack."

"Night, boss."

Oliver jotted down a note to call in another server to cover tomorrow, then closed down his laptop. He checked through the restaurant to ensure everything was ready. He wished he could leave everything as it was and not have to be a perfectionist about it all. He reasoned that because he'd sunk all his money into the place, he didn't want to miss anything and have it blow up in his face. Other people might see him as someone who didn't trust anyone else. He didn't care; it was his livelihood, after all.

Ignoring the thought that it was acceptable to check everything since Rikki had proved him right, he drove home with the reminder he was visiting the doctor in the morning. He had no idea what would come from the visit, but time would tell.

Which it did, six hours later. Oliver had grabbed an appointment first thing that morning and was waiting for the doctor at eight o'clock. Before he'd left for the doctor's surgery, he made as much food as he could, which meant he'd only had roughly three hours sleep, but he'd been worse.

"Mr Collins?" The doctor stepped into the waiting room, then turned back and retraced her steps while Oliver followed.

When they sat, the doctor looked expectantly at him. "How can I help?"

"Well, I don't know, in all honesty. I wondered if you could give me a check-up because I've been tired, exhausted really, and though I know I work long hours, I wanted to rule out anything else." He clasped his fingers together, feeling like he was wasting the doctor's time.

"Okay, let's have a look at your history." Dr Raines was silent as she read through what Oliver assumed was his file on the computer. "All right. Your health has generally been good, although as I'm sure you know, you could do with losing some weight. That won't help your tiredness, but other than that, nothing to show anything wrong." She clicked a few more times, then pulled a blood pressure cuff from a drawer. "Let's get some basics down for you for now, and I'll arrange for some blood tests."

Oliver went through the usual blood pressure, temperature and other checks, which Dr Raines seemed cheerful about. He answered questions about his routine and lifestyle.

"I can't see anything that would indicate a reason for your tiredness, but I'm going to test you for a few things to rule out certain possibilities."

Oliver nodded. "Do you have any ideas?"

Dr Raines leaned on her desk. "It could be several things, but I'm wondering if you might have chronic fatigue syndrome. You've mentioned several symptoms which could point to it, but they are also common in other things too. I don't want to guess until I have the results from the blood tests."

"How long will the results take?"

"Approximately two weeks. If you speak to the receptionist before you leave, they can book you in for a test."

"All right. Thanks."

"You're welcome."

Oliver left the surgery with no more answers but plenty more questions. He had a blood test appointment for Tuesday and had got an early one again. There was nothing he could do until he had the results, and he put it to the back of his mind and drove back home. The final preparations for the shelter's food didn't take long, and he arrived at the restaurant only a little later than normal.

The soft chatter and laughter distracted him enough to get through lunchtime, then he ducked into his office to finish the paperwork he needed to and ordered the food they'd need for the following day. Jack brought him a coffee, which he gratefully drank, even though it wasn't his favourite. By the time the dinner crowd started, Oliver felt drained. He wanted nothing more than to drop into bed and sleep for a week, and he couldn't understand why he was feeling like this when it hadn't been a problem for the last three years. Nothing had changed in that time, except for doing the food for the shelter, and that didn't take as much time as people thought.

Draining a glass of water, he refocused on the food, making a quick appearance in the dining area, then stayed with his station. He expected nothing less than perfection from his staff; therefore, he couldn't do anything less himself.

But as the staff closed the restaurant, Oliver dropped into the chair at his desk and rested his head in his hands. The paperwork would have to wait.

"Oliver?"

He lifted his head, eyes blearily seeking the source of the voice.

A hand slid across his shoulder, someone crouching next to him. "Oliver, are you okay?"

Oliver rubbed at his face, finding it wet. Once he'd woken himself a little more, he focused on the person. "Dean?"

"Yeah, I'm here. Are you okay?"

Oliver closed his eyes briefly when Dean squeezed the nape of his neck. "I'm okay. I'm tired. An early night for me, I think."

"I agree. Can you put up with the restaurant not being checked over tonight? I can help you in the morning."

Oliver hesitated. His stomach churned, and his hands clenched. He wasn't sure whether he could leave it—he'd be too wound up to sleep. "I'm not sure. I know that sounds ridiculous, but I don't know if I'd be able to sleep knowing some things needed checking."

"What are the most important things?" Dean's gaze didn't waver. He didn't roll his eyes at Oliver's over-the-top need.

"Um...the doors and windows, the tills and the cookers."

"Okay, then. You check the cookers and the tills; I'll check the doors and windows. Would that put your mind at ease enough to sleep?"

Oliver's heart thumped hard, but he inhaled through his nose and nodded. It wouldn't hurt if, for one night, things weren't perfect. At least the restaurant would be secure, and Oliver could come in a little earlier the next day to check things over before he had to start prepping.

He said goodnight to the remaining staff, then Dean locked the door behind Jack. Working silently, they checked the few things Oliver knew he couldn't leave for the next day. When Dean finished the last check, he wandered over and cupped a hand under Oliver's chin.

"Are you okay with this? Is it enough?"

Oliver licked his lips. "I feel like I need to do everything, but I can manage until tomorrow."

Dean dropped a kiss on his upturned lips and steered Oliver to the back door. "Is Zee dropping by tonight?"

"Yeah, she should be here already." They opened the back door, and there she was. They transferred the bags.

Once they'd bid goodnight to Zee, Dean held out his hand. "Let me drive you home."

"I'll be fine."

"I don't want you to drive when you're tired. I can come back for my bike later."

"You don't want to leave your bike here. It's not protected."

Dean stared at him, grazing his teeth across his bottom lip several times. "Okay, but I'll be right behind you. If you start to feel too tired, pull over."

Oliver smiled. "Deal."

Dean kissed him and helped him into the car. "Don't leave until I'm ready." He closed the car door, and Oliver watched through his mirror as he jogged over to this bike.

His hands trembled when he started the car, and he clenched them into fists, then spread his fingers wide several times. He had never vocally acknowledged his anxiety about certain aspects of his life, but he had a feeling it was of the obsessive-compulsive disorder strain, though not bad enough to warrant a complete routine that could never be broken. Many people had it worse than he did, but it still put a strain on his mind. He'd never had someone who had helped him previously.

Lights flashed in his rearview mirror, and he snapped his seatbelt into place. He reversed out of his space and drove home, all the while aware of the man directly behind him. There was a tug of something he had not experienced before. Something he wanted to explore. Something he couldn't explain. He couldn't remember feeling like this for anyone before. It was a little scary—all right, a lot scary because it meant he had further to fall should it not work out.

Dean pulled in behind him at his house, and they carried the food into the kitchen, working side by side in silence while they put away the food, locked the house up and climbed the stairs. With each creaking step, Oliver's energy levels fell, and by the time he'd reached his bedroom, he was dead on his feet.

Arms slid around his waist and helped him to the bed. While he sat, Dean knelt at his feet, pulling his socks off before reaching forward and unfastening the buttons of the chef jacket he'd forgotten to remove. They exchanged no words as Oliver watched Dean tend to him. His emotions were close to the surface, and he couldn't talk because of the lump in his throat. No one had ever done this for him, and he closed his eyes to both stop his grateful tears from overflowing and memorise every moment to bring out on his darkest of days.

Dean tugged him to standing, lowering his trousers but leaving his boxers in place. The covers swiped across the back of his legs when Dean pulled them up for Oliver to climb in. When he was tucked in, Dean crouched next to him.

Oliver opened his eyes and whispered, "Stay?" but knowing Dean would refuse.

"I'd love nothing more." He leaned forward, pressing a kiss to Oliver's forehead, and stood, moving to the opposite side of the bed and removing his clothes at the same time.

The mattress dipped, and Oliver rolled to face Dean, keeping the covers tight around him. Dean smiled and held out his arm. Oliver wasted no time and scooted into his embrace, resting his head on Dean's chest and sighing when his arm came around him.

"Sleep," Dean murmured, pressing a kiss to his head.

Oliver closed his eyes and inhaled the scent of smoke, leather and something earthy. Sliding his arm over Dean's stomach, he held tight and succumbed to sleep.

He woke up overheated and sweaty, cocooned in his covers and spooned by a furnace. At least, that's what it felt like. His eyes blinked open several times before they would stay that way for longer than a second. Pushing the cover off his shoulders, he exhaled, trying to cool himself down, but the heatwave from behind him didn't help. He refused to move. Feeling the gentle ebb and flow of Dean's breathing on his neck was something he wouldn't deny himself.

"What's that smile for," Dean rasped, making Oliver jump.

He chuckled. "I thought you were still asleep. How did you know I was smiling?"

"A guess. I was asleep until you pushed the covers off. I don't mind, though." He kissed Oliver's exposed shoulder. "It gives me more time to taste you." He left a trail of kisses up Oliver's neck to his ear.

Oliver pushed the side of his head further into the pillow, trying to give Dean more room. "Taste away," he groaned when Dean pulled his earlobe into his mouth.

Dean's hand skimmed across Oliver's chest and stomach, Oliver automatically clenching his stomach muscles to make them seem smaller.

"Shh, relax. It's me."

Oliver inhaled and let go. He flinched when he felt his stomach expand further than he'd have liked but tried to ignore it. It wasn't easy, but Dean did a pleasant job of distracting him when his hand slid over his boxers and cupped his rapidly hardening cock.

"Is this for me, Oliver? Do you like it when I touch and kiss you?"

"Yes," he breathed, canting his hips to press harder against Dean's hand.

"You're good for me. How do you want it? Do you want my mouth on that gorgeous dick, or do you want my cock in your ass? Your choice, sweetheart."

The endearment sank deep inside Oliver, and tears welled up. "Please, Dean! I need you inside me!" He wanted Dean to be inside him like his words were. He couldn't do anything but beg; his emotions were all over the place.

"I can do that."

Dean shoved the covers from their bodies, the chill washing over Oliver as Dean rolled him onto his back. Oliver tucked the pillow further beneath his head, lifting his upper body. When he was positioned, Oliver smiled at Dean as he drew nearer and nearer, closing the distance between their mouths. He'd never tire of kissing this man.

The tongues tangled, sliding alongside each other's in a sensual caress Oliver felt in his lower stomach. The kiss deepened, and Dean smoothed his hands down Oliver's body to the waistband of his boxers. Oliver helped Dean to push them off, discarding Dean's at the same time. He had a feeling this first time would be quick, and he couldn't wait.

"Condoms? Lube?"

Oliver pointed to the bedside table. Dean moved off him, much to Oliver's disappointment, but returned with supplies. They moved in sync, Oliver rolling to his hands and knees, and Dean kneeling between his legs. Dropping his forehead and chest to the bed, Oliver closed his eyes and concentrated on the feeling of Dean's hands all over him.

"Are you ready, Oliver?"

"Yes, please!"

Dean's finger pressed against his pucker at the same time a hand encircled Oliver's cock. He groaned into the covers, gripping with both hands while Dean prepared him for the coming intrusion.

When Dean pulled his fingers free, Oliver whimpered. "Shh, give me a second."

A blunt pressure against his hole had him opening his mouth and exhaling in a rush. He relaxed and focused on every single inch that was driven into him. The drag on his insides had his eyes rolling into the back of his head. Once Dean was fully seated, he paused. One hand rested on the mattress by Oliver's hips, the other reached around and stroked Oliver's cock.

"Oh, fuck! Please move!"

Dean withdrew the tiniest amount, then moved forward again. He repeated the action several times until Oliver moaned and pushed back, taking Dean deeper.

"Jesus, Oliver. Fuck."

"Please! Fuck me! Harder!"

Oliver writhed beneath the muscular body, wanting everything Dean was willing to give him. Everything.

Chapter 14

Dean

Dean would deny Oliver nothing. He repositioned his hands at Oliver's waist and picked up speed, slamming into Oliver and sending delicious sensations through his body. He could feel his orgasm barrelling down on him, and he wanted Oliver there with him.

"Come for me, Oliver! Come *with* me."

Sweat dripped down his forehead, back and chest, not only from their activities but also because of the heat in the room. The slapping of their skin and their heavy breathing were the only sounds, sending Dean higher.

"I'm coming! Ah, fuck!"

His body convulsed, his hips stuttering out of rhythm. His hands gripped Oliver when Oliver's body clenched on his sensitive cock, pulling more from Dean's spent dick as Oliver tipped over the edge. Dean rested his forehead on Oliver's back, gasping into his skin. His cock slid free, but he stayed where he was, kissing and licking the sweat from Oliver's body while they came down from their high.

"I needed that," Oliver mumbled.

"As much as you needed to sleep," Dean retorted with a chuckle. "How are you feeling?"

Oliver pushed upright, no doubt keeping himself out of the wet patch, and smiled over his shoulder at Dean. "Much better, thanks."

"I'm glad to hear it. Shower?"

"God, yes, please. It's bloody hot already, and it's not even seven in the morning."

"The joys of summer."

They stumbled to the bathroom and ducked under the spray alternately. They did nothing more than kiss and touch, but it felt like much more. Much deeper. More intense. Dean pushed the thought aside and concentrated on Oliver. Once they were decent, they descended the stairs for breakfast and to cook.

"You told me about your plans to extend the restaurant. Do you have a time frame in mind for that?" he asked once they finished eating, and Oliver had given him a knife, a chopping board and some vegetables.

"Business is booming. I don't think it will be too long unless something happens. Maybe two years. It's difficult to tell because I need to ensure I have money set aside in case anything big breaks like the ovens or something. There's no telling if or when that would happen, so I need to be careful."

"Understandably. Hopefully, two years, though, if everything goes to plan." He was hoping it would be sooner because Oliver needed a break. He wished he could take some of the burden from him, but Dean knew nothing about running a business.

Oliver nodded. "Yes." There was a lull in the conversation until Oliver said, "What were you doing at the restaurant last night?"

Dean grinned. "I wanted to surprise you. I'm in the middle of my shifts and wanted to see you."

"I hope you're going to get some more sleep before you start work tonight?" Oliver narrowed his eyes at him.

"Yes. Once we've checked over the restaurant, I'll head home for a nap."

Oliver frowned. "I forgot about that. I can do that, no problem."

"No, I promised to help, and I will. I can sleep after. There's plenty of time." Dean leaned over the counter and puckered his lips.

Oliver shook his head with a smile and kissed him. "Thank you."

Dean wasn't sure if Oliver was ready to share any information, but this was as decent an opening as he might get. "Is there some reason you won't allow someone else to check on the restaurant?"

Remaining silent while Oliver pondered his question was hard, but he concentrated on chopping the veg. Dean had a feeling he knew what Oliver was going to say, but he wasn't certain.

"There are several reasons, I think," Oliver began. "The restaurant is my life, my livelihood. I have sunk everything into the business to make it a success. It's difficult leaving something important to you in the hands of someone who may not realise *how* important it is. I don't want to be let down."

"Let down? Who let you down?" Dean tried to concentrate on what he was doing as well as listen to Oliver's words, but the pain in the chef's voice was difficult to bear.

"When I first started the restaurant, I was in a relationship. We'd been together for around two years. It was during that relationship that I'd been increasing my hours at work and trying to save enough money to begin my dream."

Dean watched as Oliver spoke, the vegetables forgotten in front of him. Oliver moved swiftly from doing one thing to doing another with no issues.

"I'd spoken to David about it before, and he'd agreed it was a terrific idea. We didn't see each other much in those two years, which is why it lasted as long as it did, but six months after opening the restaurant, David gave me an ultimatum. He'd obviously had enough of the relationship."

"You'd explained it to him, though. How could he turn around and draw a line in the sand?"

Oliver shrugged, but Dean could tell it hurt him, even now. "The worst thing was that he took me to court and tried to take me for what money he could get, saying I used *our* money to start the restaurant. What he hadn't realised was that I was meticulous with my accounting at that point. I knew where every penny came from and went to. He drew me through the mud, but he got nothing. Then dared to say I owed him." Oliver sighed.

"Asshole. Does he still bother you?"

Oliver shook his head, still moving around the kitchen. "He moved away from what I heard."

"You said several reasons. What are the others?" Dean tried to change the subject.

"Well, on a similar subject to what happened there, I found out yesterday that one of my servers has been skimming money from the till for the last six months." Oliver huffed. "I guess I'm going back to checking all the figures in minute detail again, which is a good thing and a curse."

"What do you mean?" Dean began chopping again.

Oliver set a pan of pasta on the hob to boil, then stared out of the window. "The need to check everything is an ever-present need in me. I don't know if I have OCD or something similar, but my mind won't rest if I allow someone else to do something without making sure they've done it right."

"And that's why you work such long hours," Dean surmised.

Oliver nodded. "I can't let go of it. The restaurant is everything to me."

Dean put the knife down and strode over to Oliver, sliding his hands around his waist and linking his fingers together, and rested his chin on his shoulder. "You are amazing. After everything life has thrown at you, you are still standing and fighting every day."

"It doesn't feel like enough some days. Like this." Oliver pointed to the food. "It's all I can do, but it doesn't seem to be enough. The shelter needs more, other places need more, but I can't do anything else."

Dean spun Oliver around, holding him. "You are doing everything you can, and that, to me, is fantastic. Few people around here will go to such lengths, at the expense of their time—and sleep. You are one in a million."

"No, I'm not."

Dean cupped his chin, bringing their mouths together. "Talented and modest. I like it."

Oliver snorted, smoothing his hands over Dean's arms. "Did you finish those vegetables?"

Heat crept into Dean's cheek. "Almost?"

"Is that a question or an answer?" Oliver's eyes shone.

"An answer?"

They laughed and turned back to the table, where Dean had plenty of work to get done. He didn't mind, but an idea had been seeded, and he couldn't wait to get to work that night. Plans were afoot.

After dropping off the food at the shelter and following Oliver to work, they checked through the restaurant, and Oliver was pleased to see nothing needed changing. Some of the weight seemed to leave Oliver's shoulders, and Dean realised how much he carried, especially when his insecurities pressed close. He understood exactly why Oliver was like he was after what that asshole put him through.

Dean drove home and slept the afternoon away, rousing again when his alarm woke him at four in the afternoon. His apartment was an empty space he'd not decorated or filled with personal belongings, but after spending time with Oliver, he realised he needed to unpack a few more boxes and make it a home. He jotted "boxes" on his calendar for his next day off while he ate some toast.

Pulling out his phone, he debated sending his message but did, anyway.

DEAN: *Would you be able to drop by the station later? I'd like to talk to you about something.*

He got ready for work, then climbed on his bike, roaring down the street. He was going to have to get Oliver on the back of his bike one day. He was certain he'd enjoy the freedom, although his concerns about his weight would no doubt stop him from agreeing.

Oliver had given him a lot of trust that morning when he'd laid himself bare to the wounds of his past. Had he been able to close himself off again before he left for work?

Wandering into the station, he called out greetings to Blue Watch and headed for the changing rooms. Niall and Scott were already there, and they spoke for a while—well, he and Niall did. Scott brooded. Once they were ready, they strode back to the main area to get the handover from the previous watch and to get the information from Paul at the start of their shift. All in all, it had been quiet, although he knew better than to say that aloud.

As soon as they completed the necessities—checking over the engines, getting everything ready to go—Dean dashed up the stairs to Paul's office and knocked.

"Come in!"

He entered, finding Paul behind his desk and Quinn waiting in a visitor's chair. "Evening." He nodded and sat beside Quinn.

"I spoke to Quinn about what you told me the other day. The fundraiser for the shelter. Is this what this is about?"

Dean leaned forward, resting his elbows on the arms of the chair. "Yes and no. Did you know Oliver has been helping the shelter out with food?"

"Yes. It's common knowledge, I think," Paul said.

"Do you know he's about killing himself to do it?"

Quinn sat forward. "What?"

Dean sighed. "This is Oliver's day. He gets up around six in the morning, cooks for the shelter and delivers the food to them around ten o'clock. He heads to the restaurant and works from then until it closes, then helps to clean and set the place to rights. Then he goes home to bed, although not always sleeping straight away. Rinse and repeat." They both frowned at him. "Okay, let me say it again in times. Gets up at six, cooks for two to three hours, delivers it, goes to the restaurant by ten-thirty. From ten-thirty in the morning until one the next morning, he's working at the restaurant. He sleeps for, on average, four hours a night. I'm worried."

"I didn't realise how much he was working. I thought he took a break in the middle or left someone else in charge at some point. Why is he doing it all by himself?" Quinn asked.

"His reasons are personal, but I had a thought about it while I was talking to him." He turned to Quinn. "Would you be interested in helping him to cook for the shelter?"

Quinn grinned. "I'd love to. I never thought about it before." He stared at Paul. "What do you think?"

Paul smirked. "You're already going to do it. Why are you asking me?"

"Because we're a team."

The words settled inside Dean, and he sat back, staring at the far wall. A team. That's what Oliver needed. A team he could rely on.

"Dean?"

He came back to the conversation. "Sorry. What did you say?"

"I was asking if you were all right," Paul said.

"Yeah, I'm good. Oliver has trust issues, which is all I can say. I need to prove to him that his staff and his friends have his back. That they're a team. That we're a team. I don't know how to do that."

Quinn rested his hand over Dean's. "Talk to him. Like I do with Paul, talk to him. Tell him your ideas. Show him, and he'll begin to see."

"What if he doesn't trust me?"

Paul chuckled. "I would say he already did if he's told you things he's told no one else."

"Why are *you* doing this, Dean?" Quinn asked, gazing at him.

"His restaurant means more to him than anything else. He means a lot to me, but I can see his struggle every day. The struggle he hides from everyone. I hate it."

Quinn smiled. "Show him you care by talking to him and including him in everything. Going behind his back will have the opposite effect."

"Why?"

"He'll believe you think he's not capable of dealing with things by himself when that's what he's been doing for years. You need to include him in every way so he doesn't feel left out or less than he is."

"He'll think I'm trying to take over," he murmured.

Quinn nodded. "Yes, and you don't want that."

"Thanks. I'll speak to him about it and let you know if that's okay?"

"Of course. As a side note, I'd love to cook for the shelter, whether it's every day or some days. I don't want to take anything away from Oliver, but I'm there if you need me."

"Thanks, Quinn." He glanced at Paul. "The fundraiser?"

Paul and Quinn shared a look. "How about a firefighter calendar?"

Dean's eyes widened. "What?"

Paul smirked. "You wanted to know. I asked around, and from what information I could find, a calendar provides double the funds to any other fundraiser we do." He paused. "What do you think?"

"I think the firefighters are going to kill me."

Paul and Quinn laughed. They spoke for a little longer, then Dean was called out of the office by the alarm. He wouldn't mention the calendar to anyone yet. He needed to finalise some details with Paul before he said anything.

The night continued in the same vein. They had several hours of downtime until a call came in, then another hour before another call. It wasn't continuous, but it kept them on their toes, and they got little sleep.

OLIVER: *Just a quick message to say goodnight. I'll see you soon x*

The message came through during one of their calls. He didn't reply straight away, not wanting the noise to rouse Oliver from any sleep he might have been getting, but as soon as the clock ticked closer to six in the morning, he chanced a reply.

DEAN: *I'll see you in my dreams as corny as that sounds x*

The handover was quick and simple, though Jason caught him before he could leave.

"Dean!" Jason shouted before he could climb onto his bike and escape. "We're going for breakfast. Do you want to come?"

He wanted to sleep. "Sure. Where are we going?"

"Duck & Waffle."

Dean blinked at him. "Excuse me?"

Jason threw his head back in laughter. "I can't believe you've not heard of the Duck & Waffle. How long have you been here again?" He didn't wait for Dean's answer. "Anyway, it's near one of the university campuses. Popular with students for obvious reasons—it's open twenty-four hours. They serve delicious waffles and full English breakfasts for those who want it."

"Sounds tasty. Are you heading straight there?"

"Yeah."

"All right. I'll meet you there."

Jason gave him the address, and he typed it into his phone and got on the road. It was around twenty minutes away but closer to his apartment than the station was. He couldn't complain. As soon as he'd parked in the car park and swung off the bike, Jason had caught him in a headlock and dragged him towards the building.

The Duck & Waffle reminded him of an old-style American diner with booths and stools at the counter. All that was missing were the roller-skating servers.

They dragged two long tables together, so everyone had plenty of room. The server came and took their drink orders first—everyone asked for coffee despite needing to sleep soon. The menu had a broad selection, but Dean supposed they needed to cater to the different mealtimes. He decided on a full English breakfast, hoping it would fill him enough that he'd sleep even with the coffee.

"What's this I hear about a charity calendar?" Jason asked, pointing his finger down the table at Dean.

Dean's eyes widened, and he held up his hands. "The calendar wasn't my idea!"

"Yeah, yeah. I'll believe that when I see it. You want to see us bare it all, don't you?" Valerie pressed her finger into his cheek, her tone teasing and melodious.

"It was Chief's idea! Raising money was my idea, but not the calendar." He dived into giving them details about the shelter and how it received little funding from anywhere. He left out Oliver's link to it. "Chief said the calendar raises double the funds of any other type of fundraiser the station has ever held. I think that speaks for itself."

"Well, I'm up for it."

Dean raised his eyebrows. The voice had come from the person he'd least expected to be a fan of it all—Scott.

"Seriously?"

Scott nodded but said nothing further, tucking into the food that had arrived while he'd been talking.

"Yeah, I'm in, too," Niall said.

"I'm all in for getting naked!" Jason sing-songed.

Scott threw a napkin at him. "How did you ever get the crew commander position? You're juvenile."

"Aww, you love me, really," Jason teased, puckering his lips across the table and making kissing noises, though Dean could see his eyes dim.

Everyone laughed. As the conversation continued, Dean studied the occupants of the table. He'd never been happier.

Chapter 15

Jason

Jason loved the idea of posing for a calendar. He wasn't shy about his body, and he was always up for raising money for good causes. Maybe he could persuade the photographer to do some extra photos of him for his personal collection. Jason's collection, not the photographer's. Although that idea had merit. Maybe the photographer was gay, and he'd be up for a get-together.

He'd worn out his welcome at the pubs and clubs around Cambridge, not because he was an asshole, but because he had a voracious appetite and never spent more than a few nights with someone. Not for want of trying, though. He didn't need to be in someone's life, causing trouble.

"What are the plans for the photos? You know, poses and outfits?" he asked, then cut into an enormous pile of pancakes and shoved it in his mouth.

Dean waved his hands around. "I don't know, to be honest. I think it will be up to the photographer within reason. Definitely not nudes, Jason."

Jason pouted as best he could with his mouth full, then grinned and chewed. As much as they thought he'd want nudes, he didn't. He was confident about his body but not confident about his cock. He'd make sure that would never see the light of day in photos, especially ones that the public would no doubt see.

He swallowed and chased it down with a gulp of tea. "Nah, nudes are so last season," he joked.

Scott rolled his eyes, and Jason chuckled. He'd worked with the man for several years now, but he still couldn't figure out if Scott was stuck up or sex-deprived to give him his gruff demeanour. Regardless, Scott was a great firefighter, and he wouldn't wish for anyone else to be on his team. Except maybe Nash from Blue Watch because he was fine with a capital F.

Having to lead this bunch of misfits was a dream come true for Jason, and it had surprised him when Paul offered him the position. He'd expected Scott to get it, as he'd been there longer than Jason had. When he'd asked Paul, his station commander had waved him away, saying Scott was where he needed to be, then changed the subject. It had been something that had bothered him since he took over the position three years ago.

"Do we know if the pictures are going to be singles of us or two or as a group?" Valerie asked.

Dean held up his hands. "I don't know anything yet. I don't even know if Paul has agreed to go ahead with it. He said they were supporting other charities this year. It might not happen."

"Which charity would the calendar be for?" he asked.

"For the shelter that Benny runs."

"I know that place. It's close to Paul's heart. I doubt he'll deny the opportunity."

Scott leaned on the table. "He might have his hands tied, though. If he can't do it, there's nothing to stop us organising it ourselves."

Jason raised his eyebrows. "You'd go against the chief?"

Scott shook his head in what Jason knew was exasperation—it was an expression he threw in Jason's direction regularly. "No, but we wouldn't be going against them. Just because they can't organise it doesn't mean we can't. They might not have the manpower to do it."

Jason tilted his head. "Fair point."

"Oh, my god! The world's going to end!" Valerie said, clapping her hands over her cheeks.

"Why?" Niall asked, shoving some waffle in his mouth.

"He agreed with Scott! That never happens! Quick, everyone, under the tables." She pushed her chair back and went to climb underneath when Scott pulled her up and pushed her back onto the chair.

Niall choked on the food he'd eaten, and Dean pounded his back to help him.

The crew laughed, and the conversation continued.

Excluding the asshole that shall not be named because, thankfully, he had been turfed out, Jason had a fantastic crew, and he wouldn't change anything about it.

Chapter 16

Oliver

The heat combined with it being a Bank Holiday kept Oliver busy at the restaurant all day, a mixture of people not wanting to cook and being out of the house. The suffocating heat of the kitchen overwhelmed them all, but he made sure everyone had plenty to drink and took more breaks than usual. He didn't want any of his staff keeling over from heat exhaustion. As for himself, he was a sweaty mess, but there was nothing he could do about it. Even when the sun went down, it was still stifling. Thunderstorms were no doubt on the horizon.

"Boss? Dean's here. Thought you'd like to know." Jack winked before ducking back out of the door.

A smile crept across Oliver's face as he finished several orders. He wouldn't have time to sit with him that night, but he'd nip and see him for a few minutes.

A server came in with orders. "Dean wants—"

"Beef fajitas. Yeah, I know. He's going to look like a beef fajita one of these days," he grumbled good-naturedly. A ripple of laughter went around the kitchen.

"I doubt he's going to change much doing the job he does. He obviously burns a lot of calories as a firefighter," Serena said.

Oliver glanced over at her, seeing the twinkle in her eye. "Keep your hands to yourself, madam."

Serena held up her hands and chuckled. "Hey, I look but don't touch. Sue me!"

Oliver grinned. "Yeah, he is something to look at, I agree."

Their conversation turned to people they found attractive, and soon the kitchen staff was arguing over the best-looking celebrities. Oliver finished the plates he had, then handed the kitchen over to Serena for five minutes while he delivered Dean's food. He wiped his face and hands, swapping his chef's jacket around so he looked cleaner and carried the food to Dean's table.

Oliver's stomach fluttered when he caught sight of him. Dean was rugged, not traditionally gorgeous, but he was Oliver's type. When Dean saw him, his face lit up, and Oliver's stomach swooped. No one had ever looked at him like that. It made him want to trust in Dean's words that Oliver's appearance didn't matter to him. It was difficult, though.

"Here you go." He slid the steaming plate in front of Dean, then sank into the opposite seat. "I can't stay for long. The kitchen is crazy tonight."

Dean glanced around. "I can see that. What's caused this?"

"The weather and the Bank Holiday, I think. I usually see an uptick in customers when it's hot because most people don't want to be locked in a stifling kitchen when they could get someone else to do it."

Dean chuckled. "Yeah, that's true. How are you managing the heat?"

"We've got some air circulating, but it's not pleasant, that's for sure." Oliver shrugged. "I'm used to it, don't worry."

"I do worry." He laid his hand over Oliver's and squeezed. "I don't want you getting ill."

"Honestly, I'm fine." He stood. "I have to get back."

"Hey." Dean crooked with his finger, and Oliver leaned down. Dean lifted his head, pressing a kiss to his lips before moving back. "I want more than that, but I know you're working."

Oliver licked his lip, savouring the brief taste of him. He hated having not seen much of him in the past couple of days, but he was glad Dean was there now. If Dean was true to form, he'd stay until Oliver closed and follow him home.

"Stop looking at me like that," Dean groused, shifting in his seat.

Oliver sucked in a breath and stepped back. "See you soon."

The rest of the evening passed by. Oliver didn't get the chance to sit with Dean again, but his staff told him when Dean moved from the table to the bar. While he cleaned up his station, he thought about their relationship. He had gone from not wanting anyone to be in his life because he couldn't give them the time they deserved to not wanting Dean to leave him. As busy as he and Dean were, they seemed to have made strides to see each other as much as their working hours allowed. Sometimes, he felt like he was taking more than giving because his hours were inflexible, but he had to hope Dean would say something if that was the case.

"Hey," Dean said. "I was thinking…"

"That's always dangerous." Oliver smirked.

Dean narrowed his eyes. "Could you write down everything you need to check at night before you go home? I thought we could go through it and work out which are more important to you, and maybe I could help with the things less important? The things that won't cause too much upset if you don't check them yourself."

Oliver stared at him, his heart racing. When he didn't reply, Dean squeezed his hand. "Sorry, um, that sounds good. No one has ever…everyone believed I was a control freak."

Dean shook his head. "No, you're not. You have a lot riding on this business. It's okay to want to protect it."

Oliver swallowed hard against the lump in his throat. "Thanks."

Though it took extra time, he went around the restaurant with Dean in tow, writing down what he checked and what he was looking for until it was all done. They exited out the back door in time for Zee to pull up. Transferring the bags, he pulled Zee into a hug.

"Thank you for this, Zee. I know it messes up your sleeping, but it's better than getting you into trouble."

She waved her hand. "It's not a problem for me. I barely sleep as it is. It's unlikely, even if I didn't do this, that I would sleep before 3 a.m. anyway."

"Still, you go above and beyond to help. Thank you."

"Thank you, too. You do all the work with what I give you. I'm glad we can do this for the shelter. They deserve the help."

She smiled at them both and climbed back into the car, waving as she drove off.

"Is she likely to get into trouble for this?" Dean asked, his forehead creased.

Oliver shrugged a shoulder. "It's possible. I think most people won't bother about it and will turn a blind eye, even if they're not already doing it, but she could lose her job over it because, technically, she's stealing from the company. Though most people wouldn't see it that way because the stuff would go straight in the bin, anyway."

"You would've thought the supermarkets would be delighted the food wouldn't waste."

"I believe that's why they pretend they don't know. It is a wonderful thing, but the company could get into trouble because the food is out of date on that day, and therefore, not good for consumption. But as we all know, dates have a little leeway in them, but companies who sell the food do not."

"That's crazy, but I can understand the legal aspects of it."

"It's a similar reason I can't cook the food in the restaurant's kitchen. I could, but if inspectors ever found out, there *could* be repercussions. I can't take the chance of them shutting me down, so I do it at home instead. Not ideal, but it still works."

Dean smiled. "I want to talk to you about that, but can we get home first?"

Home? "Yeah, sure. Let me lock the back door." He wandered over to the restaurant to lock and double-check the lock before heading back to the car. "I'll see you there."

"With bells on."

Oliver chuckled. "I wouldn't. It might wake the neighbours."

Dean laughed and swung his leg over his bike, with Oliver ogling his body as he did. There was something about the movement that made him quiver inside. The journey was brief, but fatigue was seeping in. He stifled a yawn when he parked in his drive and climbed out. Dean opened his boot before he got there and began lifting bags out. Oliver grabbed a few and strode to his door, opening it wide to let Dean through before backtracking to get the last bags and lock his car.

Dean was already putting the food away when he entered the kitchen, and it took him a few seconds to stop his heart from racing. At that moment, he realised how deep he was getting with Dean, how perfect he looked in his kitchen, in his home. He shook off the images and focused on his bags. Zee had outdone herself that night. There would be plenty of food for the following day, which reminded him of something he needed to tell Dean.

"I have to nip to the doctor's surgery tomorrow morning, but I'll be back quick enough to do the cooking."

Dean frowned. "Is everything okay?"

Oliver nodded. "A blood test, nothing to worry about." At least, he hoped that was the case.

"What time is your appointment?"

"Eight o'clock. I'll get up a little earlier, make a start on some of the cooking, then finish up when I get back." Dean nodded. "What did you want to talk to me about?"

"Oh, yeah." Dean smiled. "I had an idea that I wanted to run past you. What if I could find someone to help you with cooking for the shelter? Either doing some days for you to give you a break or taking over?"

Oliver's stomach dropped, and he stepped back. "I thought you were content with the way things were? I told you how long it would be until I could do anything about my long hours. You said you were happy with that, and now, you're telling me you want me to change things?" Oliver shoved the last items into the fridge and stuffed the empty bags into one before hanging it on the wall, ready to put back in the car. He shook his head, annoyance flowing through him.

"That's not what I was saying! I'm worried you're doing too much, Oliver. I'm trying to help."

"Yeah, trying to help me by taking away the one thing I said I could do to help the shelter. Or did you not listen when I was talking about it the other day?"

"I know you want to help the shelter. Surely, you can understand me trying to make things easier on you." Dean stood in front of him, holding his shoulders. "I don't want you to give anything up, but I'm worried you're doing too much."

Oliver pulled away. "I told you in the beginning what my time was like, and you agreed it was doable. Obviously, it isn't." Oliver swallowed. "I think you should go."

"Oliver, no. Let's talk this through."

"Why? So you can try to change my mind? So you can try to convince me to give up doing what I want to do? No. You didn't listen to me. You need to go. I have to think."

Oliver pivoted away and strode to the stairs, dragging himself up and shutting Dean out. He didn't hear Dean leave the house, but he heard his bike roaring off several long minutes later. Ignoring the tears trailing down his face, he got ready for bed, pretending he was back to where he'd been before Dean invaded his life. Back to being single.

Despite knowing he wouldn't sleep, he climbed into bed after his shower and lay staring at the ceiling. He had no idea how long he'd been lying there when his phone rang. Checking the screen, he saw Dean's name and sent the call to voicemail. It rang several times after that, and he ignored them all. It was only when someone began banging on his front door that he understood something was wrong.

Pulling on a pair of joggers, he raced to the front door and flung it wide. Dean stood there, eyes wide.

"I'm sorry, Oliver. The restaurant...it's on fire."

"What?"

"The restaurant is on fire. The crews are trying to put it out now, but I think you need to get there."

Oliver stared at Dean, not quite comprehending. "But we locked it up. Everything was fine. I switched everything off. There's no way..."

Dean stepped closer, resting his hands on Oliver's biceps. "I'm sorry. Let's get you dressed."

Oliver followed Dean's instructions without saying a word, still trying to wrap his mind around what Dean had said. How could his restaurant be on fire?

"No one knows yet. I'm waiting to hear from the crew, but we might get some more information when we get there."

It was only when Dean answered that Oliver realised he'd said the words aloud. He didn't understand what was happening. He switched off when Dean had bundled him into the passenger seat of the car. As they got closer, he could smell smoke and saw an orange glow in the distance. It still didn't make sense until they parked, and Dean helped him from the car, holding his hand as they walked the remaining distance to where several fire engines were.

The first glimpse of the restaurant stopped him in his tracks. He covered his mouth with one hand, staring at the flames consuming his livelihood. He dropped to his knees, a keening cry escaping him. Dean held him, rocking him, but Oliver couldn't hear a word he said. There were people between them and the restaurant, but Oliver didn't need to see the destruction to know it was gone. Everything he had worked for was gone. He'd lost everything.

He stared at the flames reaching for the sky, mesmerised, and lost all sense of time. Only when his legs began cramping did he move to stand on trembling limbs. He couldn't say anything, no matter how many times Dean asked him questions or asked him to tell him he was okay. He wasn't okay.

At least he had plenty of free time now. He snorted.

"Oliver?"

He glanced at Dean, sighing, and shook his head. He sank onto the kerb, sitting with his legs stretching out into the road and dropped his head into his hands. Dean was right next to him. After their fight earlier, he was surprised by

Dean's appearance and willingness to stay with him. He would've expected him to leave him alone as Oliver had asked him to, but once again, Dean was proving how much more he was than the men who came before him. It made Oliver see Dean's earlier comments in a different light.

While his world crumbled around him, Oliver focused on the one thing that hadn't changed. Dean.

"I'm sorry," he croaked.

Dean wrapped his arm around his shoulders. "What?"

"I'm sorry. For earlier. I can see now what you were trying to do. I'm used to being in charge of my own life. I forget people want to help." He swallowed. "It goes against my insecurities to ask for help."

"You don't need to worry about that now."

"Why not? It's all I have left. The fire has taken everything from me except you. I'm sorry for how I acted. I couldn't see past what had happened in my previous relationships. I put you in the same box as them, but you're nothing like them. You make the world a better place."

Dean held him tighter, bringing him into his chest and cradling him. "As do you. We can get through this together, Oliver. I promise."

"Oliver, Dean."

Oliver glanced up at his name, seeing Paul standing with a grim expression. "Hey." Oliver felt a little spaced out, but he could concentrate enough to hear what they were saying.

"We're not sure how the fire started yet, but as soon as the flames are out, we'll go in and look." He stared at Oliver.

"I'm sorry, Oliver. It's all gone. The fire was too big and spread too fast."

Oliver lifted his head. "Did everyone get out of the homes above?"

Paul nodded. "Everyone's fine. A bit of smoke inhalation, but they got clear in plenty of time."

"Well, at least I've got time to come to a barbecue now," he joked, huffing a little.

"I'd have preferred it was under better circumstances," Paul replied.

Oliver shrugged. "What's done is done."

Paul and Dean shared a glance, and Oliver knew what it was about. "I'm fine." He wasn't. "Do the fire crew need me to do anything?"

"No. You can talk to them tomorrow if they do."

"Okay." He rolled to his knees, then scrambled to his feet before holding his hand out to Paul. "Thank them for me and tell them to ring me tomorrow if they need me."

"Will do."

"Are you coming with me or staying here?" he asked Dean.

Dean glanced at Paul. "I'll come with you."

Oliver didn't wait. He strode to the car, climbing into the passenger seat because his hands were still trembling. He must be in shock or something because everything seemed far away. His body settled when Dean sat in the driver's seat and reached to clasp his hands.

"Are you okay? Oh, stupid question, Dean," he mumbled. "I'm sorry, Oliver. What can I do?"

"Take me home, Dean. Stay with me."

"I can do that."

Dean squeezed his hands and let go, and it was all Oliver could do to stop himself from reaching for Dean and crying for him to hold him. He could do that when they were in the safety of Oliver's home. When he hid behind closed doors. When people weren't looking at him with pity.

When he was secure and cocooned from the rest of the world.

He could wait a few more minutes.

Chapter 17

Dean

When Dean received the call that the restaurant was on fire, he hadn't been able to get to Oliver's fast enough, especially when he'd not answered his phone. He'd taken his car instead of his bike because he knew Oliver would be in no fit state to drive. Oliver had gone quiet, and Dean hadn't been able to coax anything out of him until Oliver had started talking while they were watching the flames take over his business. Oliver hadn't said what Dean had expected him to. Nothing about the fire; it was all about them and the disagreement they'd had earlier.

When Paul came over, they'd both worried about Oliver's behaviour, though neither said the words. Dean knew Paul would ring him the next day to make sure they were both okay.

In the car, it had taken everything to let go of Oliver's hand because he could feel how Oliver held him and knew he was holding on by a thread. Apart from the initial cry when he'd seen the fire, Oliver had shown no emotion to it, and it worried Dean.

He parked the car in Oliver's driveway, and they climbed out. Dean took Oliver's keys from his pocket where he'd put them earlier, not wanting Oliver to have to think about anything. When the door closed behind them, Oliver turned to him.

"Make love to me," he said, his eyes pooling with tears.

"I don't know if—"

"Please. Let me feel you."

Dean swallowed back his words and threaded his fingers through Oliver's, leading them up the stairs. He would do whatever Oliver needed.

Closing the bedroom door behind them, he faced Oliver, cupping his jaw and lowering his lips to feast on the man's mouth. Oliver gripped his hoodie and moved closer. Dean slid his hands behind Oliver's head and deepened the kiss, tasting tears along with Oliver's usual flavour. He contemplated stopping, but he thought Oliver might need reassurances before he could finally let himself feel everything he was bottling up at that moment. Pushing thoughts of stopping aside, he began divesting Oliver of his clothes.

One item at a time dropped to the floor until they were naked. Dean stepped forward, pushing Oliver back onto the bed. Oliver moved until his head was resting on the pillows, then Dean crawled over him, reaching to the bedside for the lube and a condom. He dropped them to the bed and kissed Oliver, sliding his hand over his body while bracing one by his head. As much as he wanted to take his time, he knew Oliver needed the release.

He picked up the lube, squirting some onto his fingers and rubbing against Oliver's hole. The pucker trembled as much as Oliver's body did, and Dean pressed inside. By the time Oliver was prepared enough to take Dean's cock, Oliver's shaft was a deep red and leaking precome onto his stomach. He rolled on the condom, slicked it, then lifted Oliver's legs over his forearms. They'd never tried this position, and he wasn't sure if Oliver would be comfortable, but he knew the man would say something if he wasn't, even distant as he was.

"Ready for me?"

"Always," Oliver breathed.

He breached his entrance and kept driving forward, inch by inch. Sweat dripped down his back from withholding. "Are you okay?"

Oliver nodded. "Make love to me," he repeated.

Dean pressed a kiss to Oliver's leg, then pulled back. He sank inside again, repeating the process several times when Oliver keened his agreement to the angle. He picked up speed, watching Oliver's responses to make sure he was okay.

"You feel good," he groaned, speeding up until he was slamming into Oliver. He couldn't lean down and kiss the man in this position, but he gripped him and brought him to the edge before he encircled Oliver's cock and stroked in time with his thrusts.

"I'm...I'm..."

Oliver shouted Dean's name, and his cock emptied over his chest and stomach. The sight of it and the clenching of his ass muscles had Dean seconds away. Three thrusts more, and Dean was over the edge, his focus hazing out as his body released.

"Fuck," he gasped.

When Oliver whimpered below, he pulled free, discarding the condom over the edge of the bed while he rearranged their bodies until they were on their sides, facing each other. He wrapped his legs and arms around Oliver as tears began streaming down his face.

"It's okay. It's okay. I'm here."

He murmured nonsense in Oliver's ear while the man grieved at what he'd lost that night. Dean's heart broke for him.

Oliver's phone alarm went off at six-thirty that morning, but neither had slept for long. Oliver had several breakdowns during the night, and Dean had held him through them all. The man looked drained.

"Why don't you rearrange your appointment? You can get some more rest."

Oliver swung his legs over the edge of the bed, sitting upright. "I need to get it done. I won't sleep anyway. I might as well go." He stood, shuffling across the room to the bathroom and disappeared inside.

Dean stood, pulling on his clothes. "Oliver, I'm going to get the coffee started," he called through the closed door.

"Okay, thanks."

Dean sighed. He didn't know whether last night had got everything out of Oliver's system or whether it would continue to hit him now and again. Luckily, Dean had several days off now and could help him out—if he would let him, that is.

He wandered into the kitchen, filled the kettle and flicked the switch, grabbing two mugs from the cupboard and adding instant granules. While he waited for the kettle to boil, he emptied the bags of food they had left on the table, those that wouldn't spoil from being left out. He placed the empty bags in the bag Oliver had used the previous evening and sorted the food to make it all visible at a glance. There was a lot of food this time, but it would give Oliver something to do.

Pouring boiling water into the mugs, he stirred the contents as he considered his options. He didn't know what Oliver intended to do today, other than go for his blood test and cook for the shelter. He certainly couldn't go to the restaurant. Dean wasn't sure whether the restaurant's accounts and other paperwork had gone up with the building. He hoped not.

Oliver shuffled into the room. "Thanks," he said when Dean handed him the mug.

They sipped in silence until Dean couldn't take it any longer. "Do you want me to drive you to the doctor?"

Oliver shook his head. "I'll be fine. I'm sure you have other things to do."

Dean inhaled and put his mug down. Crossing over to Oliver, he grabbed his hips. "I have nothing planned for today except spending time with you. Helping you with whatever you need. Doing whatever you want me to." He winked.

"That sounds promising." Oliver smiled, small but there, nonetheless. "There is plenty of cooking to do."

"Then we'll do that." Dean dropped a kiss on Oliver's mouth and turned back for his coffee. "There is a lot of food here."

"Let's go through and see what we have, and I'll start making a plan."

They worked side by side for several minutes, dividing the food into different piles depending on the meal Oliver would be cooking. There was enough for seven different meal choices, which seemed to please Oliver.

As usual, he relegated Dean to chopping the vegetables and potatoes. He didn't mind. As long as it helped Oliver, it was a blissful experience to spend time with him. When Oliver said he needed to leave, Dean almost asked again if he wanted him to drive but refrained, not wanting to upset him.

Therefore, it surprised him when Oliver said, "Dean, will you drive me?"

Dean raised his eyebrows but schooled his surprise. "Of course."

The drive didn't take them past the restaurant, for which Dean was glad; he didn't think Oliver could deal with that right then. Within minutes of arriving at the surgery, Oliver was out again, blood test done and sent off, and they were driving home.

"What do you want to do after cooking and delivering for the shelter?" he asked.

Oliver was quiet for a minute, then glanced over at him. "I think I need to deal with the questions from whoever needs to speak to me, then I'll contact the insurance company and see where I stand. As much as this has broken my heart, I had enough insurance to cover in case this happened. I'm hoping I can start rebuilding quickly."

"You're planning on rebuilding. I wasn't sure if you'd find a different location instead."

Oliver canted his head. "Why?"

"Pure convenience, I suppose."

Oliver nodded, his gaze distant. "It would be convenient, yes, but I love where the restaurant is...was. It's the perfect location, and everyone knows where it is...was." He rubbed a hand over his face. "I'm going to rebuild."

"Okay. Do you want me to contact Paul and see who you need to speak to?"

"Yeah, that would be great. I have no idea who needs me."

Dean reached across to link his fingers with Oliver's and pulled his hand for a kiss, his gaze on the road ahead, though his attention was firmly on the man beside him. Oliver went back to cooking while Dean called Paul.

"Hey, how're things?" Paul asked.

"All right. Oliver wants to know who he needs to speak to about the fire."

"The fire inspector went through the remains and found it was arson. Someone had set a fire in the main dining area, and with the accelerant, the fabric didn't stand a chance. It spread too fast to be held back."

"Fuck. Who would want to do that to him?"

"No idea. The police need to speak to him." Paul rattled off a number, and Dean wrote it down. "How is he holding up?"

Dean fiddled with the pen. "Better than expected. He's talking of rebuilding already."

"That's a good thing. He's looking to the future."

"Yeah, but…"

"What?"

Dean sighed. "I don't know. I'd expected him to be more of a mess. Don't get me wrong, last night was difficult. He was distraught, but it's as if he's ignoring his pain. I don't know. Forget about it."

"You know him, Dean. You've become close in the last few weeks. Give him time and be there for him. He'll lean on you if he needs to."

"Yeah, I suppose."

"Get the police out of the way, then ring me later. Quinn would like you both around for dinner tonight."

"Okay. I'll ask and let you know."

He said goodbye and wandered back to the kitchen, where several pans were bubbling away on the stove, and Oliver was chopping the vegetables with a speed he would never hope to match.

Oliver glanced up and smiled. "Is Paul okay?"

"Yeah, he's fine. Quinn has invited us for dinner tonight if you'd like to go."

Oliver hesitated for a second, then nodded. "That would be nice."

"Great. Paul's given me the number for the police. That's who you need to speak to."

"All right. I'll do that as soon as I've done this cooking and delivered it."

They worked together—well, as much together as Dean could when he couldn't cook anything—and soon it was all piled into the boot of his car. The drive to the shelter would usually take them past the restaurant, but Dean went the long way around instead. He parked outside the shelter as a little drizzle started.

"Why does it always rain when we're delivering food," he joked.

"It thinks you need a shower." Oliver grinned at Dean's open-mouthed expression.

"Oliver!" They smiled at Benny as he raced towards them, throwing his arms around Oliver. "I'm sorry to hear what happened. Are you okay?" he said when he pulled back.

Oliver nodded and gave a small smile. "I'm good. I'll be back up and running soon. I'll let you know when the opening night is. You and Leona can come."

"Can't wait. You didn't have to cook today, you know."

Oliver shrugged. "I already had the food. I may as well do what I love to help others while things are up in the air."

Dean rested his hand on Oliver's nape and squeezed. "Shall we take these inside?"

They each grabbed a couple of containers, and Dean locked the car while they carried them to the kitchen; then Dean and a volunteer went back for the final few items. Benny and Oliver were deep in conversation when he returned, and he left them to it, not wanting to intrude, though he watched Oliver's body language for signs of stress. Despite Paul's words, Dean was worried. Oliver was effective at hiding things from him.

The drive home was quiet, and Dean stopped himself from filling it with questions or inane talk. When they pulled up to Oliver's drive, there was a police car outside and two officers at the door. Oliver climbed out and greeted them; Dean followed behind.

"Good morning, Joey. Morning, Kade." Oliver held out his hand and shook before slipping between them and unlocking the door. "Come on in. I'll make a brew."

With the front door closed, Dean removed his shoes and wandered down the hallway. He needed to check if Oliver wanted him there for the questions, but he didn't know these officers like Oliver seemed to.

"Hey," he said, "do you want me to go somewhere else while you're talking?"

Oliver glanced at him, eyes wide. "No, stay. If you can, I mean. If you have other plans, that's fine."

Dean slid his arm around Oliver's shoulders and pressed a kiss to his temple. "I'm staying then. I didn't want to overstay my welcome."

"You're always welcome here." Oliver lifted his mouth for a kiss, which Dean kept brief no matter how much it pained him.

"All right."

He carried two teas over to the officers and sat down on a seat opposite. Oliver placed his cup in front of him, then sat next to Dean. Not wanting him to feel alone, Dean rested his arm on the back of Oliver's chair, his fingertips against him.

"I'm sorry about what happened, Oliver. I can't believe it myself," Joey said.

"Thanks. It is a bit of a shock."

Joey nodded and glanced at Kade. "We've received the report from the fire inspector. I'm sorry to say someone set that fire. Now, we need to figure out who."

Oliver's face paled, and he gripped his cup hard enough his knuckles were white. "Who would...?" He dropped his head and closed his eyes, rubbing his hands through his hair.

"Can you think of anyone who might have a grievance against you?"

"The only person I can think of is Rikki Long. I fired her after I caught her stealing money."

"When was this?" Kade opened his notebook.

"Thursday night. Jack saw her off the property afterwards."

Joey nodded. "Anyone else?"

Oliver frowned but shook his head. "No. I've not fallen out with anyone recently." His gaze flicked to Dean, then to the table.

"Except me," Dean said.

"Dean! I know you wouldn't do this."

"It doesn't matter, Oliver. They need to know." He turned to the officers. "We had an argument on Monday night. Oliver asked me to leave, which I did. I only returned when I'd been told about the fire and came to tell him."

Kade stared at Oliver. "Do you want him present while we question you?"

Oliver rolled his eyes. "I know he didn't do it, Kade. He's a firefighter. He can stay."

Joey pursed his lips. "What did you argue about?" he asked Dean.

"I was trying to persuade Oliver to get help with the shelter cooking. He didn't agree with my suggestion and asked me to leave, which I did."

"What time was that?"

Dean frowned and sighed. "Um, I don't know. I didn't look at the clock when we closed the restaurant. Maybe around one-thirty or two o'clock."

"And what time did you return?"

"Three-twenty."

"That's very specific," Kade mentioned.

"I received the call at three o'clock. It took me twenty minutes to get dressed and drive to Oliver's."

"Kade, stop. Dean wouldn't do this."

Dean rested his hand on Oliver's arm. "It's okay, Oliver. They're doing their job. They need to rule me out. Being a firefighter does not mean I'm incapable of setting a fire. If anything, that goes against me. I didn't do it, though. I would never do that to you."

Oliver cupped his cheek. "I know you wouldn't."

"There's no one else you can think of who might have a grudge against you?" Joey asked.

Oliver shrugged. "You know my history, Joey. David is the only one who caused me any hassle before this. I doubt he would have returned to continue."

Joey nodded. "Okay. We'll keep looking into it. Do you have remote access to the CCTV cameras that are at the back of the building where you usually park?"

"No, but the security company should."

"All right. If you can get me their details, we'll contact them to ask. It might show something."

Oliver rose and left the room, leaving Dean with the officers.

"Don't hurt him," Joey said, staring at Dean with a fierce determination.

"I won't. Not intentionally. The argument came about because he thought I was trying to change him, when in fact, I was trying to get him to go easier on himself. He's been working himself into the ground, and I'm worried about him."

Joey opened his mouth to say something, but Oliver returned. "Here's the number."

"Thanks, Oliver. We'll be in touch, okay."

Oliver saw them out while Dean cleaned the mugs, putting them to dry on the draining board.

"Now, I need to call the insurance company and begin making plans. I have an idea."

Chapter 18

Oliver

Oliver withheld his idea from Dean until he'd spoken with the insurance company. They said they'd look into it and be in touch once they had completed the initial investigation. The person he spoke to had advised that if the claim was successful, the payout should happen within a few days, but the investigation into the claim could take two to four months. It wasn't what Oliver had wanted to hear, but it meant he could get his plans in place before that happened.

"Are you going to tell me your plans or make me guess?" Dean sipped his tea, though his eyes twinkled at Oliver.

Oliver cradled his mug. "I'm going to see if I can extend the restaurant. The small building to the back of it used to be a café, but it's been sitting empty for a while. If I can buy that place, then I could hire someone or several people to cook the food for the shelter there. It won't happen for a while yet, but I can at least look into it."

"That sounds like a great idea. What made you decide to do that?"

Oliver held out his hand, palm uppermost, and Dean put his hand on top. "You did."

Dean frowned, then his eyes widened. "No, I didn't mean you had to stop providing for the shelter, Oliver! I know it means a lot to you. All I wanted to do was help you. I wanted you to not be as tired or stressed. I promise that was all. I never wanted you to stop doing what you love."

Oliver waited patiently while Dean finished. "All done?" Dean nodded. "I know you didn't. At first, I thought you were trying to change me, but this fire made me realise I had several people who would care if something happened to me, and I wasn't giving them the time I should. I am tired. I am stressed. That is why the doctor gave me a blood test. When I get the results, I'll know whether it's something wrong with me or if it's because I'm working too much." He squeezed Dean's hand. "I want to spend more time with you than snatches of minutes here and there."

Dean smiled. "I'd love that. But wouldn't buying that extra building put a strain on your profits?"

Oliver tilted his head from side to side. "Potentially. I still have to run the numbers, but I think I'll be able to do it, especially if the only thing I have to do is pay a wage. Hopefully, Zee can continue bringing the food. If that stops, I'll have to rethink."

Dean stood and rounded the table, crouching by Oliver's side. "You are amazing." He pressed a kiss to Oliver's hand. "Before, when I spoke about getting someone to take over for the shelter, I had already spoken to Quinn about it. I didn't make any promises," he hastened to add, "I told him you might like the help, but he said I needed to speak to you first. I'm sorry for going behind your back. I was trying to help."

Oliver shifted in his chair until he faced Dean, sliding his fingers over the man's head. "It's okay. You did it with my well-being in mind. I didn't understand that at the time because nobody had ever done it before. If Quinn is interested, then we can discuss it. At the moment, though, I may as well keep doing it myself because I don't have the restaurant to think about."

"It won't be long before it's up and running again." Dean dropped his eyes and rubbed his nose as he slid into the seat closest to Oliver. "You're taking this very well. I don't mean you should shout and scream about the injustice of it, but apart from that one time, you've not said anything about what happened. You've not cried. Nothing. I'm worried you're holding it in."

Oliver sighed and turned back to his tea, sorting through his emotions. "I don't know how to answer that. When it happened, it felt like my whole life had been torn apart, and I'd lost everything. But then I thought about the shelter and the people who need that place, and I realised I still had a lot. A lot more than they did, and a lot more than I thought I had. It put things into perspective. Yes, I'm upset because the fire took away something I'd worked hard to make a success. But some people don't have insurance, don't have people helping, don't have any kind of support network or financial aid. I'm *lucky*." His breath caught on the last word.

Dean took his hands again. "You amaze me more every minute." He bowed his head to kiss Oliver's knuckles. "Shall we get ready to go? I know Paul and Quinn are eager to see you."

Oliver smiled. "Sure. It'll be strange having someone else cook for me."

"You'll be able to check out Quinn's talents and see if you can deal with him helping with the shelter food later on." Dean winked.

"I'll tell him you said that."

Dean drove to Paul and Quinn's house a little later than planned after fooling around in the shower turned into something more. By the time they arrived, they were pleasantly relaxed. Paul opened the door with a flourish and invited them in. Oliver had never been to their house before, having only met Paul when he'd been one of the crew members who had visited the restaurant before it opened to ensure it had the smoke alarms and everything needed for it to be reliable to work in. Oliver hadn't needed to have them check it out, but he'd wanted to be sure. After speaking with Paul for several minutes about food, Quinn and the fire station, they'd become firm friends. It had been a busy time in Oliver's life, and he'd never had the chance to visit, though Paul and Quinn often visited the restaurant.

"How are you both?" Paul asked as they wandered down the long hallway to the kitchen at the back of the house.

Oliver studied the photographs lining the hallway. There were pictures of the fire station crews, Paul and Quinn's wedding day, several other photos of them and their kids, but it was the images of the buildings which caught Oliver's attention. There was a set of eight photographs depicting the fire station, the veteran centre, a bar called Crush, a bakery called Sweet Tooth, the hospital, the nursing home, a university building and...Oliver's restaurant.

"This reminds us of the places that mean a lot to us as a family."

Oliver didn't jump at Paul's voice but kept his focus on the pictures. "Thank you," he whispered.

"We change them out as things change in our lives, but those that are taken down get put into an album instead."

"It's a lovely idea. I might have to steal it when the restaurant gets back up and running."

"Feel free." Paul clapped him on the shoulder. "Come on. Let's eat."

They wandered through to the kitchen where Quinn was finishing up, it seemed. "Hi! I'm glad you could come." He wiped his hands on a towel at his waist and pulled Oliver into a hug.

Oliver felt a prickle in his eyes, but it was more to do with how much time he'd wasted not getting to know these people as well as he could. That would change. "Hey, thanks for having me."

"You're always welcome. Open door policy for family."

Oliver frowned. "I'm not family."

"Chosen family, not blood family." Quinn smiled. "I hope you like ratatouille."

Oliver grinned. "Love it."

"Grab a drink and go join the others on the back porch. It'll be ready in five."

He chose a beer bottle and exited onto the enclosed back porch. Paul and Dean were already deep in conversation about the fire station. He sank into the seat next to Dean, staring across the back garden. With the free time he had now, he'd be able to get his garden sorted and maybe put in the herb garden he always said he'd do. He might even add some raised beds and grow some vegetables or something. He could use the food for the shelter.

"What do you think, Oliver?" Paul asked.

Oliver snapped back to the conversation. "Sorry. I was miles away. Think about what?" He glanced at Dean, whose cheeks were flushed.

"Dean had an idea to do a fundraiser. When he came to me about it, I wasn't sure, but I asked around. A firefighter calendar raises more money than anything else. We were thinking of doing one and giving all the proceeds to the shelter."

Oliver stared at Paul, swallowed and turned his gaze to Dean. "Why?"

Dean smiled but ducked his head. "I know how much the shelter means to you. I wanted to help."

Closing his eyes didn't stop his emotions from rising to the surface. How the hell had he been as lucky to have Dean want him? He blinked open, eyes watery, focusing on Dean. "I think that would be fantastic."

"Food's ready!"

They rose and headed for the door, but Oliver tugged on Dean's arm to get him to stop.

"Everything okay?"

Oliver said nothing, just cupped his jaw and kissed him, hard and deep, then soft and gentle. When he pulled back, they were breathing hard, and Oliver smiled. "Thank you." He kissed him again. "For everything."

Dean gave a bemused smile. "You're welcome."

They sat at the dinner table with Paul, Quinn and their twin sons, Eddie and Toby, who were both at university. The conversation was rife with teasing and laughter, and Oliver had never felt more at home as he did then. The food was delicious, and he would gladly accept any help Quinn wanted to give with cooking. When Paul asked about his plans for the restaurant, he explained his thoughts, and Quinn came on board with the idea. They brainstormed some more ideas and, before he knew it, four hours had passed, and it was getting dark.

"Thank you for having me, us," Oliver said to Quinn, glancing at Dean. "I'll be in touch about the plans."

"Make sure you do. I'm excited to help. I love cooking, but I would never stand the pressure of doing it in a busy kitchen. But cooking for the shelter would be my idea of heaven."

And Oliver believed it because Quinn's face lit up whenever he spoke about it. He knew there, and then, Quinn would be in charge of the shelter food. Now, he needed to persuade him to take a wage.

Oliver woke up, cocooned in warmth and smiled at the soft breath on his neck. There was no longer a rush to get up in the morning, so when Dean wasn't on shift, they lazed about in bed, but Oliver refused to wake him until he was ready to get up. It gave him time to think about everything and had become a ritual of sorts.

The past week had been filled with paperwork, claims, phone calls, cooking, organising, and everything else that needed to be done to ensure the restaurant would reopen as soon as they had given him the insurance money to pay for it. A builder had given him an estimate of the time it would take to rebuild—six months—which meant it might be open in time for next summer. It had seemed like a long way away to him, but once he got started on researching and planning, he knew he didn't want to rush.

One thing he hadn't done yet was visit the restaurant since the fire. He couldn't bring himself to do it and drove the long way around to avoid seeing it. Today was the day he was going back because he wanted to view the small property behind it, too. Dean was coming with him, which he was thankful for.

He'd been considering changing the opening hours for Nourris Moi when it reopened. After looking at his figures, he'd found the mid-afternoon made little money if he considered the number of staff. He still made a profit, but it was a much smaller margin than other times of the day. Lunchtime would stay the same because he had many people who came for business meetings, but he might close at two o'clock, then reopen at five o'clock. He needed to fill out the spreadsheet and see what the costs looked like with that business model, but it would mean he would have some spare time in the afternoon.

He wanted to make Serena head chef for the lunchtime hours, but presently, she was working for another restaurant. He didn't know if he could entice her back when the time came. If not, he would find someone else, and it would allow Oliver to start work at four in the afternoon. Again, it was something to think about. He wanted to discuss his ideas with Dean, Paul and Quinn first. Not that he couldn't decide himself, but he wanted to involve them, especially as he'd confirmed Quinn could take over the shelter cooking for five days out of seven. The other two days, he'd cook himself because he didn't want it to be a full-time role for Quinn when he had his family to think of.

"You're thinking awfully hard over there," Dean mumbled, rubbing his lips over Oliver's back.

Oliver smiled. "Plans are afoot, kind sir."

Dean huffed. "Aren't they always?" He moved closer, fitting their bodies together and tightening his arms around him. "How are you feeling?"

Oliver considered his answer. "Nervous. A little melancholic." He chuckled. "Impatient."

A breath of laughter filled his ear. "You? Impatient? Never would've guessed."

"Hey!" Oliver rolled over to face him, wrapping his arm around his waist. Dean kissed him once. "Thank you for coming with me."

"We haven't got there yet."

"I know. I..." Oliver shrugged. "It means a lot, that's all."

"Everything's coming together. You're doing a fantastic job of sorting everything out. There's not much more you can do. This is something I can help with, even if it's only as emotional support. I wouldn't want you to have to deal with this on your own."

Oliver's eyes fluttered shut when Dean kissed him slowly and meaningfully. Despite his need to feel Dean in every way possible, they needed to get ready, but he let himself enjoy this time before breaking the spell.

"Rain check," Oliver said.

Dean growled and rolled Oliver to his back, peppering kisses all along his neck and chest while Oliver laughed and pushed at him.

"I insist on the rain check taking place as soon as we've finished at the restaurant." Dean narrowed his eyes, although Oliver could see the spark behind them.

"Agreed."

Dean pulled back, pouting, and climbed off the bed, pulling on Oliver's hands to lift him upright. They stumbled to the shower, which in hindsight, wasn't the best choice because they ended up wasting more water when Dean dropped to his knees.

Dishevelled and late, they arrived at their destination, and Oliver's heart wrenched. The empty, smoke-stained building was nothing like the vibrant, busy place he'd made it into. For a second, everything seemed impossible, but then he remembered what the contractor had told him. *"You can make it the same or different, but either way, the building will remember what came before. It will never be forgotten."*

It took him a few minutes to notice the group of people milling around near the front of the building. He glanced at Dean and received a shrug and a frown in response.

Wandering closer, he saw Ave and George sitting behind a small table, talking to several other people standing on the other side. When Ave saw him, she excused herself and came over to them.

She enveloped him in a hug. "Oliver, my boy. I'm glad to see you. How are you doing?"

He smiled. "Not too bad, Ave. We're coming to check out what it looks like so we can know where to go from here."

"This place will be up and running in no time if I know you well enough." She grinned.

Oliver indicated the table. "What are you doing here?"

"Ah, well, we had a thought and decided to see what other people of the city thought, too."

What was she talking about? "A thought about what?"

"How much Nourris Moi meant to us. We asked around, and people are showing their support."

"Support for what?"

Ave tilted her head. "The refurbishment. People want Nourris Moi back, Oliver. We have donations of both money, time and abilities to help the restaurant get back on its feet."

Oliver blinked at her, unable to say anything. Dean came up beside him and slid an arm around his shoulders. Oliver clenched his hands, trying not to cry. He had never realised how many people had his back until he'd experienced a crisis of sorts, and they'd all come out of the woodwork from behind the scenes. It was a crazy way to think about it, but there it was.

"Thank you, Mrs Oxford. This means a lot," Dean said.

Ave waved her hand. "I think you can call me Ave, dear. Now come and have a look at the list of people with abilities and skills you can use. It's quite extensive."

They spent several minutes with Ave before Oliver saw Paul, Quinn and Roman, the estate agent. They said their goodbyes and promised to see them before they left, then followed the three into the small café behind his beloved restaurant. He was still trying to get his head around what Ave and George had done for him, but he put it aside to think about later and concentrated on what Roman was saying.

"The owner has declined your offer to purchase the property."

Oliver's heart sank. "Did they say why?"

Roman smiled. "They are signing the property over to you, free of charge, on the understanding that you will use it for the shelter only and anything else the shelter needs it for. That is the stipulation."

Oliver felt himself guided into a chair, and he dropped his head into his hands. He couldn't believe what a community this city was. It was too much. Dean crouched in front of him, and Oliver lifted his gaze, the man blurring through his tears.

"This city is more than I ever imagined it could be," Dean said. "Never have I ever seen something like this before, but do you know something? You deserve every bit of this."

Oliver burst into tears and threw his arms around Dean, sobbing into his chest. He'd always felt alone in the world, despite his brother being alive. But here he was, surrounded by those he loved and those who loved him back. He made a promise to himself. He would do everything within his power to pay everyone back for their support during this tough time. Not financially, but by doing what he could for the community. Giving back.

Everyone deserved the world.

Chapter 19

Dean

When Paul called Dean into his office at the start of the next shift, he was confused. He had no clue what his boss might want.

"Dean, come on in and sit."

He did, closing the door behind him before taking a seat opposite Paul. "Everything okay?"

Paul leaned back in his chair and crossed his hands over his stomach. "Yes and no."

Dean frowned. "What is it?"

"The police have been in contact about the fire at Nourris Moi."

"What did they find out?"

Paul sighed and rested his arms on his desk. "They have the CCTV footage from behind the restaurant the night of the fire."

"Did they see who did it?"

Paul nodded. "Evan."

Dean reared back. "Evan?"

"While you and Oliver were talking to Zee and taking the food, Evan slid into the restaurant through the open back door and waited until you'd gone to start the fire. Not long after it started, he kicked the back door open and came running out."

"Why would he start the fire? What did he have against Oliver?"

Paul shrugged. "They don't know. They picked him up this morning to question him. Hopefully, we'll have more information soon."

"Oliver never mentioned Evan. I don't know if he even knew him, although it was likely as the crew had been to the restaurant before."

Paul frowned, and Dean remembered the words he'd overheard Evan say as he left the station that day. *"This is fucking shit! I don't deserve any of this, you fuck!"*

"Do you think he was doing it to get back at us?"

"Why?" Paul glanced at him.

Dean tried to follow his thought process. "He was mad at me because I'm gay. He was mad at you for firing him. Is he likely to have started the fire as a way of putting us in danger?"

"He knew what shifts we worked, though. He would've known we wouldn't be the ones on call."

"But we would've been upset if it hurt anyone else. He could've not wanted to hurt us physically—maybe he did like some of us from working here so long—but to hurt us emotionally might last longer."

"It's possible. We won't know his motivation until the police ask him."

Dean rubbed a hand across his face. "I can't believe he'd do it. Although I really should. I had a similar conversation with Oliver the other week."

"What do you mean?"

"The police came to speak with Oliver and me the day after the fire. They began questioning me because Oliver and I argued that night. Oliver said there was no way I'd do it because I was a firefighter. I told him firefighters were as likely to start a fire as anyone else."

Paul nodded. "That's true. The stress of the job doesn't make a firefighter immune to bouts of ego or hero-worship."

They were quiet for a minute. "I can't believe it was Evan."

"Keep this quiet for the moment. I shouldn't have told you, but I wanted you to be aware in case anything comes up. I believe Kade or Joey were going to speak to Oliver today."

"I'll ring him in a bit and check on him."

Paul smiled. "I'm glad you found each other. I'd worried about Oliver for years. Since he's been with you, he's changed."

"I have, too." Dean grinned.

"Hmm, maybe. Get to work."

Dean chuckled. "Yes, Chief."

He left the office and went straight to work, checking the engine and making sure everything was where it needed to be. Within minutes, the alarm blared, and they jumped into action.

"Car crash. Riverside. Three vehicles involved, one precariously perched on the edge of the River Cam. Fuck.

Ambulances and police will join us there," Jason read off tablet as they entered the cab.

Scott peeled out of the station, sirens wailing while they pulled on their gear. Car crashes could be difficult or easy, depending on the circumstances and location. By the sounds of this call, one car was ready to go into the river, which was terrifying for those inside.

They didn't say much on the ride over. They couldn't say who would do what because until they knew the situation, they didn't know what needed to be done. Scott parked the engine on the bend of the road, blocking the way to stop other cars from getting through. A police car had already blocked off the other end of the road. A police officer came up to them as they exited.

"From what I can get from witnesses, a car lost control as it came around the bend, over-corrected and ended up crossing the line to the other side of the road. A van was coming up that side and veered into the other lane to miss the car, crashing into another one behind the first and taking it forward until it rested over the edge of the river. The fencing gave way. We're not sure if the van is holding the car in place or if the car is balanced by itself. I've told all occupants to stay in the car and not move."

"Good job, thanks." Jason turned to them. "Dean, see if there's some way we can get the car secured. We might be able to hook a cable onto the tow bar or something to stop it from going over. Valerie, check the van and car for any leaks. Scott, get hold of the water rescue team. We may need their help. Niall, speak to the passengers. Keep them calm."

Everyone dispersed to fulfil their orders. Dean moved over to the car. The driver's side was bent inwards, with the van's nose in place. He walked around the back, noticing the back driver's side wheel was several inches off the ground. As he reached the edge of the road and the start of the river, he struggled to keep his expression neutral so that he didn't alarm the passengers of the car. The front passenger wheel was hanging over the edge, and when he lay on the floor to see underneath, he could see the front driver's wheel was barely on the road. Any movement could send that wheel off, and the car could fall.

He stood again, heading to the engine. The car had a tow bar, but he wasn't sure it would be enough to keep the car from going over. It might buy them some time, though. Unwinding the cable, he approached the car but didn't attach the cable. He approached the river again, looking at the height of the potential fall. It wasn't far, which gave him an idea.

"Jason," he called as he jogged over, noticing Pearce, the watch commander for Blue Watch, had joined him. "Can we get a barge over here?"

Jason frowned. "Why?"

"The drop to the water isn't that far, but if we could get a barge to come close enough, it might be able to prop the front of the car while we at least get the passengers to safety. I'm uneasy about trying to attach the cable now. The car is balanced about half and half at the minute."

"All right. Hold on." Jason spoke into his radio, contacting the control centre, asking for information on anyone who may own a barge in the area. Dean heard them respond with, "We'll let you know."

Jason turned back to him. "We're going to have to try to secure that vehicle. There's no guarantee anyone will do it."

Dean nodded. "I need someone at the engine ready to give tension on the cable as soon as I attach it in case it moves the car."

"I'll do it," Pearce said.

Jason nodded. "Stand by the cable controls. The minute Dean gives the go-ahead, tighten it enough that the car doesn't move. Don't try to pull it back."

"Understood."

Dean strode over to the car and lifted the cable. He inhaled and stepped closer. Reaching his hand forward, he hooked the cable into the towing eye hook, every scrape and slight movement of the car sending his heart racing. The passengers screamed when the car shook as the cable slotted into place. Dean lifted his hand for Pearce, and the cable tautened enough to take the brunt should the car slip. He stepped clear, breathing as if he'd run a marathon.

"A barge is on its way. It'll be about ten minutes," Jason said.

"Is the car handbrake on, do we know?" Pearce asked.

"Not sure."

Pearce jogged towards the car where Niall was talking to the passengers, then dashed back. "Handbrake is off. If we are using the barge, we need to get the handbrake on once the barge is beneath the car; otherwise, it will roll straight off the other side."

Jason nodded. "As soon as the barge is in place, we'll get them to put it on. By that point, it should be secure enough to get the passengers out, then pull the vehicle back onto the road with the cable."

Pearce moved back to speak with the passengers of the car. Several minutes later, a barge came into sight, along with a water rescue boat. The barge pulled up close but not too close, and Jason went to speak to the owner and the water rescue crew. When he came back, he clapped Dean on the shoulder. "Ready?"

"Why did I come up with this idea?" he groaned.

"Because you're fucking clever," Jason deadpanned.

Dean grinned. He watched as the barge manoeuvred in front of the car, then slid closer. Niall was still with the passengers, who were understandably freaking out, but Pearce had stepped back.

"Valerie, get to the cable and be ready to wind in if need-ed," Jason shouted.

Dean held his breath as the barge brushed against the car, lifting it with a screech of metal on the edge of the road. The front wheel turned as it rested against the top of the barge. The car slid forward, the cable becoming taut and holding it back.

"Everyone, hold steady! Niall, Scott, get those passengers out! Now!"

The front passenger door was hanging over the water, and the driver's door was caved in. They instructed the occupants to pull on the handbrake, then climb into the backseat one at a time. From there, they could exit through the back passenger door. The car slid some more with the movement from the first person, and screams filled the air. The cable held. The first person climbed free of the car and was whisked off to the ambulance. The car screeched forward again. The remaining passenger held tight to his seat, pleading with them not to let him die but refusing to move. The car slid again. It was going down.

Dean stepped forward, pushing Scott aside, and he rested his knee against the back seat, grabbed hold of the man's arm and yanked him backwards. The man tried to fight, which had the car moving further.

"Stop flailing and get your ass out of the car!" Dean shouted.

He moved the guy to the side enough that he could grip under both arms, then yanked him through the gap between the seats. Dean's knee was still on the seat when the car dropped. He fell forward, still gripping the man, not wanting to lose him in the water if they both fell in.

Fortunately, Dean fell to his stomach. Unfortunately, the man dangled over the edge of the road. Dean used all his strength to keep hold of the man while the other members of the team held onto him. He watched as the car rolled over the top of the barge and into the water. Luckily, it hadn't taken the barge with it, although the small vessel had taken on water and floated further away, leaving them close to falling straight into the River Cam.

Jason sprawled next to him, grabbing onto the man, then helped pull him up. They took the man to an ambulance. Dean laid on his back, staring at the sky, panting.

"You're a fucking asshole, you know that, don't you?" Jason said, his breathing as bad as Dean's. "I thought I'd fucking lost you."

Scott appeared in his vision, face dark, eyes narrowed. He held out his hand, and Dean grabbed it. Scott hauled him upright, holding him close. "You ever push me aside like that again, I will have your head," he growled.

Dean could see the worry in his eyes, despite his words. "Duly noted."

They set about clearing their equipment from the scene, though Dean was a little slower than usual. His legs were trembling like a newborn foal, and his head was killing him. Jason's words ricocheted in his head. He'd thought he was done for, too.

They stayed around until they handed everything over to the police, then Scott drove them back to the station, where Paul was waiting.

"Great job, everyone." He stepped closer to Dean and pulled him into a hug. "You scared the crap out of me, Dean. Don't do it again."

Dean chuckled. "It's my job, Chief."

Paul narrowed his eyes and pursed his lips. "That may be, but you need to stick around longer." He clapped him on the back. "Rest up and get some food and drink, Red Watch. You need it after that." Paul turned to walk away, then pivoted back. "Dean, call Oliver."

He nodded and hurried to get things put to rights for the next call. Climbing the stairs, he wandered to the windows while the call connected.

"Oh, thank fuck," Oliver said in answer. "I saw what was happening on the TV."

"How?"

"Someone was filming the whole thing from the other side of the river. I thought...fuck, I thought you'd gone over when the car did. You scared the shit out of me!"

"I've heard that a lot since I was hanging over the edge of the water," Dean joked through a lump in his throat. "I didn't realise people cared."

"Don't you fucking...you little...Dean!" He couldn't help but laugh at Oliver's outburst but sobered when he heard the next words. "I love you, you asshole. Don't fucking play with your life. I know you're a firefighter, and things are dangerous but don't find trouble. I need you here. You're it for me, Dean. Never do that again."

Tears pooled in his eyes, and he closed them, letting them drip down. "I can't promise to never put myself in danger because it's part of the job I do. What I can promise is to love you with everything I am. Is that enough?"

"I suppose." Oliver's reply was soft and wet, as if he was crying, too.

"Good. I'll see you soon, sweetheart."

He ended the call and blew out a breath as a roar sounded behind him. Whirling around, he saw the entire crew standing, applauding and shouting for him. He thought it was to do with the river call until Jason started singing, "Oliver and Dean up a tree, k-i-s-s-i-n-g!"

Dean rolled his eyes but smiled. "And don't you wish you had what I've got!" he yelled in response.

"Fuck, yeah!" Jason said. "Mine will be cuter, though."

"I'll remember you said that."

They sat down to eat, chatting and joking amongst themselves. There was nothing Dean could change about his life as it stood at that moment. Except for what happened with Nourris Moi.

"Dean?" He looked up and saw Paul at the door. The man jerked his head, and Dean nodded.

"Ooh, someone's in trouble." Valerie smirked.

Dean grinned, then followed Paul up to his office. Once more, they sat in their respective seats, and Paul crossed his arms on his desk.

"They charged Evan with arson." Dean's eyebrows rose. "He admitted the fire was a way to get back at *you*."

"For what?"

"The police said Evan blames you for me transferring him. I didn't fire him. I told him he had a choice. Evan didn't enjoy being told no. Instead of aiming his hatred at me, he aimed it at you."

"But why torch Nourris Moi?"

"He saw how close you were to Oliver. He thought Oliver would end things with you. I don't know why he thought that unless he had known all along that someone would catch him. The only thing I can think is that Evan believes when Oliver finds out he torched the restaurant because of you, he'll break up with you. He obviously doesn't know Oliver."

Dean didn't think Oliver would do that either, but he wasn't certain he wouldn't. The tiny seed of doubt was planted, and Dean couldn't let it go. Would Oliver break up with him because the fire had been his fault? He'd have every right to. Dean wasn't sure he wanted to find out.

"When will Oliver find out?"

"The police were going over there after they'd spoken to me."

Cold snaked down Dean's spine. Oliver didn't know yet. Would his declaration of love change when he heard?

"You okay?"

Dean glanced up at Paul and tried to smile. "Yeah. Tired." He huffed a laugh. "I'll speak to you later."

Paul said nothing, but Dean saw the frown on his face as he closed the door. Dean rubbed his nose, then his entire face and stepped outside the station, leaning his back against the wall. As he stared at the blue sky, he wondered whether his life was about to change. There was no way Oliver would be happy staying with him when it was his fault Nourris Moi burned down. Who could ever forgive someone for that? He doubted it.

When the shift ended, he'd go to Oliver and apologise, then grab his stuff and leave. He'd stay out of Oliver's way after that. It was only fair, after all. Why should Oliver put up with seeing Dean's face every day, which would remind him of everything he'd lost?

Chapter 20

Paul

Paul watched Dean exit the office and knew something bad would happen. He had no idea what Dean would do, but his expression told of his misery. He hoped Oliver could help him. Oliver and Dean were perfect for each other, but they needed to believe it themselves, and sometimes, they couldn't see it. From the short time he'd known Dean, he'd figured out that the man would sacrifice himself to save others.

He rubbed a hand over his face, unable to follow the trail of thought that Dean might have gone down to make his expression go from being delighted they had caught the arsonist to being despondent.

Paul picked up his phone and dialled. "Hey, sweetheart. How are you doing?"

"Busy, busy as always. The ideas for the cooking are coming along nicely, and it's something we should be able to manage between Oliver and me, which is great. I know Ave will volunteer if we need help, but she had enough to do with those three boys of hers." Quinn laughed, the sound musical through the phone. "What about you? I saw what happened at the river."

Paul exhaled and chuckled. "Yeah, that was torturous. More for those who were there. I saw it on TV myself and itched to be there helping."

Quinn hummed. "I know you do. You can always go back to it, you know."

Paul snorted. "No. I'm too old, sweetheart. As much as I'd love to be in the thick of things, I have to leave that for the younger ones now."

"You're only as old as you feel, my dear."

"In that case, bring on the nursing home."

They laughed.

"How is Dean doing? That scene must've scared the wits out of him."

"Dean is surprisingly okay. It's the rest of the crew that was shaken. I'd never heard them curse as much as they did when they unloaded from the engine on their return." He paused. "I told Dean about Evan."

Quinn was quiet for a moment. "Do you think that was wise?"

"At the time, yes. Afterwards, I'm not sure."

"What did he say?"

"Not much. It shocked him, obviously, but it was almost as if he pulled a cover over himself and pushed it aside. I don't know, Quinn. Something is going on in his head, and I'd like to know what it is."

"Keep an eye on him. That's all you can do. Maybe mention something to Jason, so he can do the same. You have...four hours until the end of his shift. Watch him and see what happens."

"Thanks, sweetheart."

"You're welcome. Do you want pork chops for dinner?"

Paul's stomach rumbled, even though it hadn't been long since he'd eaten. "Perfect."

"I'll see you soon, then. Love you."

"Love you back."

Paul hung up and rested back against his chair, the squeak of the springs loud in the otherwise silent office. Quinn had things right. He needed to watch and ensure Dean was okay. It was nothing less than he'd do for anyone else. He had a feeling it had to do with Oliver, but what, he didn't know.

He stood, intending to find Jason and ask him to watch out for Dean when the alarm blared again. Jogging down the stairs, he caught Jason before they left.

"Keep an eye on Dean for me. He's had some bad news, and I don't know if he's feeling off-kilter, especially with what happened earlier."

"Will do, boss."

Jason raced off, and Paul held his hand up as the engine left the station. He stepped into the forecourt and watched it disappear down the road. He hoped Dean's issue was something easy to fix.

Chapter 21

Oliver

When the live footage of the rescue played, Oliver abandoned the cooking and sat watching. He'd never seen Dean—or any of the firefighters—in action before, and it was harrowing. They were far away, and he could do little to help. He stared helplessly at the screen with his hands clenched together. When Dean almost fell into the water, Oliver fell to his knees and screamed at the TV. By the end, tears were streaming down his face, and he had to sit on the floor and take deep breaths before he could compose himself.

Several long minutes later, he went back to the cooking and finished up. As he was pouring the last of the soup into a container, the doorbell rang, and he opened the door to Kade and Joey.

"Morning. To what do I owe the pleasure?" Oliver asked with a smile.

Joey grinned back. "We have some news on the restaurant."

Oliver's heart rate increased. "Come on in. Do you want a cup of tea?"

Both police officers agreed and followed Oliver down the hallway.

"Wow, you have quite the production line going here," Kade commented.

Oliver laughed. "It looks a mess, but there's order within it."

He made tea for the three of them, clearing off a few containers so they could sit at the table. When he sat, he stared at them expectantly.

Joey cleared his throat. "The fire at the restaurant was arson, without a doubt. We arrested someone this morning after we found evidence on the CCTV cameras."

Heart in his throat, he asked, "Was it Rikki?"

Joey shook his head. "It was Evan Rhodes."

"Evan?" Oliver frowned, trying to figure out where he'd heard the name before. "The only Evan I know is the firefighter." Joey nodded. "What?" Oliver stared at him and shook his head. "Why?"

Joey glanced at Kade, who sighed. "Evan had a grudge against Dean, and he thought it would hurt more by attacking your restaurant than the man himself."

Oliver sat back. He couldn't believe a firefighter had done this. His conversation with Dean the previous week sounded in his head. He'd lost everything because of his association with Dean. What the hell?

"The night of the fire, Evan had been hiding in the back car park, and when you both came out to speak to Zee, he slid into the building. It was almost two hours later when he kicked out the back door and ran."

Oliver stared at the mug cradled in his hands. "Why did it take this long to figure it out?"

"The security company stalled a few days before handing over the video."

"I don't know what to say."

Overwhelmed didn't even begin to describe how he felt. He'd thought for sure it was Rikki or someone he'd wronged in the past. To find out it was nothing to do with him, just the person he'd been seeing, was mind-blowing.

"What happens now?"

"Evan has been detained, and we're awaiting information about his bail and court hearing. I'm sorry, Oliver. I know it's not brilliant news."

"What's not? You found who did it. Why is that not good?"

Joey stared at him. "I meant that it was because of Dean it happened."

Oliver waved his hand. "It's not Dean's fault. Although I'll be having words with him about not telling me about Evan's problem with him." Joey frowned at him. "What? You think I should blame Dean?"

Kade waded in, "No, that's not what he's saying. It's surprising because most people *would* blame Dean because he's the link."

"That's ridiculous. Now, if Dean had told Evan to do it, then that's a different matter. Dean, however, had nothing to do with it. This is going to hurt Dean and make him feel bad for bringing me into it. I know what he's like." His phone rang, and it was the man himself. "It's Dean."

"We'll see ourselves out. Call us if you need anything."

"Thanks," he said to the officers, then answered the call, "Oh, thank fuck!"

As he listened to the voice on the other end of the phone, he let his fears out. Tears pooled in his eyes, and he sniffed to keep them at bay, mostly unsuccessful. He was glad Dean was okay, and everyone else was, too. His heart filled with love for the man, and he finally let him know exactly how he felt. It was far too soon, but he couldn't help loving this amazing man. It surprised and elated him to find Dean felt the same. He couldn't wait to see him that evening.

After the phone call, he cleaned himself up, more relaxed now he'd heard from Dean. Carrying the food to the car, he drove to the shelter and deposited it with Benny.

"Are you sure you're still okay doing this?" Benny asked.

Oliver grinned. "Yes, and I have some news." They wandered to Benny's office after he'd delivered the food to the kitchen.

"What's this news?"

"There's two pieces of news. The first is that I'll be handing some of the cooking over to Quinn Thompson. He's agreed to come onboard cooking for you five days a week, and I'll do the other two days. On top of that, I have acquired a small building right next to Nourris Moi to use as a base for cooking for the shelter. The building can be used for anything related to the shelter as we see fit."

Benny was speechless, and Oliver stayed quiet, letting the information sink for the older man. "You shouldn't have used your money to buy the building!"

Oliver held out his hands. "I didn't. I had planned to, but in the end, the owner signed it over without payment on the condition we would use solely it to benefit the shelter. You could even hold cooking lessons there or something like that. It's something to think about. For the moment, though, we're getting it up to scratch, and then I'll be doing the cooking there instead of at home. It's a win-win because I'll be able to monitor the restaurant rebuild too."

Benny rubbed his hands over his freckled face and beard. "I can't believe it."

"You do wonderful things here, Benny. It's time things were made a little easier for you."

They moved the conversation onto other things, and before Oliver knew it, it was lunchtime. He said goodbye and drove home, grabbing some food for himself and sitting down with the paperwork and laptop to go through some more numbers and plans. There were many things he needed to look into, but he was most interested in the new design. On the walls, he wanted to add some photographs as Paul had in his hallway—places that meant a lot to him and the people around him. As for the layout, he wasn't sure whether to keep it the same or try something new. He had an appointment with an architect the following week, but he wanted to have some ideas before he met him.

As it got later, Oliver packed away his work and began making dinner. Dean would be home soon, and he wanted something ready for him. He wanted something special to remember the day they had first swapped the three little words. He decided on a homemade pasty with mashed potatoes and honey-glazed oven-roasted vegetables. If it was the last thing he would do, he'd get Dean to like veg-etables. So far, he'd not had much luck.

When a knock sounded, he raced down the hallway and threw open the door. Dean gave a small smile, and Oliver dragged him inside.

"I'm glad you're back." Dean said nothing. Oliver raised his hand to cup Dean's jaw but paused when the man flinched. "Are you okay?"

"I came by to pick up my things. I'll be quick. You don't have to put up with me for longer than necessary."

Dean brushed past him, leaving Oliver standing there with raised eyebrows and an open mouth. What was he on about? Then Oliver closed his eyes and gave a smile. Here was the man who was willing to be unhappy to ensure Oliver was happy.

"Dean. Stop what you're doing, right now." Oliver's voice came out stronger than he'd thought it would with the amount of emotion bottled up inside him.

Dean glanced across the room at him. "You don't need to say anything, Oliver. It's my fault this happened, and I'll get out of your way."

"Stop!"

Crossing the living room, he stood toe to toe with Dean, never wavering his focus. "You are not going anywhere un-less you want to go. I want you here. Nothing that happened with the restaurant was your fault." Dean grimaced and looked away. Oliver turned his face back again. "It was not your fault. It was Evan's fault. He is the only one to blame here."

"But if it wasn't for me—"

"I'd be alone and killing myself working too many hours. You make me want to be better. To be more. To be here. You make me want to make changes and find a balance. A balance I wasn't bothered about before I met you. It took meeting you to realise nobody else would've been able to get through to me, to make me see what I was doing to myself." Oliver inhaled. "If you want to leave, then leave. I won't stop you. Don't leave because of what *Evan* did. He's inconsequential. If you don't love me after all, then leave. If the idea of leaving me fills you with dread or makes your heart feel like it's being ripped in two...stay."

Dean blinked, and tears trickled down his cheeks. "I don't want you to regret being with me."

"I can't because you are the best thing to ever happen to me." Oliver cupped his jaw, wiping the tears with his thumbs. He pulled Dean closer, telegraphing his intent. Their lips met in the softest, briefest kiss in history, then Dean burrowed his face into Oliver's neck and encircled his waist. Oliver held the back of Dean's head and slid his hand up and down his back, soothing him as best he could.

"I do love you," Dean murmured into his neck.

"I love you, too."

They stayed that way until the oven timer beeped, and Oliver disentangled himself. "I refuse to burn dinner. I've not done that in years." He laughed and strode to the kitchen, Dean on his heels.

They sat down and enjoyed the meal. Dean tried the vegetables, and although he didn't eat them all, Oliver took it as a win. Funny thing was, Oliver had grated some vegetables into the pasty filling, and Dean didn't complain about that. He was keeping that secret close to his chest, though.

A week later, Oliver was finishing up the shelter cooking when the doorbell rang. Cursing, he wiped his hands on a towel as he shuffled down the hallway, hoping it hadn't woken Dean. He was in the middle of his shifts and needed to sleep later today so he could start nights that night.

Oliver opened the door and stared at the five-foot-ten brown-haired, super-tanned man.

"Not even a hello for your brother after months of not seeing each other?" Andrew said, raising one eyebrow. His lips twitched as he no doubt withheld his smile.

"What the hell are you doing here?" Oliver closed his mouth and ushered the man and his family into the house. "I'm glad to see you."

He hugged Andrew, holding on for much longer than normal. Then moved on to Stacy, his wife, and shook his head in awe at their two boys, Aaron and Taylor. They had grown a lot.

"Why didn't you tell me what happened?" Andrew asked, hands on hips.

Oliver sighed. "I didn't want you to worry. Everything's fine. Would you like something to eat?"

"Yeah!" the boys shouted, as six-year-olds were wont to do.

Oliver didn't want to curb their enthusiasm, but he told them about Dean sleeping upstairs as a voice said, "Don't worry, I'm up."

Oliver glanced over his shoulder, seeing a ruffled but gorgeous Dean smiling at them. "You were supposed to be sleeping," he chided.

"I can have a nap later. I'm good." He dropped a kiss on Oliver's lips and wrapped an arm around him. "Are you going to introduce me?" Dean said with a twinkle in his eye.

"This is... Hold on a minute." Oliver narrowed his eyes at Andrew. "How did you know what happened?"

Andrew grinned and held his hand out to Dean. "Nice to put a face to the voice."

"Nice to meet you."

"This is my wife, Stacy, and my kids, Aaron and Taylor."

Oliver pulled away from Dean. "Hold up. When did you speak to Andrew?"

Dean fidgeted on the spot and rubbed his nose. "I may have sneaked his number from your phone last week and messaged him, then we chatted, and voila." Dean held out his hands and smiled sheepishly.

Oliver squinted at him and stepped into Dean's body, wrapping his arms around his back and tucking his head into his neck. "Thank you." He hadn't realised how much he needed his brother until he was on his doorstep.

"You're welcome. Now, sit and speak with your family. I've got a delivery to make."

"No, I'll do it."

Dean cupped his face. "It's why I got up." He kissed him and waved at Oliver's family. "I'll see you again in a little while." He turned to Oliver again. "I'll drop by my house and take a nap, so you don't have to worry about keeping those two boys quiet," he said with a smile.

Oliver lifted onto his toes and kissed him again before turning back to his family.

"He's a good man," Andrew said.

"One of the best." Oliver cleared his throat. "Would you like a drink?"

"Yes, please!" Stacy said, laughing. "All I've had is the horrible plane and airport coffee. I need something better. I'm begging!"

Oliver chuckled. "You'll have to take a supply of it back with you."

"I intend to."

The adults drifted down the hallway after Oliver had shown the boys how to work the TV and on-demand remotes.

"Gosh, it smells delicious in here. What have you been cooking?" Stacy asked as she sat at the dining table.

"Bolognese, beef casserole, chicken chasseur and minestrone soup."

"Don't think I could eat them all together, but individually...yum."

Andrew snorted. "He cooks for the shelter, remember."

Stacy backhanded his chest and rolled her eyes. "I know. I'm teasing."

"How you ever put up with him, I don't know," Oliver joked.

"Me neither."

"Hey, I'm right here!" Andrew pouted.

Oliver closed his eyes briefly and thanked whoever was listening for bringing Dean into his life. Dean had somehow known Oliver needed this, even when Oliver hadn't known himself.

He carried the mugs over to the table. "How come you came back after so long?"

Andrew looked at Stacy and threaded their fingers together before turning to Oliver. "Stacy's pregnant, and we've decided to move back. This is a double trip—to get the ball rolling on finding a place to live and to see what we can do to help you."

Tears pooled in Oliver's eyes. He never used to be emotional. "I'm pleased for you both. How far along are you?"

"I'm past the first trimester, but if we want to be back here before the baby's born, we need to move fast. They won't let me fly too close to my due date. If they delay things for whatever reason, we'll have to wait until after the birth."

"Well, if things get delayed, you can always move in here, to begin with. I'd love to have you."

"Thanks, Ollie."

They spent the entire day together, the kids playing in the back garden with a ball Oliver had found tucked away in his shed. Dean arrived for an early dinner, and everyone got along well. Oliver couldn't believe his entire family was united. The only thing that would make it better was having Paul and everyone else joining in, which gave him an idea.

"We should have a barbecue." He turned to Dean. "Tell Paul to spread the word. Barbecue here, on Saturday. I'll invite Ave and George, Serena and the staff from the restaurant. It'll be a celebration of family."

Dean lifted Oliver's hand to his mouth and kissed his knuckles. "Sounds like a plan."

The boys crashed and burned after eating enough for an army, and Stacy tucked them into bed in the spare room. The slight time difference must've been too much for them. Dean went off to work after Oliver had given him a kiss to remember for the night, then Oliver, Andrew and Stacy argued over what film to watch.

All in all, Oliver had the best day he'd experienced in a long time.

Chapter 22

Dean

"Red Watch, I have an announcement to make." Paul stood before them with his hands behind his back while the crew stood at ease. "There has been a new position created to help new recruits to get a better feel for the station and have someone they can go to who is not in management if they have any problems. We know new recruits don't like to cause issues with older recruits—"

"I'm not old," Jason called.

Paul glared at him. "And I hope this will give them someone else they can approach first. I have thrown Dean in the deep end." That ended with several bouts of laughter and teasing about the river incident. "As always, make sure you help him out should he need it. We don't have any new recruits tonight, but tomorrow one will visit to see if this is a good fit for him. I expect you all to be on your best behaviour because, as you know, we need another crew member."

Dean raised his hand and spoke when Paul nodded to go ahead, "Oliver is having a barbecue on Saturday and has asked me to invite you all."

A loud cheering rose to the rafters, and Dean smiled.

Paul waved his hands to calm the noise. "That sounds great. Count us in."

They received the last instructions for the shift and dispersed to their respective jobs. It wasn't long before Control called them out to an incident involving a fire in a wheelie bin. Then a house fire, followed by a garden fire. By the time they were back at the station, Dean was dog-tired. Luckily, it wasn't his turn to cook; it was Scott's. They finished the meal before being called out again to help an ambulance crew gain entry to a house.

This happened regularly, especially with older people who lived on their own. If they fell upstairs, then there was no one to let the ambulance crew inside, and they called the fire crew to help.

This time, the neighbour had called the ambulance because he'd heard the occupant shouting and banging on the wall separating their houses. The ambulance crew had arrived, but they couldn't gain access to the property. Hence, the fire crew had turned up. They tried taking out the lock on the door first. That would usually give them access and was the cheapest item to replace. If that didn't work, they would move on to using the "red key," which is another name for a metal, hand-held tube that gets rammed into the door to force entry.

Unfortunately, they needed the red key, and the ambulance crew were able to attend to the patient. The fire crew stayed to help them remove the patient from the property.

Once the paramedics strapped the patient into the ambulance, the fire crew secured the house as best they could and returned to the station. Scott, Jason and Valerie all went to the bunks to sleep, whereas he and Niall holed up in the break room, playing cards.

Dean's phone rang, and his stomach churned. It was three o'clock in the morning, and no one he knew would call him at that time unless it was an emergency. He dropped his cards and panicked when he saw it was his dad.

"Dad? What's wrong?"

"Ah, stop your worrying. I'm fine. I couldn't sleep. Thought I'd call for a chat."

"Jesus Christ, Dad. You scared the life out of me."

Clark chuckled. "It benefits your soul to be shocked now and again, I'm told."

Dean's heart calmed. "Why can't you sleep?"

"I think it's this heat. It's too much for an old man like me."

"You're not old. You've got Sadie to keep you young."

"That I do. Anyway, what's been happening at your end of the country."

Dean chuckled. "I'm not that far away, Dad." Clark made a noise. "Well, I have a new job which I officially start tomorrow."

"What do you mean a new job? Are you not firefighting anymore?"

"Slow down. Give me a minute, and I'll explain." Dean rolled his eyes at Niall, who was trying to smother his laughter.

"Well, hurry up about it, boy. I'm not getting any younger."

That brought a laugh out of Niall, and he stood and headed out of the room with a wave.

Dean explained to his dad about the new recruit liaison position and what it entailed. It wasn't much more than he was doing now, except it might change when they have a new crew coming in. He filled his father in on what was happening with Oliver, including the results of the arson investigation and Evan's involvement. His dad had never cursed as much as he had then.

"I'm thinking of coming for a visit. Would that be okay?"

Dean grinned. "Of course, it would! When were you thinking of coming? If you're free this weekend, we're having a barbecue on Saturday. You'd get to meet a lot of people."

"I think we could manage that. Sadie said she'd happily drive us to you, so I wouldn't have to worry about getting a train."

"You can stay overnight if it would be easier on you."

"I'll ask Sadie in the morning and see what she says. I'll let you know tomorrow."

"No rush. If you can get here, great; if not, we'll see you when you can."

Dean loved the idea of sharing his life with everyone important to him. The number of people who fit that description was increasing every day. He spoke some more to his dad, then signed off when Clark started yawning. Wandering down the stairs, he aimed for the door to outside, picking up a folded chair to take with him. He wanted to see if he could see the stars.

As he sank into the chair, he rested his head back and stared into the clear night sky. There wasn't even a whisper of a cloud marring the perfect black and sparkle sky. He easily found Orion and several of the other constellations.

A noise caught his attention, and he lifted his head, withholding a flinch when two shiny eyes stared back at him from five feet away. Foxy had finally come to say hello, it seemed. Dean lowered his gaze, not wanting to be seen as aggressive, but kept his focus out of the corner of his eye. Foxy—they needed a better name for him than what Jason picked—stepped a little closer, then paused. Dean made no sudden movements, leaving his arms on the arms of the chair while he kept his gaze on his hand nearest to the fox.

There had been many tales he'd been told about this fox. Some members of the other crews say they had tamed him, and the fox would allow them to touch him and pet him. Dean didn't quite believe that, but he would like for it to be true.

Foxy moved closer in small, slow increments until he was about a hand's width away. He didn't know what to expect, but he hoped the sirens wouldn't startle the fox too much. Although if that were true, the fox would never be around.

A wet nose nudged his hand, but Dean didn't move. He knew foxes could be vicious—he wasn't stupid—but he wouldn't stop this one from exploring and scenting him if it made the fox feel better. He had no idea how long he'd stayed in the same position, except for the fact his neck was aching from holding it in the same position.

He tensed his whole body when the coarse fur of the fox rested against the back of his hand. Swallowing hard, he froze, then ever so slowly lifted his head to the stars again. They made a sight if anyone had seen them. A firefighter sitting on a chair, perusing the stars, while a fox laid its head on his hand. He would've loved to have a picture. Maybe one day, the fox would be comfortable enough to be stroked or something.

Something slammed in the distance, and Foxy lifted its head, staring in the direction, then turned and moved back towards the hedges surrounding the station. Dean stared after it with a bemused smile.

"Wow," a voice whispered nearby.

Dean glanced over his shoulder to see Niall stood there with his phone. "I know, right? That's the first time he's come to see me."

"I got it on video."

Dean raised his eyebrows. "You did? Fantastic. I was thinking I wish I could have a picture."

"Not sure how it came out with it being dark, but hopefully, you'll see something."

Niall sent the video through to Dean's phone. "I can't believe how clear the sky is. There's something magical about nighttime," Dean murmured.

"I agree."

The following night, he was introduced to the new recruit, Felix. He showed him the ropes and helped him get acquainted with everything. Things were a little different from working a shift than what they went through as trainees. Felix would join them on the calls but wouldn't be working them. That first night, he was there for observation only.

Felix seemed like a nice enough kid. He was twenty-three years old, had a brother who was a firefighter in York and lived with his parents until he saved up enough for a deposit on a house for himself. He appeared to have his head screwed on. Before they finished the shift, Dean invited him to join the barbecue this weekend. Whether Felix would turn up was anyone's guess, but the invite stood regardless.

When he got to Oliver's the next morning, everyone was already up and about. Andrew's kids were watching TV and eating breakfast on the sofa, Stacy was helping Oliver cook, and Andrew was supervising while drinking coffee and scrolling on his phone. Although he didn't live with Oliver, it was nice to come back to a busy house instead of an empty one.

"Good morning."

Oliver set the pan aside and reached for him, automatically pulling him in for a kiss—another thing he could get used to.

"Morning," he rasped. Despite not being too close to the fires he'd helped put out last night, he'd still inhaled a little smoke, as they all did from time to time.

"Hold on, sweetheart." Oliver moved around the kitchen while Dean dropped into a chair and rubbed his face. He needed to sleep. "Here you go."

A cup appeared before him, and he could smell the lemon. He smiled at Oliver and received a hand sliding over his head. Dean sipped the hot lemon water, then rested his head against Oliver's stomach, wrapping his arm around Oliver's waist and closing his eyes.

There was nowhere else he'd rather be.

"Drink up, then get yourself to bed."

"I'll head home. You don't need to worry about me." He drank some more, the concoction soothing his throat as it always did.

"No, you will not. You'll go upstairs, have a shower and go to bed." Oliver crossed his arms over his chest.

Dean chuckled. "All right, boss."

"Good." Oliver pecked him on the lips and refocused on his cooking. "Do you want anything to eat before bed?"

"No, I'm all right, thanks," he said, standing.

Oliver peered at him through narrowed eyes. "Take that with you and finish it all."

Dean picked up the cup and toasted him. "Yes, boss. Night, everyone."

"Get some rest, Dean," Stacy said with a wave.

He climbed the stairs, sipping his drink, and closed the bedroom door behind him. Resting the cup on the bedside table, he stripped out of his clothes and stood under the hot spray, hoping to wash away some of the smoke and dirt that accumulated through his shift. When he was as clean as he was going to get, he slid between the covers and hugged Oliver's pillow to his side.

Several hours later, Dean nuzzled into the pillow beneath him and sighed. He felt a warmth at his back and an arm around his waist, and his mouth curled. Clearing his throat, he whispered, "Are you awake?"

"Yeah, enjoying the calm," Oliver murmured.

Dean kept his eyes closed and enjoyed the silence. He threaded his fingers with Oliver's and held it close to his chest. Oliver kissed the back of his neck, and Dean hummed. He felt languid and sleepy, but his cock was taking an interest in Oliver's actions. Goosebumps flowed over his skin, and he tilted his head to the side to give Oliver more access. Oliver nibbled at his earlobe, then removed his hand from Dean's grip and palmed his cheek, turning his head towards him. Their lips met in an unhurried kiss but soon became frantic.

"Will you fuck me, Oliver?" he broke away to ask.

Oliver paused, eyes wide. "I...um...yeah, if you're sure."

"I'm sure."

Oliver's cheeks darkened as much as his eyes did. *Oh, yeah, he liked that idea.* Bottoming wasn't something he did often. For him, it took a lot of trust to put his body in someone else's hands. He had that trust in Oliver, and Dean wanted to give something of himself to the man who had made him believe he could make a balance of his work and personal life.

"How do you want to…?" Oliver waved his hand around, and Dean laughed.

"The question should be, where do you want me?"

"On your back."

Dean rolled to his back and spread his legs. Oliver smoothed his hands up his legs, crawling forward on his knees, and stopped before he touched him where Dean wanted him to. Oliver kept glancing at Dean as if to make sure he was okay with the direction he was moving in. Dean tucked both hands behind his head and got comfortable, opening his body for Oliver to do whatever he wanted to.

Oliver biting his bottom lip had Dean standing to attention faster than ever before. Combined with the fact Oliver would soon be inside him, Dean wasn't sure how long he'd be able to hold out. Oliver leaned over him, their stomachs touching as he bent down for a kiss. When Oliver pulled away, Dean tried to follow, but Oliver reached into the bedside table for supplies, then returned to sitting on his heels.

"Are you sure?"

Dean grinned. "Extremely sure."

Oliver licked his lips as he squirted some lube onto his fingers and threw the tube onto the bed. He pushed against the back of Dean's thighs, spreading him wider. The cold of the lube made him flinch, but it soon warmed up. Oliver massaged his pucker until Dean was ready to push his hands aside and do the job himself. When Dean grumbled, Oliver smirked up at him and pressed a kiss to the red, swollen head of his cock.

"You are such a tease," he panted.

Oliver encircled the base of his cock and held it away from his stomach. Dean watched as his tongue came out and repeatedly flicked against the bundle of nerves beneath the head. At the same time, he breached his hole and sensation sparked along Dean's nerve endings. There was a slight burn that accompanied the penetration, but it was to be expected when it had been several years since he had last done this with anyone.

Oliver slid his finger in and out while his tongue worked magic, keeping Dean on the edge. When Oliver added a second finger, he sucked the head of his cock into his mouth. After that, Dean lost all sense of time. He could only feel what Oliver was doing to him. A whimper escaped when Oliver withdrew his fingers and mouth simultaneously. Dean squirmed on the bed as the feeling of emptiness surrounded him.

It was only when he heard the crinkle of foil that he blinked open his eyes to watch. Oliver rolled a condom down his shaft and slicked it.

"Ready?"

Dean nodded and crushed the sheets in his fist. Oliver held his thighs back and nudged the head of his dick at Dean's entrance. Dean inhaled and relaxed his body, bearing down to allow Oliver to slide past the tight ring of muscles of his ass. Oliver continued, pressing forward at a slow but steady rate until he was fully seated.

"Jesus."

Oliver paused with his hands braced on the bed beside Dean, his breath coming in short, sharp pants.

"It feels good."

"Go ahead, Oliver. I'm ready."

Oliver took a breath, then withdrew. He was almost out when he pushed back in, fast and hard. Dean groaned. The feeling of his insides being stimulated was something he'd forgotten. He kept his bottom lip between his teeth as Oliver set a fast pace. Oliver slid one hand to Dean's stomach, then his rhythm faltered, and he grumbled.

"Sorry, I can't reach. My stomach is in the way."

To begin with, Dean didn't know what Oliver was talking about, then he understood.

"You don't need to do anything," he gasped. "The friction...is amazing. Keep going."

He doubted Oliver believed him, but what he said was true. Sandwiched between both his stomach and Oliver's, he knew he wouldn't need any other touch to go over the edge. Oliver picked up his pace and cursed.

"I'm almost there."

"I am..."

Dean exploded beneath Oliver. He distantly heard Oliver curse again, then felt the tremble of his body as he held himself deep. Dean lay panting on the bed with his eyes closed. He grimaced as Oliver pulled out, then sighed as the gentle flood of endorphins flowed over him. A warm wet cloth jerked him from his stupor, and he blinked open to watch Oliver clean him. Oliver put the flannel on the bedside table and climbed back onto the bed, scooting himself closer and resting his head on Dean's shoulder.

"When can we do that again?" Dean asked.

Oliver chuckled. "I'm glad it was good for you." He paused and sighed. "I'm sorry I wasn't able to stroke you."

Dean pulled Oliver closer, kissing his forehead. "You don't need to apologise. It was fucking fantastic. I need to do that again soon."

Oliver squeezed his waist and settled in. They laid there for several long minutes, enjoying the silence and being together with no rush to do anything.

The front door slammed shut. "Uncle Oliver! Where are you?"

Oliver exhaled a chuckle. "Yeah, that didn't last long."

"Every minute I get with you is worth it," Dean whispered against his mouth.

Chapter 23

Oliver

Oliver, Dean and Stacy spent the morning cooking up a storm while Andrew took the kids out of the way. Dean was still learning to cook, but he'd come a long way since they'd first started the "lessons." It had been almost a month since the fire, and Oliver was trying to get used to his new normal. He could see the reasons Dean had worried about him. Now that he had an excessive amount of free time, he understood he'd been doing too much.

The insurance company had yet to confirm anything about the case, so he was hanging, but he'd already begun cleaning up the mess the fire had left behind. After speaking with Ave and George and finding out exactly what the community had offered, he'd taken people up on their skills, and the building was being cleared out and checked to make certain it was structurally sound before they went any further. Oliver had decided that even if the insurance company didn't pay out—they should, but in case—he would rebuild, regardless. He'd built the business up from nothing the first time; he could do it again. It would be tight, money-wise, but he'd manage.

The doorbell rang, and Dean wandered off to answer it, wiping his hands on a towel as he went. Oliver smiled after him.

"I'm glad you found him," Stacy said, grinning over the counter. "You're much more relaxed than you were before."

"He tried to make me see what was happening to me before the fire, but it took losing the restaurant to understand. It's stupid, but I get a second chance. Things will be different this time around."

"I'm glad. You deserve happiness."

"Hey, hey! There's no party until I get here!"

Oliver peered over his shoulder and snorted as Jason walked through the door, brandishing a bottle of wine. "What would we ever do without you?" Oliver's sarcasm rolled off his tongue.

"Exactly!" Jason pointed at him.

Oliver raised his eyebrows. "Are you already drunk?"

Jason looked offended. "No! I'm high on life."

"Hmm." Oliver studied him, the lines around his eyes more pronounced than when he'd last noticed. Jason was larger than life, but Oliver had always thought he was hiding a lot of pain. This wasn't a day to dig into it, though. "Go outside and get the music set up, please."

"Aye, aye, Captain!" Jason saluted and exited.

"He's a character," Stacy murmured.

"That he is."

"Oliver!"

He switched off the burner and turned in time to catch Ave in his arms. "I'm glad you could come, Ave." He glanced over her shoulder to see George and the three boys they were currently fostering. "Hey, George. Hi, boys. There are plenty of drinks outside. Music should be playing soon, and if you check out the garden, there should be a few balls and other stuff that might interest you." He winked at the boys. They were fourteen, twelve and nine years old, all from the same family, and from what George had told him, they had settled in well over the past few months, considering the reasons for them needing to be fostered in the first place.

Music blasted through the open windows until it lowered to a more manageable level. A heavy beat filled the air. He should've known better than to let Jason choose.

Hands slid around his waist, and Dean rested his chin on his shoulder. "Everything sorted here?"

"Yes, all done. I'm going to put these into containers, then put them on the table under the nets. Could you—"

Jason popped his head back in. "Did you make your sauce?"

Oliver shook his head, feigning sadness. "I didn't think you'd want it." Jason's expression had Oliver laughing. "You should've seen your face. Yes, I've made the sauce."

"You're horrible!" Jason pouted and left.

"He's not going to talk to you all day now," Dean said, standing upright after dropping a kiss on Oliver's cheek. "I'll help you take the food out."

"Thanks."

More guests arrived until the garden was teeming with people. Oliver stood by the back door, observing his friends and family with a small smile. He hadn't realised how many people were in his life—well, his and Dean's—until he saw them all together like this. There were more people than chairs, and the majority had to stand, but it didn't seem to stop their enthusiasm to mingle. Conversation and laughter filled the air, and he promised himself this would become a regular thing.

Many of the firefighters from Cam fire station were there. White Watch was working, but the rest of the crews had come, most of them anyway. Paul and Quinn were present with their boys, who had taken an interest in Andrew's boys and Ave's kids, even though they were older than the others. Pearce, Blue Watch's Watch Commander, was there with his wife and new baby, Delilah. Maddox, Green Watch's Watch Commander, was there alone, as always.

His restaurant staff had all arrived—every single one of them had turned up, which surprised him. Oliver hadn't been able to pay them to keep them on staff because of how long the business wouldn't be running; therefore, most had found new positions within the city. It was a shame to have them leave but understandable under the circumstances. It was lovely to see them outside of the busy restaurant, though. He hadn't realised some of them were in relationships. Serena was there with her girlfriend, and Jack was alone.

He narrowed his eyes, transferring his gaze from Jack to Maddox. "I wonder..."

"You wonder about what?"

The voice in his ear made him jump, then laugh. "I was going to try my hand at matchmaking."

"Who?" said Dean.

"Jack and Maddox."

"Hmm. That might work."

Oliver threaded his arm through Dean's, then leaned his head against his shoulder. "I love this," he murmured.

"What? The cattle making a mess?"

Oliver snorted and tapped his arm in mock telling off. "Having everyone together. I've decided this will be a regular thing. We all need it."

"Sounds like a plan."

"I'm sorry your dad couldn't come."

Dean shrugged. "It happens. Sadie couldn't have predicted her brother would get ill, but he'll come and visit soon, I'm sure."

A shrill whistle rent through the air, and conversation stopped as they faced where the noise had come from. Paul stood on a plastic box, resting his hand on Quinn's shoulder for stability, no doubt.

"I would like to say a toast. Oliver, you had been a huge part of our lives for many years, even before Nourris Moi started. You're kind-hearted and always want to help others, even to the detriment of yourself. We want to thank you for being there for us when we were too tired to cook for ourselves. For being there when we needed a shoulder to cry on, even if it had to be done at the bar in your restaurant." Everyone chuckled. "You have made such a difference in people's lives, especially those at the shelter. Because of your care and compassion, the shelter has fed more people than ever. I hope to one day say that I did something worthy of being remembered. To Oliver!"

"To Oliver!" guests shouted.

Tears pricked at the corners of his eyes, but he smiled through them. To find out how everyone saw him was overwhelming, and he couldn't speak. Dean kissed his temple.

"I told you…you're amazing," he mumbled.

Oliver laughed, then straightened and cleared his throat and raised his voice. "Make sure you eat the food!"

"As if we'd miss out on your cooking!" someone shouted back.

Oliver inhaled and let it out slowly. He was in high spirits.

"Oliver, Quinn mentioned to me you were considering creating a vegetable garden or something similar here, is that right?"

He nodded at Nash, Blue Watch's crew member. "I was hoping to use it eventually to supplement the shelter food we get."

Nash shoved his hands into his pockets. "Well, my brother is a landscape gardener, but he specialises in vegetable gardens that also work as a normal garden. He could help you out if you're interested?"

"Definitely. Get him to give me a ring. I want to get it started as soon as possible."

"Brilliant. I'll let him know." Nash smiled and wandered back into the crowd.

"Things are looking up," Dean said.

"That they are."

Excitement coursed through Oliver as he turned the key in the newly finished "Shelter Kitchen," as they'd called it. He walked in with Quinn on his heels and studied their surroundings. There were large windows at the front, similar to what Nourris Moi had, sending lots of light through to the back of the room. The front part of the building would be the preparation area with clean stainless-steel counters, sinks for washing food and separate ones for washing hands, and cupboards beneath the counters to hold their equipment. There were several large fridges and freezers.

They wandered towards the back, through a doorway that led to the cooking area. It had four ovens, six sets of hobs and some counters surrounding them. Oliver grinned. It was set out perfectly. He stepped through another doorway, leading to where the dishwashers and sinks were for washing up. It was done.

Today was the first day they'd be using it officially. To begin with, it would be him and Quinn who would cook, then when the rebuilding of the restaurant began in earnest, Oliver would split his time, and Quinn would take over fully. Eventually, they hoped to have volunteers come in and help them with prep or cooking, depending on their abilities. It was a work in progress, but plans were coming together.

"This is amazing," Quinn said. "I'm glad I was able to see it before so I could get the immense wow factor. Fantastic job, Oliver."

He waved him away. "I didn't do anything. I told the architect what we wanted, and he delivered."

"Regardless, it looks great." Quinn rubbed his hands together. "Shall we get started?"

Oliver grinned. "Definitely."

They transferred the bags from their cars to the preparation area and emptied them. They'd already discussed the basic recipes for standard meals like cottage pie and lasagne, and they would discuss any other ideas they got. Oliver had been adamant this be a joint venture between them because he knew once the restaurant was up and running again, Quinn would be in charge. Oliver was more than happy with that.

They began washing and chopping, the conversation light and easy, although Oliver made a mental note to bring a radio in for when they were alone. They'd been working for around an hour when Ave entered.

"Good morning, Ave. How are you?"

"I'm super, thanks, boys. How's your first day working out for you?"

Oliver chuckled. "We've been at it for an hour, Ave. It's working fine. What are you doing here?"

She waved her hand. "I was in the area and thought I'd drop by and say hello."

Oliver narrowed his gaze, then flicked it to Quinn, who shrugged. He wasn't the only one to get a weird vibe from her then. Shaking his head, he refocused on the potatoes he was peeling.

"Oh, I got something you might be interested in." She ducked her head out of the door and waved at someone.

Oliver stared as four people entered, carrying several bags between them, and placed them on the prepping surface they weren't currently using. Then they left, leaving him with Quinn and Ave again.

"What's this, Ave?" He wiped his hands.

"Well, I've had a conversation or two over the last few days and weeks," she said. "I got two more supermarkets to supply you with food for the shelter with another store in talks with their management team about it."

She wrung her hands together and shuffled on her feet as if unsure what she'd done was the right thing to do.

Oliver approached her and pulled her in for a hug. "Thank you." His throat closed up, and he couldn't say anything else. He stepped back, eyeing the bags. Glancing at Quinn, he cleared his throat. "We're either going to need some help, or we're going to be cooking an evening meal, too."

Quinn rubbed his face. "Let's call Benny. He'll be able to tell us which is the better option. We don't want to overwhelm him with too many visitors to the shelter at once."

"I agree. If he chooses a second meal, what time would we be able to do it?"

"Would eight or nine o'clock be doable, do you think?"

Oliver shrugged. "I don't think it would matter to the visitors."

He grabbed his phone and dialled Benny, taking a deep breath so he'd be able to speak without choking up.

"Benny, we have a situation." He explained what had happened, and Benny had said an evening meal would be better because they were at full capacity for lunchtime with what Oliver already provided. Benny said it hesitantly, then changed his mind and said it would be too much work for them. Oliver smiled and told Benny to expect an evening meal around eight-thirty that evening. He could hear Benny's tears, and Oliver told him to rest up and that they'd see him in a couple of hours.

"Two meals it is, then. We're going to have to get people in to help," Oliver said.

Quinn nodded. "Yes, we are."

"I'm sorry. I made extra work for you. I thought it would be a splendid idea," Ave said.

Quinn pulled her in for a hug. "It is a great thing, Ave. We hadn't considered it happening. We can regroup and sort it out. Don't worry."

"Well, I can be the first volunteer." She rolled her sleeves up. "Put me to work."

Oliver did. He asked her to go through the food in the bags that had been delivered and make a list of what there was and what the expiry dates were on them, then put anything into the fridge that needed to go, and stack the rest to one side. They'd figure out where it all went after they'd done the first batch of cooking. Oliver plugged his phone into a socket and started a playlist to play in the background. By the time they had placed the food into the individual containers they had decided to use, he was smiling hard enough to make his cheeks ache.

"I can't believe this worked," he said, stacking the containers to carry to the car.

"Anything is possible if you put your mind to it."

"Thank you, Ave. We appreciate your help," he told her.

"You're welcome. I'll be back to help more. I know a few people who might give you an hour. I'll let you know."

Oliver chuckled. Ave knew everyone, so that didn't surprise him. They filled the car, and Oliver drove them to the shelter, parking in his usual spot.

"I'm excited about this, Oliver. I love cooking as you know but to have it *mean* something makes it even more worthwhile." Quinn smiled.

"It does."

They climbed out as Benny opened the door. Benny ran to him and held him as he rushed through several unintelligible words.

"Benny! Calm down. We don't mind, but we need to discuss logistics and things like that. I don't want to say we'll do it every day until we know how much food we'll be getting from each of the supermarkets Ave asked. You might need to have a sign on the door to say whether the second meal is available. I don't know."

Benny waved him away. "I'll sort that this side. I don't want you doing too much."

Oliver pointed to Quinn. "I have help now. Plus, we're going to look for volunteers as well. We'll make it work."

"I can't thank you enough."

They carried the food into the shelter and left it with the volunteers there, then headed back to the Shelter Kitchen for Quinn's car. When he pulled up, Quinn asked, "What time shall we meet back here?"

Oliver blew out a breath. "Six? That gives us two hours."

Quinn nodded. "Okay. See you later."

He climbed out of Oliver's car and into his own, driving off with a wave. Oliver stared at the front of the Shelter

Kitchen and smiled. Everything was coming together. With a last look, he drove home.

Dean was sitting at the dining table, frowning at his laptop, but he glanced up and smiled when he saw Oliver. Dean stood, wrapping his arms around him.

"How did it go?"

Oliver chuckled and explained what had happened with Ave while Dean made them a cup of tea.

"I can't believe it. I wonder if the supermarkets were able to find a loophole, which meant they could give you the food without repercussions? If that's the case, Zee won't have to worry about her job any longer."

Oliver nodded. "That would be nice. I'll speak to Ave again. See if she knows who is involved. I don't want anyone to risk their jobs for it."

"I'm sure it'll be fine. You'll be cooking again tonight, then?" Dean grinned. "I'll come and help."

"You don't need to—"

"I want to. I can spend more time with you that way. I need to nip home first."

Oliver licked his lips and stared at his hands. "What if you…brought a few extra things over here? I could make some room for you in my wardrobe." He bit his lip, not looking at Dean.

Dean lifted his chin with a single finger. "Are you asking me to move in?" Oliver rolled his lips inwards and nodded. Dean smiled. "I'd love to, but you need to be sure."

"I am certain."

Chapter 24

Dean

Dean received a call to visit Paul's office on the afternoon of one of his days off and to bring Oliver with him. He wasn't sure of the reason, but Evan's hearing had happened the previous week. He was hoping it was something to do with that.

Oliver parked the car, and they climbed out, greeting several of White Watch as they went. They'd knocked when the siren blared, and Oliver watched with wide eyes as the firefighters around them ran. Dean chuckled, gaining Oliver's attention.

"What?"

"Nothing."

"Come in!" Paul shouted.

Paul stood to hug them both before inviting them to sit down.

"You're worrying me, Chief," Dean said, only partially joking.

Paul held his hands out. "There's nothing to worry about. It's an update on the arson case."

"The hearing was last week, wasn't it?" Oliver asked.

"Yes. They've notified me of the result."

"And?" Dean asked.

Paul sat back in his chair. "He accepted a plea bargain with a reduced sentence. The judge took into consideration him not intending to physically harm you because he waited until you were out of the building before setting the fire. However, he didn't consider the people living above the restaurant, and being a firefighter, he knew the potential outcome if the fire wasn't contained."

"What sentence did he get?" Dean had a feeling it was a low one.

"Ten years."

Dean's mouth gaped. It was longer than he'd thought.

"I wasn't expecting such a long sentence for a plea bargain," Oliver said.

"He was looking at twenty years or more. Ten *is* a bargain."

"I can't believe it." Dean shook his head. "All the years he spent as a firefighter, gone because of his prejudice. Who else knows?"

Paul shook his head. "No one yet. I wanted to let you know before I made it common knowledge."

"Thanks," Oliver said.

Paul cleared his throat and smirked. "Dean, you're scheduled for your photoshoot on 28 October with Jason."

Dean groaned. "Really? Why'd you have to put me with Jason? I'll never get a word in edgeways, and you know exactly the kind of photos he's going to want."

"Good luck."

Oliver chuckled. "You'll love it."

Dean raised his eyebrows. "Maybe I should drag you along and see how much you like it when someone else is touching my naked skin."

Oliver narrowed his eyes. "Hmm. Maybe I should come along to ensure you behave."

Dean laughed. "I think you're right, Chief. This is going to be fun."

Paul snorted. "As I said, good luck. Anyway, get off with you. I know you have a long journey tomorrow."

They did. Dean was taking Oliver to see his dad and Sadie for a few days. He'd taken some well-needed days off to ensure there was no rush to get back. In theory, they could spend a full week there, but he knew Oliver would want to check on the progress of the restaurant with his own eyes instead of someone else's.

Clark's house was on the small side; therefore, they'd booked into a hotel for four nights with the potential to extend it if they chose. It would be nice to get away from their lives for a bit. To take a break and reset. It would be their first holiday as a couple, and Dean was excited to show Oliver his hometown. Hopefully, he wouldn't bump into anyone from Reading Fire Station.

The drive home was quiet, and Dean left Oliver with his thoughts, knowing he'd talk about any issues when they got back. The prison sentence was far longer than Dean had expected it to be, but he knew nothing about legal stuff like that. One mistake, and Evan was now serving ten years in prison. It was a crazy thought.

As soon as the door closed behind them, Oliver turned and pressed himself to Dean, sliding his arms around his back.

"Is it horrible that I wish Evan got a longer sentence?" he mumbled into Dean's T-shirt.

Dean rubbed a hand up and down Oliver's back. "No, it's not horrible. It's understandable when he took everything away from you."

Oliver pulled back and lifted his head. "Not quite everything." He smiled and kissed him.

Dean allowed the slow exploration until it was almost more than he could bear, then he broke away. "We have work to do."

Sighing, Oliver pouted and drifted away from him. "Such a shame. Maybe later."

"Definitely, later."

They spent the afternoon packing and making sure everything was in place for them not being there for a few days, and the evening making love until they were both spent and worn out.

When the alarm went off the following morning, they both groaned.

"Whose idea was it to leave early to miss the traffic?" Dean mumbled.

"Yours," Oliver said, sounding as chipper as always.

"We need to arrange some sort of time that fits us both instead of you being an early bird and me being a night owl." He rolled onto his back and covered his face with his arm, shutting out the dim morning light.

"Isn't that around mid-afternoon?" Oliver was already out of bed and heading for the shower. "Wouldn't it be easier to offer to blow you in the shower to get your arse in gear?"

Dean was lost in the powers of returning to sleep when Oliver's words registered. He shot upright. "What?"

"Better hurry!"

Dean scrambled out of bed, almost falling when the blankets wrapped around his feet, and dived into the bathroom. "I'm here."

"Thought that enticement might work."

Dean took a long, slow perusal of Oliver's wet calves, thighs, ass, back and shoulders, then stepped under the spray behind him, nestling his cock into Oliver's crack and wrapping his arms around him.

They had brought a special padded bath pillow so Oliver's knees didn't hurt him as much. Dean had said they could do it in bed, but Oliver had protested, saying he wanted to do it in the shower. Not wanting to argue too much, Dean had searched for something to make it easier and had found the pillow by chance.

Oliver spun in his arms, smoothing his hands up and around Dean's neck and leaned in to join their mouths in a kiss that started slow and explorative, then deepened until they were both gasping for breath.

Oliver dragged his mouth away, panting, and sank to his knees. His hands smoothed around to grab Dean's ass and squeezed. Dean tried to stay as still as possible, wanting to enjoy every second, but the moment Oliver's mouth touched him, it did him in. Dean rested one hand on the tiles beside him; the other pushed Oliver's hair away from his face. He would never grip Oliver's hair, but he found stroking his fingers through it to be as addictive as his mouth.

Watching his cock disappear into Oliver's mouth sent his arousal sky high. He wanted to look away, to keep his orgasm at bay, but whether or not he watched Oliver, the images were still in his mind. Oliver flicked at the bundle of nerves as he lifted off, then licked over his head before taking him deeply once more. One of Oliver's hands wrapped around the base and stroked in conjunction with his mouth, and his other hand worked between Dean's legs until he was pressing a finger against his pucker.

"I'm not going to last," Dean gasped.

At his words, Oliver increased his speed and tightened his grip. Dean dropped his head back, clenched his fingers against the tiles in a useless attempt at support, and groaned loudly as he shot down Oliver's throat. He could hardly keep himself upright with his knees trembling and acting like jelly.

He felt Oliver move off and reached down to help him stand. When he had him within reach, he took his mouth, tasting himself alongside Oliver's unique blend of flavours.

"Thank you for that." He rested his forehead against Oliver's and held him closely.

Several minutes later, Dean reached for the soap and began washing every inch of Oliver he could reach. He paid special attention to his cock until Oliver was making a mess of Dean. Once Oliver had recovered, they swapped sides, and Dean washed himself while Oliver climbed out.

"Apart from breakfast, we have everything we need for the journey, don't we?" Dean asked while they were dressing.

Oliver nodded. "I'm making cheese toasties." It didn't take them long to get ready, have breakfast and climb in the car. Dean was driving, but they had chosen to use Oliver's car due to it being in better condition than Dean's.

When they finally reached his father's house, Dean could tell Oliver was nervous. Despite them having spoken on a video call, Oliver was worried his dad wouldn't like him, but as soon as he turned the engine off, Clark was out of his house and down the steps, waiting for them to exit the car. Taking a deep inhale, Oliver did.

Dean climbed out and smiled when he saw his dad with Oliver in his arms. He waved at Sadie and came to stand beside his boyfriend.

"Hey, Dad."

"I'm glad you're here. How was the traffic?"

"It wasn't bad, actually. I think we missed most of the motorway rush hour." He pulled his dad into a hug. "How are you?"

"Good, good. Anyway, come in. Sadie wants to see you."

Clark shuffled up the path to the front door and stood beside his girlfriend. "Sadie, this is Oliver."

"Nice to meet you, Oliver." She held out her hand.

Oliver shook it. "You too. Thanks for having me."

"Sadie!" Dean enveloped her in a hug and pressed a kiss to her cheek, causing her to blush. "How did you find someone this sweet, Dad?"

Clark pushed at Dean's forehead, knocking him back a step. "Pfft. He says the same thing every time he sees her."

Dean laughed. "Too true." He smiled at Oliver, who seemed to have relaxed a little at their banter.

"Who wants a cuppa?" Everyone raised their hands at Sadie's question. "Come on, then."

"We'll be there in a minute."

Oliver hadn't wanted to come empty-handed, and he'd cooked something yesterday that they could heat up to save them from worrying about providing for them. Dean had told him it wasn't necessary, but Oliver couldn't be dissuaded.

They retrieved the food from the boot and the bag containing a bottle of wine for them all to share and entered the house. Dean led the way to the kitchen, which was the primary hub of his dad's house—always had been, likely always would be. It was a kitchen and dining room in one, and Clark would sit at a chair at the table and read his newspaper or do his crossword puzzles while Sadie did similarly. It was where they did most of their talking. Dean couldn't understand why it couldn't happen in the comfortable seats of the living room, but each to their own.

"Oh, you didn't have to do that," Sadie exclaimed with a hand on her chest when Oliver showed her what he'd brought.

"I know, but I love to cook." He shrugged a shoulder.

"Thank you. We can have this for dinner."

Sadie set the food in the fridge, then turned back to make the drinks. Dean and Oliver sat at the table.

"How is the restaurant coming on since I last spoke to you?"

Oliver sat forward, a small smile on his face. As he spoke about the rebuilding efforts and the new layout and design, Dean saw his expression light up, as it always did. No matter what had happened, excitement visibly coursed through Oliver whenever he spoke about the plans. Some of their friends had friends in high places and had been able to fast-track some certificates and approvals they needed to get the building work started. Instead of a June date, they were looking at April, maybe even March, if things stayed on track.

After they had drunk their tea and had a light lunch, the four of them went for a walk around the back of the houses, where a small river ran. It wasn't anything like River Cam, but it was still called a river, though Dean would have said it was more like a brook.

"How is the new position working out for you?" Clark asked.

Dean smiled. "It's terrific. All the new recruits start on our crew with me as their liaison. Once we think they're solid enough, they get sent wherever they need to be. It feels a little like babysitting sometimes, but it's good to meet a lot of new people."

"Sounds like you've finally found some roots." Clark smiled. "I'm happy for you."

"Thanks."

"Oh, Clark, Sadie. My brother and his family are moving back into the area, and we're planning another get-togeth-er. Not a barbecue this time, but a party of sorts. It won't be until January, but I wanted to let you know in advance," Oliver said.

"I'll write it on the calendar."

"Your sister-in-law is pregnant, isn't she?" Sadie asked.

"Yes. She's about four months at the moment. The airlines won't allow her to fly after thirty-six weeks. She and her boys are coming to stay with us at the end of January, while Andrew finishes up in Dubai. He should only be a couple of weeks behind her."

"Let's hope so. I'd hate for him to miss the birth." Sadie smiled.

"It's my brother. He will," Oliver deadpanned.

Dean enjoyed the conversation and company as they returned to his dad's house. They stayed for dinner, then headed to their hotel to check in. They both sank into the bed when they laid down for a rest. Dean rolled his head to the side, smiling when Oliver did the same. He linked their fingers and squeezed.

"This is perfect," Oliver said, moving to his side and resting his head on Dean's shoulder. "You can't hear the traffic outside. It's quiet."

"Let's see if you can make me wake the world up, shall we?" Dean whispered, lifting Oliver's chin and kissing him.

Oliver gripped his T-shirt and held him close, opening his mouth wide and tangling their tongues. Their clothes were torn off within seconds, and Dean was eager to feel every inch of Oliver inside him. When Dean rolled over to his stomach, Oliver scrambled off the bed and rummaged through a bag, making a frantic noise when he couldn't find what he was looking for. After a cry of happiness, Oliver returned to the bed, pushing Dean's legs wide while he crawled between them. He peppered kisses over Dean's lower back. For some reason, they both seem to have a frantic need to feel the closeness of the other.

Dean lifted to his knees, keeping his legs wide, and stroked his cock. Oliver pressed a lubed finger against Dean's hole, pressing inside. Dean's eyes rolled into the back of his head as Oliver worked him open. The room was not warm, but Dean could feel the sweat beading on his skin while Oliver drove his fingers against his prostate.

Dean whimpered when Oliver removed his fingers, but his cock was there, ready to impale him. Oliver thrust forward an inch at a time, and Dean muttered incomprehensible words of encouragement. Still stroking his dick, Dean felt more and more precome coat his hand and slick his way.

"Jesus Christ, you feel good like that. It's going to be quick," Oliver said.

"More. Later," Dean panted.

"Agreed."

Oliver sped up, driving into him, and Dean worked his hand faster until he clenched around Oliver's cock and spurted across the sheets beneath him. His ass cheeks and stomach muscles ached by the time he'd finished. It was only the slight sting of a slap on his ass that made him realise Oliver hadn't come yet.

"Come on, finish in me," he growled. "I want you inside me." They had done away with condoms after being checked over a couple of weeks ago, and it was the best feeling ever.

"Fuck, Dean." Oliver gripped his hips tight enough Dean was sure to have bruises, but he didn't care. "Ah, fuck!"

Oliver held himself deep, his hips only moving a little as he pumped his release into Dean's ass. No doubt it would make a mess later, but at that moment, it felt divine.

When Oliver collapsed to the side, his cock slid out, and Dean immediately turned around to hold him. He pressed kisses to Oliver's gaping mouth, taking advantage of the fact to explore his mouth with his tongue. He released him with a sigh of contentment and climbed out of bed to clean them up.

Despite the early hour, he tucked them both into bed and didn't set the alarm for the morning. While they were here, there was no rush to do anything, and Dean would make the most of it.

Oliver fell straight to sleep, but Dean was satisfied to watch the rise and fall of his chest, the shadow of his eyelashes on his cheeks. They had come such a long way since he'd first met the man in Nourris Moi ten weeks before. Neither had been expecting to find a relationship, and both had been adamant it wasn't the right time. Love had its way, though, and they made it work. Oliver refused to allow the same thing to happen this time, and Dean was there to help him.

While the restaurant was being rebuilt, they were making plans and arranging a timetable that would suit them both. Although Dean wouldn't be working with Oliver, Oliver wanted to work around Dean's shifts so they could spend as much time together as possible. Life wasn't set in stone, but Dean knew if something happened, they'd weather the changes together.

After all, a relationship was not just about one person. It was about family.

Chapter 25

Oliver

Six months later

O liver inhaled and exhaled while he surveyed his surroundings. Nourris Moi was re-opening the following day, and tonight was for those he called family. Over the last six months, there had been many people who had chipped in with their time, money and efforts to get the restaurant back up and running, and he would forget none of them.

The restaurant looked a little different from the previous incarnation, but he loved it all the same. After speaking with many of his previous customers to get an idea of what aspects they had liked and disliked about the previous design, Oliver had kept the full-length windows running the length of the building and the colour scheme of red and cream with wooden accents. The layout had changed the most. He'd used a third of the space for larger tables, meaning bigger parties could come without it causing too much of an issue moving tables around as they'd often done before. The rest were the smaller four or two-person tables with a long bench with stools for those dining alone if they wished.

The bar had stayed the same, although he had extended it further around the back of the building to open up more space for people to sit and have a drink. When Jack had found Oliver advertising for employees, he'd come right up to him and asked for his old job back. Oliver hadn't hesitated. A similar thing had happened with several of his ex-employees, including Serena, who was now the head chef when Oliver wasn't working.

"Are you happy?"

Oliver glanced over at Dean and smiled. "Ecstatic. I can't believe we got here."

"And a month earlier than even we thought possible." Dean chuckled.

"Yeah." Oliver stared around the room at the people he had brought for the first meal in the new restaurant before they officially opened. "It wouldn't have happened without all these people."

"This community knows what it means to be a family." Oliver slid his arm around Dean's waist and rested his head on his shoulder. "Are you tired?" Dean asked, kissing his head.

"A little, but I'm fine."

The doctor had diagnosed Oliver with hypothyroidism or underactive thyroid. It wasn't as common with men as women, but it wasn't unheard of or rare. He had medication to take, and although he still tired easily, the other symptoms he hadn't known were to do with the same illness were beginning to reduce. His steady weight gain over the years was one of the symptoms, as was feeling cold, having dry skin and aching muscles. He had never realised that putting those symptoms together, along with a blood test, could show an illness that hadn't been on his radar.

The diagnosis had made working fewer hours a simple choice to make. Now, he worked his shifts around Dean's. Sometimes, he would work from before the restaurant opened to mid-afternoon, and sometimes, he would work from dinner time to closing. It gave Serena the chance to vary her shifts and work around her family as well.

Quinn had taken over the shelter meal management, which he was delighted about. He'd been content cooking for his family before, but now he loved it even more because it helped people who needed it. He had several volunteers throughout the day and could provide a lunchtime and dinnertime meal for the shelter, thanks to the supermarkets getting on board. He was even considering branching out once he found out if he'd have enough volunteers and food.

"Come on. Time to celebrate."

Dean grabbed his hand and tugged him towards a table. Oliver had planned to have a long table so everyone could see everyone else, but there were too many people for that to work. In the end, he had pushed several tables together in groups, kind of like a wedding reception layout, and let them sit wherever they wanted.

The servers began bringing out their food. Oliver hadn't wanted them working that night, but Serena had waved away his suggestion they hire out. Instead, Serena had taken to the kitchen with several staff and servers and declared they would join the festivities once the meals were delivered. Oliver tried to argue, but Dean had intervened and told him this was their gift to him. After that, he'd backed down.

After the servers had placed the food in front of the guests and sat down, Paul tapped his knife against a glass. "Oliver, you need to do a speech."

"No, you don't need to hear from me."

He waved them away, but they banged cutlery against the table until he submitted. He stood, trying to gather his thoughts. Dean squeezed his hand and smiled up at him.

"What keeps circling my head," he started, "is the thought of how many people came to my aid when I needed it most. Sometimes, when you keep to yourself, you believe there is no one to support you, that you're alone in the world, that what you do doesn't matter because if you disappeared one day, no one would remember. Losing the restaurant showed me it wasn't true. Despite the heartache it caused, losing the restaurant was one of the best things to happen to me." He inhaled again, keeping his emotions bottled up. "I had taken my business for granted, and when it wasn't there anymore, I believed no one would care about it. Many of you proved me wrong, and for that, I am forever in your debt."

"Free meals for life, right?" Jason shouted with his glass in the air.

Everyone laughed.

"What you have given me is more than a restaurant. It's more than a business. It's more than friendship. It's a family." He caught Andrew's eyes. "Besides the family I already have," he added. "Life certainly sends you on a wild ride. Finally, I want to say thank you to Dean." He stared at his boyfriend. "You kept me going when I wanted to quit. You held my hand when everything was too much. You put yourself second more times than I can count. You mean the world to me, and I would like to ask...will you marry me?"

Oliver hadn't planned on asking right there, but he felt it was the right time. Dean's eyes overflowed with tears as he nodded and stood to wrap his arms around Oliver as everyone cheered and clapped. He gripped Dean, wanting nothing more than to be his husband as soon as possible, but there was no real rush.

Pulling back, he kissed his lips, then smiled and whispered, "Your ring is at home. I hadn't planned on asking until later." Dean chuckled, wiping his tears. Oliver turned to everyone. "Right, eat before it gets cold, and Serena has my hide."

"Oh, were we supposed to wait to eat?" Jason asked.

The guests threw several napkins his way, but everyone dug in, and conversation flowed.

Oliver ate the delicious meal and studied the photographs on the wall. He'd commissioned a set of photos from the photographer who had done the firefighter calendar. It was something the photographer, Harry, was known for—more so than the calendar—and the results had pleased him. He glanced at the man sitting between Paul and Jason, catching his eye and giving him a nod.

The pictures were of Oliver's favourite places: the fire station, the shelter, Shelter Kitchen, River Cam and Oliver's house. There was also a picture of Dean's motorcycle with him on it, his head covered by the helmet. And finally, in place over the entrance, a picture of what Nourris Moi had looked like previously. He'd borrowed the photo from Paul and had it copied and blown up as best he could. It was a daily reminder of what he now had.

"Are you okay?" Dean murmured.

Oliver grinned. "Never better."

Dean

To say Oliver had surprised Dean was an understatement. He never imagined Oliver would propose, especially in front of this many people, but Dean's answer would never change. The idea of marrying Oliver had always been in the back of his mind, but he hadn't wanted to push too fast, and instead, he'd held back. Obviously, too much because Oliver had beaten him to it. He didn't mind, though.

Oliver hadn't been wrong when he'd said life was a wild ride. Nothing much had changed in Dean's half of their life. He loved working with Red Watch, more so because there had been no more issues since Evan's arrest. Paul had cracked down on the station for inclusion and several other areas, explaining—and demanding—everyone was welcome, no matter who they were or what they looked like, and if anyone didn't like it, they could leave. No one did. Niall had become one of the crew with no problems; it felt like he'd always been there, and Red Watch worked well together.

His dad had sprung a surprise on them a few weeks ago. Clark and Sadie were moving to Cambridge to be closer to Dean. He'd argued with them, to begin with, not wanting them to go through the upheaval, but they were adamant and planned to move before the summer started. It would be fantastic to have them close, and it meant he could see them more often. They were also bringing their recent addition to the family: their golden retriever rescue called Betty. Dean was a little teary-eyed at that news, too, because they'd always had dogs growing up, but since his mum had died, his dad had not got another one. It seemed Sadie had a lot to answer for.

"Are you ready?" he asked Oliver once everyone had left except for the kitchen staff, who were tidying up, getting ready for the next day.

"Yes. I have plans." Oliver winked at him.

They said goodbye, and Oliver drove them home, flicking on the radio to their favourite station. He rested his hand on Oliver's thigh and stared out of the window.

Dean couldn't wait to see how the restaurant reopening went. He knew it would be a hit, but he couldn't help but be nervous for Oliver, even when he knew there was nothing to be nervous about. Tomorrow was the only day Oliver would be present at the restaurant for most of the day. He would be there for opening and through lunchtime, then have a few hours break in the middle, then work the dinnertime through to closing. After that, he and Serena would work between them, sharing the hours so no one became overwhelmed. It had taken a bit of working out, but they'd managed, and Dean was damn proud of Oliver and everything he had achieved.

"You're deep in thought over there," Oliver said when he switched off the engine.

Dean smiled. "Thinking about everything that's happened."

"It's crazy, isn't it?"

They climbed out. Once they locked themselves inside the house, they removed their coats and shoes before Oliver dragged Dean up the stairs.

Dean chuckled. "Are you that eager to get me to bed?"

"Yes," Oliver said as if Dean had asked a stupid question, "but I also want to do something."

When they were in their bedroom, Oliver let go of Dean's hand and shuffled over to his drawers. He rummaged around in the top one before taking something out and holding it behind his back while he turned to face Dean.

"I know I already asked, but I want to do it properly." He dropped to one knee and held out a black box. Dean felt tears gather in his eyes again. "I love you, Dean, with everything I am and everything I have. Will you marry me?"

"Yes," Dean croaked. He wiped at his face again when Oliver stood, opening the box to show two gold bands with a single diamond set in the middle.

Oliver pulled one out and showed Dean the inscription on the inside of the band.

My heart, my life, my world.

"It's gorgeous. Thank you!" Oliver slid it on his finger, then Dean did the same for Oliver.

"There's more."

"What?" Dean raised his eyebrows.

Oliver went back to the drawer and brought out another bigger box of the same velvet design. "I know in our jobs we can't always wear jewellery. I found us something to use when it isn't possible to wear them on our hands." He opened the box and pulled out two neck chains. "I wasn't entirely sure if you could even wear this, but I thought, at the least, you could hang it in your locker."

Dean smiled at the consideration. "I should be able to wear the ring, but if not, I will wear the chain under my PPE. Thank you." He stepped closer and cupped his face, kissing him with everything he had in him.

The box dropped to the floor, but Dean could feel the chains still in Oliver's hands as he rested them against Dean's head. He broke away, reaching down for the box and putting the chains back and on top of the drawers for later.

"I think we need to seal the deal, don't you?" Dean said.

"Oh, absolutely." Oliver smirked.

Their lips fused once more, and Dean walked Oliver backwards to the bed, stopping when his legs hit the edge. His hands slid down Oliver's body and grasped the hem of his jumper, yanking it over his head. The move meant their lips had to part, but Dean immediately latched onto Oliver's neck. His fingers deftly worked at the buttons on Oliver's shirt and had it off in no time.

Oliver pulled at Dean's polo shirt, ripping it over his head, all the while their hands and lips were touching as much skin as possible. Dean was glad that Oliver had lost most of his shyness about his body. He could concentrate more on the pleasure he was feeling instead of on his insecurities.

Dean pushed Oliver back, and the man climbed onto the bed, scooting himself higher while Dean crawled up and over him. He kissed Oliver's chest and stomach, then reached for his jeans, unfastening them in record time. He wanted Oliver naked—them both naked. Sitting back on his heels, he pulled the jeans off Oliver's legs before standing up to do the same with his own jeans, but he removed his underwear, too, and grabbed the lube from the bedside table.

Oliver bit his bottom lip and struggled out of his boxers, kicking them away seconds before Dean covered him. They both hissed at the sensation of their cocks sliding together, and Dean lowered his mouth. The kiss was softer but more intense than before. Oliver cradled Dean's hips with his legs, and they rocked together. Oliver's arms banded around Dean's back, and Dean cupped the top of Oliver's head.

Neither moved except for the touch of their lips and the rocking of their hips. Dean's arousal, however, was skyrocketing. Sweat beaded on his body, and he eventually pulled away.

"I need you," he whispered.

"Take me. Hard and fast. We can go again later."

Dean chuckled but wholeheartedly agreed.

He prepared Oliver with the ease of having done it many times since the beginning of their relationship. Oliver was an incoherent mess by the time Dean pressed his cock against his pucker. Sliding deep in one thrust was more difficult than most people imagined, and he took his time. He didn't want to hurt his man.

Once he was inside, they were both panting into the other's mouth.

Oliver held Dean's head. "I've changed my mind." Dean frowned and lifted, though Oliver pulled him straight back down again. "I want it slow and loving."

Dean closed his eyes and shook his head. "You had me worried for a second there."

Oliver grinned, unrepentant.

Dean wrapped his arms under Oliver and began thrusting in slow increments. A small withdrawal, a small thrust, and so on until they were a sweaty mess and Oliver was cursing for Dean to go faster. He refused. He wanted Oliver to feel everything, to take everything Dean gave him, to see what Oliver did to him before it threw him over the edge.

Time stopped, and Dean kept up the punishing, slow pace. His balls ached for release. He gave up pretending he didn't need more and slammed into Oliver, being rewarded with a cry. He braced his hands on the bed by Oliver's hips and snapped his hips forward. Within minutes, Oliver was screaming his release to the ceiling as white spurts coated his stomach, the sight of which sent Dean over the edge. His arms trembled, but he kept from falling on top of Oliver—at least until Oliver pulled him down and rolled to their sides.

While they regained their breathing, Dean thanked whatever power helped him to find the man beside him.

"Love you."

"Love you always," Dean whispered.

Did you enjoy this book? Do you want to find out how the firefighter calendar went? Check out Smoke Signals to read Jason and Harry's story.

Sign up to my newsletter to get a free stories, exclusive content and early access: https://elouiseeast.com/newsletter

About Elouise East

I am Elouise East but feel free to call me Elli. I write sweet and steamy connections in gay romance. I also touch on taboo stories under the name Elouise R East.

Books that tell the stories where friendship and family are the focal point - be it blood family or chosen - is very important to me. That's why I include a variety of personalities, talents, ages, situations and abilities as I believe a story needs, or a character needs. I want my characters to be real, to be relatable, to be free to have whatever views they tell me they have. And trust me, most of the time, I do not have *any* say in the matter!

My characters come to life on the page for me as well as my readers. Their stories unfold in front of me, and I have very little input into how they want to be shown. Just like real life, the lives of my characters change with every choice, every interaction and every conversation. And I wouldn't have it any other way.

I write books that are emotionally realistic, even if liberties are taken with other aspects of my stories. I don't know any other way to write. It comes from deep inside.

Who am I? A single parent to two children who make life worth living. An avid reader who still devours every book she can get her hands on. A student of learning about any subject that takes her fancy. An author of books she would read herself. And a romantic at heart who loves anything cheesy.

Who's in?

Stalk me here... ;-)
Website : https://elouiseeast.com
Newsletter : https://elouiseeast.com/newsletter
All links : https://elouiseeast.com/links

Books by Elouise East

Love in Flames
Fight Fire with Fire
Up in Smoke
Smoke Signals
Smoke & Mirrors

Club Royal
Royal Firsts
Rogue Royal
Secretive Royal
Grieving Royal
Disowned Royal
Trained Royal
Awakened Royal
Commanding Royal

Crush
Love Conquers
Instant Desire

Primary Seduction
Deep Down
A Crush for Christmas
Life Support
Covert Strength
Love Scene
Lawful Attraction

Just A Little Crush
First Kiss
He's Behind You
A Special Love

Daddy
Love Me, Daddy
Soothe Me, Daddy
Spoil Me, Daddy
The Complete Daddy Series

Standalone
Treehouse Whispers
Star-Crossed
Protecting the Thief
Sizzling Chauffeur
A Home for Barney
Mattie

Elouise R East (taboo)
Dark & Divergent
Forbidden Temptation

ELOUISE EAST

Too Many Secrets: A Life of Secrets
Too Many Secrets: The Lake House
Secrets in his Eyes

Collide
When Fantasies Collide
When Dreams Collide
When Pleasures Collide
When Cravings Collide
When Hungers Collide